P9-CDZ-972

One by One in the Darkness

Deirdre Madden is from Toomebridge, in County Antrim. She studied at Trinity College, Dublin, and at the University of East Anglia. She won a Hennessy Literary Award in 1980 and in 1987 was awarded the Rooney Prize for Irish Literature. She made her fiction début with *Hidden Symptoms* which was published in Faber's *First Fictions* anthology, *Introduction 9* and received much praise. She is also the author of *The Birds of the Innocent Wood,* for which she was awarded the Somerset Maugham Prize, *Remembering Light and Stone* and *Nothing is Black. One by One in the Darkness* won the Kerry Ingredients Book of the Year Award.

by the same author

HIDDEN SYMPTOMS
THE BIRDS OF THE INNOCENT WOOD
REMEMBERING LIGHT AND STONE
NOTHING IS BLACK

DEIRDRE MADDEN

One by One in the Darkness

LONDON · BOSTON

First published in Great Britain in 1996
by Faber and Faber Limited
3 Queen Square London WC1N 3AU
This paperback edition first published in 1997

Photoset by Intype London Ltd
Printed and bound in Great Britain by
Mackays of Chatham PLC, Chatham, Kent

All rights reserved

© Deirdre Madden, 1996

Deirdre Madden is hereby identified as author of this work
in accordance with Section 77 of the Copyright,
Designs and Patents Act 1988.

*This book is sold subject to the condition that it shall not, by way of trade
or otherwise, be lent, resold, hired out or otherwise circulated without the
publisher's prior consent in any form of binding or cover other than that
in which it is published and without a similar condition including
this condition being imposed on the subsequent purchaser.*

A CIP record for this book is
available from the British Library

ISBN 0-571-17551-1

4 6 8 10 9 7 5 3

for my mother, Mary Madden,
and my sister, Angela Madden,
with love

Chapter One

SATURDAY

Home was a huge sky; it was flat fields of poor land fringed with hawthorn and alder. It was birds in flight; it was columns of midges like smoke in a summer dusk. It was grey water; it was a mad wind; it was a solid stone house where the silence was uncanny.

Cate was going home.

She woke early this morning. Not surprisingly, she'd been sleeping badly in recent weeks, and she lay now for more than an hour thinking about her family. She liked to imagine them still asleep, each of the three women lying in the warm darkness of her own room: Helen in her house in Belfast, Sally and her mother at home in the country. Later, when Cate rose and moved about her flat making coffee and preparing her luggage for the journey, she thought of her family waking. Helen would stretch out her hand and switch on the radio, would lie there drowsing and listening to classical music. Sally would go downstairs, and, still in her dressing gown and sleepy-eyed, would stare blankly at the cloudy sky while she waited for the kettle to boil. She would make tea, and bring it upstairs to her mother's room. It was a ritual every Saturday morning. They would drink the tea together, and quietly talk over the week that was past, and the weekend to come; and today, Cate knew, their main topic of conversation would be her own trip home. They would discuss the meal they would cook for her arrival at lunchtime; and perhaps they would speculate as to why Cate had decided to go home at such short notice; but even allowing for that possibility, it was a comfort to her to think intensely about her mother and sisters.

In the course of the journey from Primrose Hill to Heathrow, she grew increasingly anxious. Once in the departure lounge, she checked in and then paced restlessly by the windows, watching the planes taxi and take off. Turning away, she went into the Ladies and checked her hair and make-up; took out a bottle of

French perfume and sprayed some on her wrists. Usually, looking at herself in the mirror calmed Cate. A quick glance would be enough: the thick, auburn hair, the fine, pale skin and delicate features, the wonderful clothes and jewellery which were far beyond the reach of most people: 'Whatever you feel,' she would tell herself, 'this is what other people see, and this is how they will judge you.' But lately that trick had been failing to restore her confidence, and it failed today. So she put her finger up to her brow to touch a tiny invisible scar at her hairline. When she was six, she'd run into a hay baler and cut her head so badly that she'd had to go to the hospital for stitches; and it had left a faint mark which had remained with her for the rest of her life. Touching the scar quickly, so that no one ever realised that she was doing it, restored a sense of reality, a sense of who she was, in a way that looking at her own reflection could not.

She went back to the departure lounge, and bought a newspaper. Out of habit, her eyes scanned the shelves, looking for the cover of the fashion magazine for which she worked. After that she bought a cup of coffee, but she didn't really want it, any more than she wanted the newspaper. She put sugar in the coffee, just to be doing something, and stirred it in, then put the spoon on the saucer and stared at the cup. She was terrified of what they were going to say to her at home. There would be tears, that was for certain, and some of them would be hers. There would be hard words, and she wondered how she was going to cope with that. No matter how much they hurt her, she would have to try not to say anything that she would regret afterwards.

A voice announced that the British Airways flight to Belfast was ready for boarding. Cate stood up.

In the past, she'd felt invincible. It wasn't that she didn't think about whether or not disaster might befall her: she did think, and decided that it couldn't. Her life was charmed. When she was a teenager, she would shelter under trees during thunderstorms, sure that she was safe. A train or a plane couldn't crash if she was on board. She'd been stunningly beautiful, and she'd known it. For years she believed that she could have absolutely anything she wanted in life. Her family hadn't been able to understand where it came from, this ... this – confidence, she'd called it then. Arrogance, she called it now. It had left her that night in October over two years ago, when Sally rang and told her what had happened. As soon as she had finished talking she'd broken the connection on the phone with the tips of her fingers while reaching into her handbag with her other hand for her credit card and Filofax. She'd called British Airways and quickly and efficiently booked a seat on the last flight to Belfast. Then she'd thought: who else should I ring? She had friends in London, good friends, but she'd realised that there was no one to whom she wished to tell what had happened, much less anyone she wanted around her at that moment. She had just wanted to be home. So she'd put her Filofax aside, and gone into her bedroom to pack.

What Cate called her wardrobe was so large that it was more like a small room into which she could step, as she did that night to examine the rails of clothes which it contained. She'd rummaged through the dresses and jackets and skirts looking for suitable things to wear at home, but everything struck her as wrong: too pale or bright, or stylish. The only dark clothes she had were evening dresses. Eventually she'd found a grey dress she'd only ever worn once, and a black coat of classic cut. She'd looked at her shoes. She hadn't realised she had so many pairs of shoes.

Suddenly she'd remembered being in Granny Kate's bedroom one wet day, when Granny Kate was trying on a new lilac suit she'd just bought: she'd wear it for the first time at Mass on Easter Sunday. Cate was sitting on the bed playing with a powder puff and a drum of violet-scented talc, which she'd surreptitiously lifted from the dressing table, and which Granny Kate hadn't noticed because she was so busy admiring herself in the mirror. Standing in the silent luxury of her own wardrobe, Cate remembered with uncanny vividness her grandmother's room: the crocheted bedspread, the rain on the window, a scent of violets and dust. She dipped the puff in the talc and brushed it against her face.

'Granny Kelly only ever wears black,' she said. 'Because of Grandad Kelly being dead.'

Granny Kate smiled at her own reflection and smoothed the collar of her suit with her fingers.

'I wouldn't wear black,' she said frankly, 'not if all belonging to me was dead.'

When the taxi had come to take Cate to the airport later that night, she was wearing a kingfisher-blue coat. She'd arrived at the airport, checked in and boarded as usual. But as the plane taxied down the runway, she realised that, for the first time ever, she was terrified, like a tightrope walker suddenly aware of the abyss into which she could fall at any moment. That terror forced her to believe, really believe, the truth of what Sally had told her. The spell was broken, the charmed life at an end.

During the flight this Saturday morning, she kept staring at her own name on the boarding card. When she'd started working in journalism, she hadn't liked the look of her own name in print. Kate Quinn: it was too Irish, she thought, too country, and she'd been delighted when she hit on the idea of changing the 'K' to a 'C'. Cate Quinn. It never crossed her mind that her family would have any problem with this, and she had been grieved and embarrassed when it became clear that they were hurt by what she had done, and saw in it a rejection of themselves. Not that anyone said anything, but it was years before her mother changed to the new spelling in her weekly letters to her daughter, and her father never abandoned her old name. Uncle Brian still called her 'Katie', as he'd always done: it was possible he wasn't even aware of the change she had made. For a while Helen had sent her post addressed to 'Cate Kwinn', which Cate thought was spiteful at the time, although years later she could see the funny side of it.

As they flew in over Belfast, she put her face close to the window and looked down at Belfast Lough, the gantries of the shipyard, the city itself and the dark mountains that rose behind it. She wouldn't have been happy in Belfast either. Once, she'd asked Helen if she enjoyed living and working there, to which Helen had replied, 'I don't know if I'd go so far as to say that.' 'Enjoy' wasn't a word which seemed to figure large in Helen's vocabulary. It wasn't that she didn't enjoy certain things a lot, more, Cate suspected, that she didn't like to talk about them.

The plane banked and flew low. Lough Neagh appeared, a cold expanse of grey water, and then she saw fields and farms.

Cate stared intently at the land, as if trying to wring some knowledge from it, as if she were seeing it for the first time, although in fact it couldn't have been more familiar to her, the type of landscape against which she still judged all others. A flock of sheep, stained blue as a mark of ownership, scattered in fright in a field beside the runway.

People turned to look at Cate as she walked through the arrivals hall at Aldergrove. The day Cate stopped turning heads would be the day she began to worry. Helen was waiting for her. The close resemblance between the two sisters was to some extent masked by the difference in how they presented themselves; by Cate's being so expensively dressed, so impeccably groomed. They crossed to the luggage carousel. 'Here's your bag now,' Helen said, nodding at a cracked tartan grip with two woolly pom-poms tied to the handle for easy identification. Cate laughed as she bent down to pick up what was in fact her luggage: an elegant leather suitcase.

'Sorry for the state of this,' Helen apologised, as she unlocked her car door, but Cate would have been surprised, disappointed even, if it hadn't been the familiar muddle of magazines and newspapers and stray shoes and music cassettes, the whole liberally sprinkled with sweet wrappers. As Helen switched on the ignition, opera music blared loud from the radio. She leaned over and turned the sound down slightly, but paused in what she had been saying to listen to the music for a second. 'Do you mind if we leave this on? It sounds like it might be really good.'

'Feel free,' Cate said. 'So how are things? How's everyone at home?'

'All well. Mammy's very excited about your being here for the week. She was all beside herself because you gave her such short notice.'

'There was a problem with leave in the office,' Cate said. 'I had five days to take, and they put pressure on me to take them now, or lose them.'

'Maybe you'll be able to get over again later in the summer, at the time you usually come.'

'Maybe,' Cate said, but she didn't sound convinced.

Not far from the airport, they had to stop at a security checkpoint, and Cate noticed the same sheep she had seen scatter in fright just before the plane landed. Now they were huddled together beside a hedge, their jaws flicking dumbly. Helen threw her driving licence back into her open handbag, and they drove on again. A weak sun struggled against rapid, thick clouds. It started to rain.

'So how's work?' Cate asked, and Helen frowned.

'Oh, much as usual. We're defending this guy Maguire at the moment; he shot a taxi driver. You might remember me talking about it. No? Anyway, I'm busy with him.'

'Do you still go home most weekends?'

'Almost every weekend now. It would take something really out of the ordinary to keep me away. I usually go home on a Friday night; I waited until Saturday this week so that I could collect you on the way rather than having to drive up again this morning. God no, Cate, I have to get out of the city come the weekend. It's a safety valve.'

On the outskirts of Antrim there were already houses where Union Jacks and Ulster flags were hanging out for the Twelfth of July, even though it was only mid June. Red, white and blue bunting hung across the streets. 'I thought we might as well go this way, through town,' Helen said, 'take the scenic route, rather than go by the motorway. We're in no great hurry.' On the far side of Antrim Cate noticed small pieces of wood with messages on them nailed to the trees and telegraph poles. 'WHERE IS YOUR BIBLE?' they said, 'ETERNITY WHERE?' and 'REPENT!'

Between Antrim and Randalstown was a stone wall which in the past had run unbroken the whole four miles, enclosing the estate around Shane's Castle. Like the other estates she knew of, it had fascinated Cate when she was a child, a fascination she knew instinctively to keep well hidden, especially from Uncle Brian. Life in there must be so different, she thought. She even half-persuaded herself that the trees themselves, which she could see on the other side of the wall, were not at all like the trees that grew around her father's farm. It would be like something out of a book, she thought. She imagined rooms full of beautiful things, and gilt-framed oil paintings of women with long pale faces; she thought of people riding through the estate on wonderful grey ponies, or doing embroidery by the fire and when they wanted tea, they would ring a bell and a maid would bring them in a tray with china cups and a silver tea pot. She smiled now to remember all this. Uncle Brian used to talk about the wall and the poor local people who had built it. 'Tuppence a day and a pound of oat meal, that's the pittance they got for their labours,' he said. Their father never talked about that, although he was interested in local history, much more so than his brother.

In the nineteen seventies, Cate's curiosity had been satisfied when they built the motorway to Belfast, and it cut right through the middle of the estate. The extraordinary thing was, she had been right. It *was* different, it looked like pictures she had seen of the English countryside, lush and rolling with magnificent trees, horse-chestnut and oak and copper beech, utterly unlike the frail saplings that edged her father's flat fields, even though they were only a few miles away. Sometimes on the hard shoulder of the motorway you would see a bewildered pheasant which had wandered out of the estate. You could visit Shane's Castle now, there was some sort of little railway for tourists, but Cate had long since lost interest.

After another mile or so the land began to flatten out. Helen turned off the main road, and then made a series of right and left turns into a web of increasingly narrow roads lined with high hedges. The sun had struggled through again: they could see its pale light flash on the water of the lough; and in the far distance they could see the dark blue hump that was Slieve Gallion. Cate rolled down the car window. After the heavy dead heat of London in the summer the clean cool air that smelt of the recent rain was a relief to her. Before long they could see the roof of their house above the thickly leaved hedges, and farther off, the reddish chimneys of Brian's place. The lane which led up to the farm was bumpy and rough, and Cate saw that their mother was waiting for her by the parlour window, as had always been her way. When she came out to the step, Cate hugged her and cried, suddenly afraid that she would forget her resolution and blurt out her news all at once.

'We've cooked some salmon for lunch,' their mother said when they went into the kitchen, where Sally was whipping cream in a glass bowl, 'and I got a leg of lamb for tomorrow. Take your jacket off and get settled, we'll have this on the table for you in a minute.' As she moved to sit down, Cate noticed on the dresser a large framed photograph of her father. She picked it up, and her mother paused in setting out plates on the table.

'Isn't that nice, Cate? Sally bought me the frame for my birthday, and Helen knew somebody who was able to enlarge the photo, even though we hadn't a negative for it. I like that photo the best, it's your daddy the way he was when I knew him first.'

Cate stared at the picture. 'Poor Daddy,' she said quietly after a few moments, and put the photograph back on the dresser.

'This is an unexpected treat, having you here at this time of the year,' their mother said as they all sat down at the table. 'What notion did you take to come home now?'

'I don't know,' Cate replied. 'I just got the idea in my head. I was lucky to be able to get the time off work. I had to haggle a bit with them in the office, but in the end I got the dates I wanted.'

'That was good,' her mother said.

'Yes, wasn't it?' The tone of Helen's voice made Cate turn to look at her. Helen was staring hard at Cate, and suddenly Cate remembered what she had said in the car. So Helen was the first to catch her out, Helen knew something was up. She looked away, confused and embarrassed.

'You must ring Brian,' her mother went on, as she passed Cate a bowl of carrots. 'He can't wait to see you. He was over here this morning asking what time you were due in, but we tried to put him off until tomorrow.'

'Let her get her dinner eaten first,' Sally protested, 'before we even start talking about her phoning people.'

Cate always loved the first meal with her family when she came home, and they would talk and laugh and tell each other the bits of news they had neglected in their many phone calls and letters. It reminded her of the visceral, uncomprehending emotional closeness that had bound them together over dinners of baked beans and fish fingers eaten at that same table when they were small children. Uncle Brian had always said, 'I never saw three sisters that were as close, and I never saw three sisters that were as different.' It was still true. If they hadn't been sisters, they would never have been friends. Cate knew Helen thought her life was full of empty glamour, that she spent more time thinking about cellulite and waterproof mascara than was actually the case. Cate herself viewed Helen's job as a solicitor specialising in terrorist cases and working out of an office above an off-licence on the lower Falls with a kind of horror. Both Helen and Cate wondered how Sally endured the tedium of her life as a teacher in the primary school they had all attended as children; and yet past a certain point none of this mattered. They were sisters, and that was enough.

But as they sat eating the salmon on this Saturday afternoon, Cate was aware of the other thing that bound them to each other, and that hadn't been there in childhood: the thing that had happened to their father. They wanted to give each other courage: Cate felt that just by looking at them, people might have guessed that something was wrong, that something had frightened them; and that fear was like a wire which connected them with each other and isolated them from everyone else.

After lunch, Cate opened her cases and gave the family the gifts she had brought for them: wine and chocolates, perfume, books and the inevitable piles of glossy magazines. In the late afternoon, she went for a walk alone, in a jacket and wellingtons she borrowed from Sally. She went out across the fields, wading through the long grass as one might wade in the sea. After a day of showers the sun was hidden now in white clouds which it split and veined with light; pink and blue like the opal Cate wore on her right hand. Drops of rain rolled off the heavy grass as she moved slowly through the field. What would they say to her? Her only consolation was that by this time the following Saturday, everything would be known.

Chapter Two

When Granny Kate talked about the colour of her clothes, she never just used simple words like 'red', 'blue' or 'green'. Her cardigan was 'a soft blue, the colour of a thrush's egg'. She had a skirt that was 'a big strong purple, like an iris', and a coat that was 'reddy-brown, the colour of a brick'. She was wearing a new coat at Mass this morning, and Kate was keen to have a closer look at it, for she'd heard Granny describe it to Kate's mother during the week as being 'that lovely rich-green colour you get when a mallard turns its neck and the light hits it'. The sermon had started, and Kate twisted round in her seat. Granny was two rows behind them, at the far end of the pew. She saw Kate looking at her, and smiled. Kate grinned back. Granny had a wonderful new hat too. She'd told them she got it in McKillens in Ballymena. Kate didn't know how much she'd paid for it, but it must have been a lot of money for when she told Kate's mother the price she'd leaned over and whispered in her ear, and their mother had widened her eyes and said 'No!' in such a way that the children knew she wasn't putting it on. Granny Kate had leaned back to her own side of the sofa. 'I know,' she said. 'Did you ever hear worse?' but she'd looked delighted.

Kate's mother had noticed that she was looking round, and tapped on her leg, frowned at her, whispered at her to behave. Kate turned to face the altar again. Father Black was still talking away. Even Helen wasn't pretending that she could understand what he was saying. Forbidden to look behind her, Kate now looked sideways at her elder sister, who was leafing slowly through her book. It was called *A Sunday Missal for Little Children*, and it had coloured pictures of a priest saying Mass. Helen yawned, but pretended not to: Kate could see her swallow down the yawn. Kate picked up her own book, which was about the Ten Commandments. On every page there were pictures of children and behind each child there was an angel. When the child was obeying the commandment, and doing something like giving his mother a bunch of flowers or going to Mass on a Sunday, the angel looked content; but when the children were doing bad things, like stealing and telling lies, the angels had their faces sunk in their hands, and they were crying. Helen's angel must never cry, Kate thought, yawning herself now, freely and comfortably. Not that Kate's own angel really had much to worry about: she knew she was a bit more mischievous than Helen, but she really wasn't a bad girl.

She closed the book and put it down again. Sally was asleep, leaning against her mother's hip. The rag doll she'd got for her birthday had slipped out of her grasp and had fallen on the floor. Because she was so small Sally was allowed to bring toys to church and to sleep if she wanted; their mother didn't mind so long as she didn't cry or talk out loud. Kate looked across the body of the church: she could see her daddy over on the men's side, sitting where he always did, about five rows from the front. Uncle Brian was down at the back. Their father was always one of the first of the men to go up to Holy Communion. Uncle Brian only ever went to Communion once a year, at Easter. Uncle Peter never went to Mass, not even at Christmas.

When Mass was over and the people were leaving the church, their mother would give Helen and Kate a penny each, so that they could go up and light a candle in front of the statue of the Sacred Heart. After that, they would go outside and stop briefly by Grandad Francis's grave to say a prayer for him. Only Helen could remember him, and even she had been so small when he died that her image of him was vague. She'd told Kate that she remembered when he was sick she'd gone over one day with her mother and they'd brought him a box of Meltis Newbury Fruits. She could remember him sitting up in bed turning the box over in his hands: a tiny shrunken man with eyes like black beads. Helen told Kate not to tell anybody about this, because she was afraid they would think she only remembered him because of the sweets (which Kate thought was quite possible, because Helen was very fond of fruit jellies). Usually Granny was already at the grave when they got there, because Grandad Francis had been her husband; and she was there this morning, in her new coat, which Kate stroked appreciatively with her palm as she walked beside her, down the path to where her father was standing in a group with Uncle Brian and some other men, talking and smoking.

They saw Granny and Uncle Brian again on the way home, when they stopped at McGovern's for the Sunday papers. McGovern's was in Timinstown: their daddy had once said that if you thought about it, McGovern's *was* Timinstown. There was only the shop and the petrol pump outside it and three houses: a well-furnished roadside, he said, but not to Mrs McGovern, a pale, thin woman who became a frazzle of anxiety in the hour after each of the two Masses on Sunday morning, when her shop became a mad scrum of people wanting papers and sweets and cigarettes. Aunt Lucy said that one morning when she was in there, it had all become too much for Mrs McGovern, and she'd given a big loud scream in front of everybody, and started to cry: they'd had to take her into her own kitchen and make her a cup of tea. Ever since then a nephew of hers came to help her on a Sunday morning, but you could see she still didn't like it; she preferred the rest of the week when the people dawdled in in ones or twos and made their minds up slowly.

Their mother went in to get the papers: 'I might get a block of ice cream too,' she said. 'Don't forget the wafers!' Kate bawled after her, as Uncle Brain slipped into their mother's place in the front passenger seat to continue his conversation with his brother. The two men smoked as they talked: Uncle Brian had smoked so much in his life that the thumb and first and second fingers of his right hand were a ginger colour that didn't come off, no matter how much he washed his hands. Kate didn't like this, nor did she like the back of his neck, which she studied now with distaste: a fat, pitted neck that bulged over the collar of his shirt. It was a pity, because he had a nice face, and he was great fun. But lots of men had horrible necks, past a certain age; she'd noticed that. Kate felt sorry for them: it must be terrible to know your neck was slowly becoming ugly: but then again, they couldn't see it, so maybe it wasn't such a trouble to them.

Uncle Brian drove a bread van for Hughes. He came to their house once a week, but they only ever saw him in the school holidays, because he came in the early afternoon. Kate loved going out to the van. He'd ring the bell and by the time you went out he'd be pegging open the heavy doors. When he pulled out the long deep drawers you could smell all the stuff, the Vienna rolls, the wheaten farls, the sausage rolls and the Florence cakes. There were other travelling shops which came to the house, Devlins on a Tuesday, and Sammy on a Friday. Brian couldn't stick Sammy because he didn't sell cigarettes 'on principle', whatever that meant. Their daddy said it was because he was Saved. Sammy was from Magherafelt. They could have had milk brought to the house every morning too, but they didn't need it, because they had their own cows. Their daddy set some milk aside for them every morning before the creamery lorry came and collected the rest of it. There were a few other people who came to sell things, but you never knew when they would appear, and then you mightn't see them again for months: the Betterware Brush man; a dark man with a turban, who sold clothes; and a man with a whole van full of hardware, who was always trying to persuade their mother to buy things like flower vases and tea sets. 'I really don't know what I would do with them,' she would say. 'I got all those things as wedding presents years ago, and some of them are sitting in the press to this day.' The van smelt of lavender floor polish. The most their mother ever bought off the hardware man was a few yellow dusters and a bottle of Brasso.

'Will you come over and see us later in the day?' Uncle Brian said to the children as he got out of the car. 'What about you, Miss Sally? Will you come over and see your cousins?' Sally smiled, but didn't say anything.

Aunt Lucy always took Johnny, Declan and Una to second Mass. While they were out, Granny changed out of her good clothes, and started cooking the dinner so that it would be ready for them when they got back, while Uncle Brian read the papers and kept an eye on the baby. Kate, Helen and Sally had their dinner later in the day, around five. When they went home on Sunday morning, they had a big meal of sausage and rashers and eggs and fried bread.

Kate and Helen went over to visit Uncle Brian and Auntie Lucy most Sundays, and this week Sally said that she would come too: usually she preferred to stay at home with her mother. In winter you could see Brian's house clearly through the bare trees, but now it was almost summer, and so you could only see the roof. 'Be careful of Sally crossing the foot-stick,' their mother said as they set out across the fields, which was the quickest way to get there. The only problem was the foot-stick, a frail, narrow bridge their father had constructed across a ditch for them. He didn't need the foot-stick: he could just step over the ditch, but they'd been warned not to try this. Kate didn't like to think of what their mother would do to them if Sally slipped and fell into the mud below while they were supposed to be looking after her; and she was happier when they'd got past that point, and were on to Uncle Brian's land.

Now Sally was spitting at something. 'What is it, what's wrong?'

'I swallowed a midge,' Sally said, ready to cry.

'Well, that doesn't matter, you can eat meat today, it's not a Friday. Don't be such a cry baby. Look, if you're not good, me and Helen won't take you with us the next time. We might even run away now and leave you here in the middle of the field.'

'Shush, Kate,' Helen said, taking Sally's hand. 'We aren't going to leave you here. Look, we're almost there now.'

Uncle Brian's house was much nearer the lough than their own home. It stood a short distance from a curved bay, where there were yellow wild iris and the shiny green rushes Uncle Peter used to make St Brigid's crosses every February. They pushed their way through the branches of the small trees that separated the bay from the fields they had just crossed, and stood in the wide lane for a moment to get their breath back.

Kate thought that even if you closed your eyes and tried your hardest, you couldn't imagine a nicer house than Uncle Brian's, with its two little windows sticking out of the roof and the porch and the shiny front door that was the colour of chocolate. Behind the house there were some twisted apple trees, and at the front there was a low wall which enclosed a straggling garden. Once there had been a lawn with flower-beds at the edges, but Uncle Brian had let everything just grow away to its heart's content, so that the garden had almost swallowed itself up. It was better like that, Kate thought. Granny Kate's two marmalade cats, with their hard green eyes and their whiskers like white wires, used to hide in the deep grass that took Sally to the waist. There were fruit bushes too, with squashy currants and hard, hairy gooseberries, glassy and green, that tasted bitter and made your mouth feel dry. They helped their cousins gather the fruit for Granny to make jam. A lazy rose had draped itself over the wall, and in summer it covered itself with fat yellow blossoms, and gave off a rich yellow scent. 'It's like drinking some kind of golden wine, just to smell that rose,' Granny Kate used to say.

The front door was almost never opened, and the back door was seldom locked, so they went into the house through the scullery, and then went on into the kitchen. They didn't bother to knock: nobody expected them to, for they were as free to come and go in this house as they were in their own home. If anything they were even more at liberty to do as they pleased here, for Uncle Brian and Aunt Lucy set less store by things like tidiness and good behaviour than their own parents did. The family was finishing dinner when the children went in. Granny Kate was cutting an apple pie, and they put out extra plates for Helen, Kate and Sally, and poured them mugs of hot, sweet tea. Uncle Peter had already moved over to a chair beside the stove, and Helen went over to sit beside him. Kate was more wary of him than Helen was, although she did like him. He never asked you how you were getting on at school, or wanted to test your multiplication tables or anything stupid like that. He talked to you in the same quiet way he talked to Uncle Brian or any other adult. As Kate ate her apple pie she listened in to what he was saying to Helen.

'I seen an otter down by the canal the other night. Be sure and tell your daddy when you go home.'

'What was it doing?'

'Sitting in nice and quiet by the bank, but when it heard me, it slipped into the water and swum off. You wouldn't think to look at it, the power that's in it. The jaws on that boy, if he give you a nip, he'd take the finger clean off your hand. He could bite clean through a fish, bones and all, the same as you'd eat a bit of bread and jam, and not a bother on him.'

Friday night two weeks earlier, Helen and Kate had been lying in bed ready to sleep when they heard a shout in the distance.

'That's Uncle Peter,' Kate said. Helen didn't reply.

'That's Uncle Peter,' Kate said again, as the voice came nearer.

'I heard you the first time,' Helen said. 'Keep quiet and go to sleep.'

Now he was at the bottom of their lane, they could hear him rant and shout.

'Daddy would never be like that.' Kate heard Helen sit up in bed. 'If you say one more word, Kate Quinn, I'm going to go to Mammy and tell her you won't let me get to sleep.' Kate could hear the tears in Helen's voice. The shouts gradually died away. When Uncle Peter got home, he wouldn't sleep in the house. There was a caravan out under the apple trees and Uncle Brian would take him there, and put him to bed. He'd stay there for days, maybe even weeks, and if they went to visit they wouldn't see him, he wouldn't come out until he was better. Kate felt uneasy playing in the orchard when she knew he was in the caravan. 'What does he do in there?' Kate asked Declan. 'Sleeps. Drinks. Cries. Granny brings him out a bit of dinner, but he hardly ever eats anything.' And then a day would come and you would go to the house and he would be back in sitting by the stove, lighting one cigarette off the other, quiet and shy as ever he was. Weeks and months might pass before he started to shout and had to go away again.

One day when Helen wasn't around, Kate had asked Granny, 'What's wrong with Uncle Peter?'

'Two things,' she said. 'He thinks too much, and then he drinks too much.'

'Why?' said Kate. She hadn't understood what Granny meant. Granny laughed. 'It would take a wiser woman than me to answer that.'

'Well, I don't like it,' Kate said, and now it was Granny Kate who asked, 'Why?'

'I don't know,' Kate said. 'It's just scary to hear him shouting, or to see him not able to walk properly. It's horrible.'

And when she said that, Granny had looked sad. She was quiet for a minute and then she told Kate to remember that a person might do bad things but that that didn't mean they were a bad person, and that there was no badness in Uncle Peter. The way he was made her sad and the whole family too, but the person it hurt most of all was Uncle Peter himself. 'You mustn't be afraid of him. You should feel sorry for him.'

'I do. I feel sorry for you too.' And then Granny Kate laughed. 'Oh, I'll manage,' she said, 'I'll survive.'

Uncle Peter didn't have one special job that he did all the time, like Daddy or Uncle Brian. He worked on and off at different things, fishing, or clearing drains with a rented digger or cutting back the hedges or digging holes in the road. Sometimes he went on the dole and stayed at home. He helped Granny Kate mind the baby when Uncle Brian was off in the bread van and Aunt Lucy was in the cigarette factory; sometimes he'd be doing the washing up when you went in, or taking the laundry down off the clothes airer on the scullery ceiling. Their daddy and Uncle Brian also did housework now and then, because there had been no girls in the family, and Granny Kate had made them do things when they were children because she didn't like housework herself. She didn't much care if people thought it was odd. 'If there's an hour you could spend either reading a book or washing the floor, I know which I'd rather do,' she said.

'There's a Shirley Temple film on the telly this afternoon,' Una said to Kate. '*The Good Ship Lollipop*.'

'Don't tell me you want to be sitting in watching television on a nice day like this,' Aunt Lucy said. 'It'd be far better for you to be outside playing.'

'Shirley Temple's a pain, anyway,' Johnny said, just to annoy Una, because he knew she liked her. Una was Kate's friend as well as her cousin: they sat beside each other at school. Johnny was a year older than Helen, who was in the same class as Declan.

'I could take you out in the boat,' Uncle Peter said. 'It's a good calm day for it, but I don't know that I'd have room for the lot of you.' Sally wanted to stay at home with Granny, which pleased Helen. She always felt responsible for looking after Sally and Kate, and she would enjoy being out in the boat more if she didn't have Sally to worry about. Una said that she would stay at home too, and watch the film, and Uncle Peter said that he could manage the four who still wanted to go with him.

The blue wooden boat was pulled up into the reeds. 'Get you in first, Johnny and Declan, and one of youse can start bailing her,' Uncle Peter said. The bailer was an old paint tin lying in about four inches of water at the bottom of the boat. Uncle Peter lifted Helen and Kate in, then pushed the boat hard and climbed in himself, as it slid out into the lough. Kate liked that moment, because it was frightening. She always thought for a split second that the boat was going to tip over or sink. The difference between standing firm on the shore one minute, and then feeling the boat tremble uncertainly beneath you the next was exciting. Within seconds, though, you got used to being on the water, as the boat steadied itself. Uncle Peter began to row with long, even strokes. There was a green scum of algae at the edge of the shore, but the water was clearer further out. The sky was bare and blue, but for a few high strands of fine clouds. Kate took off her cardigan, because of the sticky, prickly heat of the day, then turned in the boat to look back at Uncle Brian's house. It was strange to see from an unfamiliar angle a place you knew so well, and she wasn't quite sure that she liked it. When Helen said that you could see their own house too, she didn't want to look at it.

'Will you take us to one of the islands?' Johnny said. 'Ah, do,' he went on, when Uncle Peter didn't say 'No' straight off, and the others noticed this too, and joined in with the pleading. 'It's the breeding time,' he said. 'The chicks is hatching now, the birds'll go wild if you go out there.'

But far from putting them off, this only made the islands more attractive. Uncle Peter shrugged. 'All right,' he said, 'only youse are to behave and not stand on the nests or be frightened or anything.'

The islands were not far off the shore, in fact the alternative to landing on them and what Uncle Peter had intended when they set out would have been to row out past them, out of the bay. They were small islands, narrow and flat, with a few scrubby trees and bushes growing on them. As Uncle Peter directed the boat towards the largest of the islands, she saw why he had said they weren't to be frightened, and hoped she would be able to stay brave, for the gulls heard the boat approaching and flew up in fear and anger, to protect the chicks. They strafed the boat the way she had seen a blackbird go for one of Granny Kate's cats once, when the cat was sitting with its paws folded beside a fledgling that had fallen out of its nest. The blackbird had dive-bombed the cat again and again, coming within inches of its ears, and all the time making a racket that Granny Kate said would have raised the dead. Kate knew to look at Helen that she was frightened too, but Helen would be brave, even if Kate weakened and shrieked as the fat white birds dipped low and angry around them.

She shaded her eyes against the sun that flashed on the water, and looked up. Hundreds of gulls were flying around high above them. She'd seen this before, but from a distance, when her father would look out of the window and say, there must be someone out on the islands. She wondered if he would notice it today, and if he would ever guess who it was that was out there.

The boat juddered as it got into shallow water, and Uncle Peter told them to sit where they were until he had it properly beached and tied up. He lifted them out in turn, saying, 'Mind what I said now, mind you don't hurt anything.'

Kate had never imagined how careful they would have to be, for there were nests everywhere, crude, flat nests, she thought, not like the small, tight nest a songbird would make for itself with straw and mud and moss. The gulls' nests were just flat upon the ground, and there were so many of them you had to be careful where you walked. Uncle Peter kept warning them, Johnny and Kate in particular, to go easy. Some of the eggs had already hatched, but the fluffy brown chicks didn't interest her as much as the dark wet stunned-looking ones that weren't long enough out of the egg to have dried out and found their feet. Strangest of all were the eggs that were only partly hatched, so that when you leaned low over them you could see a tiny hole, a crack, and you knew that the bird was working away inside to free itself. Kate wondered what it would be like to be in an egg: shut up in a tiny space barely bigger than yourself, knowing nothing but that you had to tap and tap and tap until you broke into the light and fell out, uncoiling yourself. She imagined darkness and heat in the egg, and was so lost in this thought that when Helen touched her arm, she jumped.

'We won't tell anybody about this, Kate, all right?'

'We can tell Daddy, can't we?' she said.

'Oh yes, it doesn't matter if we tell Daddy,' Helen replied. 'I mean other people. People in school. We can tell them about the island, but I don't want to tell them about the birds.'

'All right,' Kate said. She glanced over at Uncle Peter, who was leaning against a tree and smoking a cigarette. Soon he would lift them back into the boat and row them away from the island. The gulls would all fly back to their chicks. They'd take Sally back home across the fields and have their dinner: chicken, and then tinned peaches with the ice cream they'd got in McGovern's on the way home from Mass. They'd get their school bags ready for the morning; and in the evening they'd have to go to bed early, so that they wouldn't sleep in the next day. And some night again when she was lying in the dark, waiting to fall asleep, she would hear Uncle Peter shouting, out there in the night. She would make herself think of the day he'd taken them out to the island and showed them the gulls' nests, and she'd try not to be frightened any more.

Chapter Three

SUNDAY

Over the years, the kitchen was the only room in the house which had not undergone significant change. Lino had given way to thick carpet in the bathroom; the red brocade curtains in the parlour had been replaced with pale blinds; the bedrooms had lost their austerity and become chintzy and floral sprigged. They'd had a conservatory built at the side of the house for their mother; they'd had central heating installed. Only the kitchen was left untouched, and that was deliberate. Their father, who had been happy with other changes made, had always held out over that. 'To tell you the truth, I can't see anything wrong with it the way it is,' he'd say to any suggestion proffered; and after he died, neither the sisters nor their mother desired to make any change to the room: they wanted it to remain as he had known it.

The kitchen was the biggest room in the house; and was dominated by a stove, on either side of which was an old-fashioned built-in press, of cream-coloured wood, with strong shelves, and thick ribbed glass in the cupboard doors. The press on one side of the stove held crockery and food; the other press held books, ornaments, and the framed photograph of their father which Cate had noticed the day she arrived home. Against the wall farthest from the window was a comfortable old sofa; over by the window itself there was a huge deal table and some straight-backed chairs. Helen was sitting on one of these chairs, drinking tea and gazing out at a stretch of grass, where a few ducks were struggling along in blustery sunshine. They'd had the birds for their father, who liked duck eggs, and after he died, their mother and Sally hadn't the heart to get rid of them, so the ducks continued to wander around the farmyard for no real reason. Because nothing had changed there was something timeless about the kitchen, and Helen liked that. In her rare moments of nostalgia she could sit there and half-close her eyes and imagine that it was twenty, twenty-five years ago, that if she were to go over to Uncle Brian's house now she would find it, too, as it was in the past; that if she listened at the kitchen door there she would hear voices: Granny Kate and Uncle Peter, and the voices of children, one of whom was herself. But she could never make the illusion last as long as she desired, and was conscious only too soon of how things had changed.

Brian and Lucy hadn't bothered doing anything with their house for years and years: the only room they had changed was the kitchen. About a year earlier they had had it completely modernised: the stove ripped out, fitted pine units installed, a vinyl floor covering laid over the red quarry tiles. Sally and their mother had gone over to see it one evening when it was all finished. Sally told Helen that their mother had baked a cake to take with her and had steeled herself before she left, but that she and Lucy had both cried and that their mother had kissed Lucy and told her that she'd done the right thing, because life had to go on. Helen had been invited over too, but she didn't go: she never went to Brian's and Lucy's house now.

She set great store by this hour on a Sunday morning when her mother and Sally were out at Mass and she had the house to herself, although strictly speaking, she wasn't alone today: Cate was still there. She told Sally she wouldn't be going out this morning as she didn't feel very well; and so far she hadn't ventured downstairs at all. Had she been well, she would certainly have gone to Mass: she always did when she was at home, and there was, for Helen, something about that which didn't add up. After Cate moved to England, Helen suspected for a long time that she only went to Mass when she came home to save face and not hurt her parents; that she probably hadn't been across the threshold of a church since she arrived in London. But then Helen had gone to visit her sister, and had been surprised to learn that not only was Cate a regular churchgoer, but that she even had a religious picture hanging in her apartment: a classy reproduction icon, to be sure, rather than a cheap, kitsch print. It was clear, however, that it was important to Cate, and that she didn't have the picture just for show.

But by her own admission, Cate's religion was a ramshackle thing, a mixture of hope, dread, superstition and doubt; upon which she depended to an extraordinary degree: or so it appeared to Helen. Sally, on the other hand, had a faith which, like much else in her life, ran in a straight and unfractured line direct from her childhood. For Helen herself, her main regret on this subject was the hurt she had caused her father; for he had had a faith which she respected, seeing in it both dignity and integrity, although it was a faith she could not share. She stopped going to Mass not long after she started university, and he had been deeply aggrieved. Was this the end result of all her study and learning? He argued and pleaded with her through that first autumn term, but when Christmas came and still she refused to go to church with the rest of the family he realised how serious she was about it. 'You're a grown woman now,' he said to her that Christmas Eve. 'We've done what we can for you; you're free now to live your own life as you see fit.' He never mentioned the subject to her again, never tried to coax or persuade her. But many years later, after he was dead, they found a little notebook in which he wrote down every month the intentions for which he particularly wanted to pray, and from which it was clear that he had constantly hoped for two things: that there would be peace in Northern Ireland, and that Helen would return to the Church. Had it been anyone else, even in her own family, who had written that, Helen would have been livid.

Sometimes she felt that this hour on a Sunday morning was the only time when she could – what? Think straight? Could she even do that now? In the past, she would have said that it was the only time that she knew any peace, when she could truly relax. But that wasn't true any more either, except in so far as the pace of her life slowed down sufficiently at the weekends for her not to be in such strict control of her own thoughts, as she was during the week. She was able to let her mind off the leash, as though it were a dog, but the difficulty was that she no longer knew how the dog would behave, whether it might not turn on her and savage her. Maybe David was right. 'You work too hard, that's the problem with you,' he said. 'The eighties are over, Helen. It's not cool to be a workaholic any longer.' But there must be more to it than that. She'd worked every bit as hard five years ago, but she'd been able then to spend her Sunday mornings thinking about movies she wanted to see or the book she was reading at any particular time, or even about work itself and the cases upon which she was engaged, with a cooler eye and more detachment than was possible when she was in Belfast. Now the thoughts that pressed in on her were the sort of things that you expected when you woke at the hour of the wolf, when your mental resistance was down and you couldn't get back to sleep again: thoughts of failure and inadequacy, of past wrongs that could never be righted; and knowing that many of them were trivial and that she was seeing them out of all proportion was no help against them. She'd said to Cate that her trips home at the weekend had been a safety valve, but it wasn't true: it was more of an entry into a danger zone, as though there were a hairline crack in her otherwise steely self-containment, and to go home was to push against that crack with her fingers and feel it yield and fear that some day it would split open completely. She realised this more fully today than ever before, and it frightened her. She got up from the chair and tried to distract herself.

The tea she was drinking had gone cold, so she threw it out and made a fresh pot. Some of the interior-décor magazines Cate had brought home were sitting on the press, and she lifted them on to her lap and started to leaf through them, but soon became bored. She'd taken no great interest in furnishing the house she'd bought in Belfast, a place to which she felt no particular attachment. She'd needed a roof over her head, there was no more to it than that; and if anyone ever spoke to her using the word 'home', her thoughts instinctively turned to her family home in the country, even though it was years since she had lived there, and she would probably never live there again. She'd bought furniture and curtains in the same frame of mind in which most people bought pints of milk and loaves of bread: she needed them. She bought clothes with the same consideration of necessity rather than pleasure, something about which Cate had nagged her for years. She gave Helen gifts of clothes, blouses and scarves much more glamorous and luxurious than anything Helen would ever have bought for herself. They'd actually had a row about it the last time Helen was over in London. Cate had tried to persuade her to go to one of those agencies where they tell you what colours suited you and what sort of clothes you ought to wear, an idea Helen had dismissed with a contempt she at once saw was excessive. 'You know I only can wear a particular type of thing because of my job,' she said, to soften the rejection, but Cate was having none of it. 'That's all the more reason why you should enjoy your clothes off duty, rather than just lie around in jeans and a jumper all the time. Hell, it's only a bit of fun, I'm not saying these things are the be-all and the end-all in life.' But Helen still refused.

It was only now, when her life had shrunk to little more than duty, coldly and honourably fulfilled, that she understood what Cate meant. She knew that her sister had been watching her since they were children; had watched her austerity close around her like a sheet of ice. Cate herself was proof of the validity of her own argument. Certainly there were women who didn't add up to much more than their jacket and lipstick, but Cate wasn't one of them. Helen could see why people gravitated to Cate, why they liked her, but also why they shied away from Helen and found her intimidating. Cate was on the side of life, and it was painful to Helen to have to admit that that was not true of herself.

On the Saturday evening Cate had picked up one of the magazines and riffled through it, saying, 'Oh, there's a letter here I saw the other day and I must read it to you. I laughed out loud when I saw it. Here we are: "Dear Décor Help-Desk, I have a needlework box with straight legs. It looks very pretty, but lately it occurred to me that it would look even nicer with cabriole legs. Can you tell me the address of a stockist, and perhaps a craftsman in my area who could do the necessary work?" ' Cate had thrown the magazine aside and chuckled, while their mother said, 'Isn't it extraordinary how little some people have to trouble them in life?'

'I can see Aunt Rosemary writing a letter like that,' Sally said, 'or at least finding nothing odd in it.'

Helen had said nothing, but she'd thought about Sarah Maguire, whose youngest son, Oliver, she was defending on charges of shooting a taxi driver. She was probably only in her mid fifties, but looked much older. She thought of her careworn face, her timid, pleading manner: Mrs Maguire probably wouldn't have been able to begin to imagine a life where she would have the luxury to think about a thing like that.

For some time now Helen had been hearing movements

upstairs. There were footsteps on the stairs, and then the kitchen door opened. Over her nightdress, Cate was wearing a fluffy white bathrobe edged in white satin.

'How are you feeling?'

'Not great.'

'Mammy'll be disappointed. I know she's planning to make you a fry when she gets back from Mass. She bought the sodas and rashers specially.'

Cate grimaced and swore gently. 'Can I have a cup of that tea?' she asked, nipping across the cold tiles in her bare feet and taking the heel of a white loaf out of the bread bin. 'This'll do me nicely.' Helen looked at her shrewdly as she passed her the tea, and Cate noticed the look. 'Cheers, Helen, I'll go and get dressed,' she said as she scampered back across the floor. 'I'm fine, really.' Helen listened to her footsteps as she went back up to her room.

Crossing to the press, Helen picked up the photo of her father and looked at it closely. In her sitting room in Belfast she had a framed photograph of herself and her father standing on the lawn at Queen's on her graduation day. How proud he'd been! She'd been the first person in her family to go to university, and in her excellent results and the speed with which she'd subsequently risen in her profession she'd far surpassed her parents' hopes or expectations. She held the photograph tightly. It was black and white, and her father was a young, smiling man in it. It was only a snapshot, but captured his kindliness. He'd had the same brown eyes as his father and both his brothers. She could see why her mother liked that particular photograph so much.

The last weekend Helen saw her father, she'd been having trouble with her car. It had developed a tendency to stall when she slowed down, but she was too busy at work to take time off and get something done about it. 'Why don't you take my car to Belfast for the week,' he'd said, 'and I'll limp into Antrim with yours and get it fixed for you.'

'Oh thanks, Daddy,' she'd said, 'you don't know what a help that would be to me. You restore my faith in men.' She meant it as a joke, but unusually, he took it quite seriously and replied, 'Well, there can't be much right with the men that's going now to make a fine woman like you say a thing like that.' The remark hurt her, as suddenly and abruptly as if he had reached out and pressed his fingers on an old wound which she had long since believed to be healed, but which his touch revealed to be as raw and painful as a fresh cut. The sudden tears that came to her eyes embarrassed her. He saw this, and for her sake pretended not to notice. 'Don't you worry, Helen, I'll get it seen to and paid for,' he said, 'and we can get it all settled between us when you're home next weekend.'

But before the week was out, he had been killed.

She set the photograph down, and from the shelf above lifted down a black book with *The People's Missal* stamped on the cover in gold. The letters were faint now, rubbed away through use, and when she opened the book a piece of brittle white palm fell out of it. The book was stuffed with memorial cards: old, dark ones, dense with print, and more modern ones which were brightly coloured. They'd put the missal for safe keeping up beside the other books which had belonged to her father. She glanced along the titles: *Flora and Fauna of Northern Ireland*, *Field Guide to the Birds of Lough Neagh*, *Monuments of Pre-Christian Ireland*, *Celtic Heritage*. The fiction was on the shelf above: *Call My Brother Back* by Michael McLaverty, Alexander Irvine's *My Lady of the Chimney Corner*, and collections of short stories by Liam O'Flaherty and Frank O'Connor. There were some of Granny Kate's books mixed in with them: *Gone with the Wind* and *Rebecca*. They'd been passed along to their father after Granny Kate died because no one in Brian's house had been a reader, and it had seemed right that any stray books in the family as a whole should ultimately make their way to their father. Even when she was at university she hadn't met anybody who loved books and cherished them as much as her father had done. When she was still a child, Helen remembered her father taking her along to hear Seamus Heaney read in Magherafelt. When was that? Sometime in the early seventies, it must have been. He'd bought at that reading one of the several collections of Heaney's poems which he owned, and as Helen reached up to lift down a copy of *North*, she noticed a figure standing at the kitchen window.

'It's only me,' Brian said, as she unlocked the back door for him. They'd long since given up the habit of leaving the door on the latch during the day. Their mother was anxious unlocking it unless she knew for sure who was on the other side, and at night even Helen was afraid when the doorbell rang late and unexpected.

'Hello, Brian, how are you keeping? Take a seat there.'

'Thanks, Helen, not so bad, and yourself? It was Katie I called to say hello to, is she out at Mass yet?'

'No, she's upstairs, but I think she'll be down in a minute or two,' Helen said, getting an ashtray for Brian and offering tea. The kitchen was full of a deep golden light now, every mote of dust showing clear as it floated and fell. Helen talked to her uncle in a desultory way about Cate's return, and the weather, but they soon fell into a silence that wasn't altogether comfortable. Whenever possible now, she avoided being alone with Brian. She remembered sitting with him on the kitchen sofa at three o'clock in the morning during her father's wake, drinking neat whiskey, neither of them speaking. He'd looked suddenly older when his brother was killed: until then, Helen had thought it was a cliché to talk about people ageing overnight.

'It was my fault,' he'd said abruptly, lifting his gaze from the floor tiles and looking Helen hard in the eye. 'It was me they wanted. I'm to blame.'

'You're never to say that again, Brian. It's not true and you know it.' He'd passed his hands over his eyes and looked away. How had he known what she was thinking? He'd never repeated those words to her but since then the idea had always lain between them like a coiled snake, making a distance, a coolness, a fear that had never been there before. She lost Brian too, that night: she did to some degree hold him responsible, and that he also blamed himself was of no real help to her.

Helen was glad now when Cate appeared, in black leggings and an oversized tee-shirt, her long straight hair pulled back into a pony tail. 'Fit and well you're looking, Katie,' Brian said, which Helen thought was flattering of him, as Cate actually looked frail and wan. She watched her sister as Cate, beaming, chatted to their uncle.

'Will you come over and see us sometime, Katie?' Brian said

wistfully, and Cate bit her lip the way she'd done when she was little and was told to do something she didn't want to do.

'Oh, Brian,' she said, 'I don't know if I can.'

'It would be great for Lucy,' he said, coaxing.

'I will, I'll come. But maybe not for a while. Maybe I'll come with Sally?'

'And your mammy, too,' Brian said. 'We'll make a night of it, I'll get Una to take a race over from Magherafelt.'

'I'd love to see Una,' Cate said. There was the sound of a car pulling up at the front of the house, and Brian at once stood up to leave. 'That's Mammy and Sally now, won't you wait to see them?' Cate said, but he waved his hand.

'Ah, sure your mammy's tired looking at me, I'm in and out of this house far more than I should be, since I can't sit at peace in my own. Tell her I was asking for her, Sally too,' and as they heard the key turn in the front door, he slipped out by the back.

'You'll have had your fill of relatives by tonight, Cate,' Sally said when she heard Brian had been there. 'You know Uncle Michael and Aunt Rosemary are coming over this afternoon to see you, don't you?'

'At least you'll get that visit out of the way near the start of your time,' Helen said. 'You'll be hearing all about the christening. Can you believe they called the baby Michael, too?'

'There's no sense in it,' said their mother. 'Three people in the same family all with the same name: four if you count my father. It's so confusing, isn't it? The son got called Wee Michael and then he was Young Michael; now they talk about Baby Michael and Daddy Michael, until you haven't a clue who's who. Talk about carrying on the family name! I never heard such a load of nonsense, you'd think they were royalty or something.'

'Or one of those people in the American Mid West that call themselves things like Wilbur E. Hackensack IV,' Helen said.

'We all got asked to the christening,' Sally said. 'It was more like a wedding, with printed invitations and a meal in the Adair Arms.'

'And do you know what Aunt Rosemary did at it, Cate? She was sitting beside Sally and when the meat was served she turns to her and says, "I'm afraid this piece of beef is rather fatty, and the doctor told me that under absolutely no circumstances should

I eat fatty meat. Would you ever mind changing with me?" And poor Sally had to hand over her dinner.'

Sally smiled. 'I didn't really mind so much,' she said.

'Well, I'd have bloody minded,' said Helen, who had been telling the story. 'If she didn't want the fat, all she had to do was cut it off and leave it. I saw the two plates and the only difference was that Sally's bit of beef was bigger. She's as bad as ever she was about her health. She's got one of those designer allergies now; I don't remember what it is she pretends she can't eat.'

'Those allergies are very real,' Cate protested, but Helen waved her hand dismissively.

'Hers isn't. She's as healthy as a clam. Honest, Cate, it's a kind of hobby for her.'

'She told me,' their mother said, 'that the only vegetables she could eat were pimentos and aubergines.'

'I rest my case,' Helen said.

'I felt like saying to her: "Aren't you lucky this has only come on you now, and not thirty years ago, when you couldn't have found an aubergine in Ballymena for love nor money?" '

Cate chuckled. 'God, you shouldn't have told me all this. If she starts to talk about her diet this afternoon, I'm not going to be able to keep a straight face.'

They arrived not long after lunch, Uncle Michael all nerves, Aunt Rosemary all effusiveness; and were ushered into the parlour rather than into the kitchen. There'd always been a tension in their relations with their mother's family, quite unlike their free and easy attitude to their father's people. Even as small children they'd known it, long before they could understand or articulate it, picking up the unease amongst the adults as horses and dogs can sense the coming of an earthquake. It was all like a foolish game, Helen now thought, a game in which their stakes had increased over the years as the sisters made good in the world. Aunt Rosemary was particularly fascinated by Cate, whom she wrongly believed to have changed out of all recognition, for Cate had never been as flighty or lazy as Rosemary had once thought her. She'd gone to London with her husband for a short holiday the previous year, and had made a point of arranging to see Cate, who knew instinctively what was required of her: tea at the Ritz, a guided tour of the shops in Bond Street and Knightsbridge, assistance in obtaining tickets for a Lloyd Webber musical. As soon as they got back to Ireland, Rosemary had phoned Cate's mother to say what a wonderful time they'd had.

'You must be so proud, with two such successful daughters,' she said, but their mother replied sharply, 'I'm proud of all three of them.' That was another difference now: how their mother's attitude had gone from timidity when she was with her family and resentment when she was away from them; to indifference when they were absent, and confidence when they were there. It was her brother and his wife who didn't know fully how to handle the changed situation. Now it was their turn to feel ill at ease and to shift uncertainly on the sofa. Helen pitied them too the horrible stale, sweet sherry that their teetotal mother kept in the parlour sideboard from one year's end to the next, and which she offered to them in mercifully tiny glasses.

As had been predicted, much of the talk was about Young Michael and Baby Michael, while Helen looked coolly at her uncle, who was frequently referred to behind his back as Oul' Michael. He'd recently retired from his job with an insurance firm; and Helen remembered how her father used to call him teasingly 'a good overcoat man'. But although they'd never been comfortable with each other, there was no real malice in his attitude towards his brother-in-law. On the contrary, it was he who had insisted on maintaining as good a link as possible with the family in Ballymena. 'Blood's thicker than water,' Helen had heard her father saying for years before she understood what it meant. Michael stared at the carpet, while his wife prattled on beside him; and Helen could find it in her heart to feel sorry for her prosperous, red-faced uncle.

Looking across the room, she noticed that Cate was also paying scant attention to the conversation around her. She had accepted but not drunk a glass of sherry, and now she was gazing into it, frowning, which, together with being withdrawn in company, was most uncharacteristic of Cate. Helen wondered vaguely how long she was going to wait before breaking her news to the family; and in thinking this, she realised how completely she'd guessed Cate's secret. It couldn't remain a secret now for too much longer.

Chapter Four

At two o'clock every Friday afternoon Miss Wilson would take a key and unlock the glass-fronted press at the back of the classroom, where the library books were kept, and they would all read for an hour. In the press there was also an exercise book covered in brown wrapping paper, and when you took a book out you had to write down in it the title and your own name; then when you gave the book back Miss Wilson would put a red tick beside your name. Usually it was the best hour of the week, but there was this problem: before you gave the book back, you had to write a composition about what you'd just read. This was to stop messers like Willy Larkin, or Helen's cousin Declan, from getting a book out one Friday and pretending to read it, then giving it back next week and getting another one out, just for the look of it. The problem with this rule was that last week Helen had made a bad choice, by taking out a book of stories about the Wild West, which had turned out to be really boring. It was the cover that had attracted her: it had a picture of a woman wearing a white buckskin jacket and skirt, with boots and a hat like a cowboy. Helen had read three of the stories, but she had only liked one of them, and she wasn't interested in trying to read any of the others. She wondered if Miss Wilson expected her to write a composition about every story in the whole book. Helen turned to the list of contents and counted how many stories there were. Twelve. She saw Miss Wilson looking at her, so she leaned over the book and pretended to read.

The story Helen had liked was about Annie Oakley, who had shot quail to feed her little brothers and sisters because they had had no grown-ups to look after them. Little Sure Shot, they'd called her. She was so good at shooting things that she'd joined a kind of circus with Buffalo Bill, and became famous and rich and made lots of money for her family. It was well seen Little Sure Shot had no mammy or daddy: it was as much as Helen dared do to look at her daddy's shotgun. He kept it on a pair of hooks, high up in the cloakroom, where only he could reach it. There were three dangerous things about which their mother frequently warned them: the lough, the hay baler, and the shotgun. But what if Helen had had to use the gun? What if something terrible happened to their mammy and daddy, and she had to look after her sisters completely: would she be able to go out to the lough shore and shoot ducks so that herself and Kate and Sally would have something to eat? She couldn't imagine it. There probably wouldn't be any point, anyway, Sally would never eat a wild duck; it was a day's work for Mammy to get her to eat anything other than fish fingers and mashed potatoes. Maybe Annie Oakley had never shot the quail either: maybe it was all just a story somebody had made up.

Daddy hardly ever went shooting now. He was too old for it, he said, he'd rather be in his warm bed on a winter's morning than out standing in the rain and the cold by the lough shore. Uncle Brian still went out though. Even he was careful about his gun: he kept it locked away in a cupboard under the stairs, and in Uncle Brian's house they usually weren't careful about anything. The last time Helen had been over there, the baby had been sitting on the floor playing with a tin opener, and she'd wondered that nobody thought anything odd about this or took the tin opener off the baby until after it had cut its finger.

Auntie Rosemary had said a funny thing a while back about Aunt Lucy. She'd said it to Uncle Michael and Helen had overheard her, but she hadn't been able to understand what it meant. She'd repeated it to her parents that night at teatime, hoping they'd explain, flinging the remark out as a statement rather than a question.

'Auntie Rosemary says that if it hadn't been for the shotgun Aunt Lucy would never have married Uncle Brian.'

At first, her parents hadn't said anything. They'd just stared at her, and then her daddy had whispered, 'Merciful God!' Her mammy went bright pink and started to shout. 'What sort of thing is that to say? Don't let me ever hear talk like that from you again, Helen!' But her daddy had quickly interrupted her. 'Don't go blaming the innocent child, Emily,' he'd said. 'Put the blame where it's due.' Their mammy stopped talking and looked at her plate. Now it was really interesting.

'What did Auntie Rosemary mean?' Kate piped up.

'I don't know,' their mammy said, but they knew this wasn't true. Their daddy had passed his hands wearily over his eyes. 'I know what she meant,' he said. Their daddy always told the truth, and he often explained things. 'What she meant was something very unkind and uncharitable, and if I told you what it meant, I'd be doing something unkind too. You must promise not to ask about this again, and you must promise above all never to say anything about it to Uncle Brian or Auntie Lucy. Promise?'

They promised.

Then their mammy had said, 'Sorry,' to their daddy, and he'd shook his head and said, 'It's not your fault any more than the child's. Let's just forget all about it.'

But Kate was bold. One day after that when Aunt Lucy was sitting plucking a mallard Helen heard Kate ask, 'Before you married Uncle Brian, did you know he liked shooting things?' She stopped working for a moment and looked puzzled. 'I don't rightly remember. I suppose I knew most men in the country went shooting then. I don't think I thought too much about it; it didn't bother me one way or the other.' Helen trod hard on Kate's toe under the table. Kate scowled at her and pulled her foot away, but she didn't ask any more questions.

The wind blew the rain hard against the windows of the classroom. Nights like this were good to go out shooting, their daddy said, and it was good weather for the men to catch eels. The best time of all for that was a stormy night in November. Sometimes their daddy would go over to Uncle Brian's house for a tea of fried eels, because their mammy wouldn't cook them. She said they stank you out of house and home for a week, and that if you'd given her a thousand pounds into her hand, she wouldn't have been able to skin an eel. Her daddy didn't mind: he said eels were probably something you had to be reared to, otherwise you wouldn't like them.

She turned the pages of her book again. Annie Oakley. Big Chief Sitting Bull. Davy Crockett. Willy Larkin wasn't concentrating on his book either. Suddenly he leaned over and whispered, 'Why has Davy Crockett got three ears?'

'Why?'

'Because he's got a right ear and a left ear and a wild frontier.'

'Willy and Helen, what are you tittering about?'

'Nothing, Miss.' They pretended to be interested in their books again. Helen sneaked a look at the watch she'd been given last Christmas. Twenty more minutes to go.

She was looking forward to the weekend, because their daddy was taking them into Ballymena to buy new water boots. They'd probably have to call and see Granny Kelly too: that wouldn't be so nice, especially if Uncle Michael was there. She wondered if Sally would be well enough to go with them tomorrow, because she'd had one of her nosebleeds this morning. Helen had been called out of class to go and comfort her. Sally's teacher had made her lie on the floor and had put the cold iron key of the school gate on the back of her neck. Sally had made a big fuss about it, but the bleeding had stopped, and she'd looked better when Helen saw her again at lunchtime.

She wished that the bell would ring so that they could go home, although usually she liked school. She was the best in the class, Miss Wilson said; she got the best marks in everything and she had the neatest handwriting. The only thing she wasn't very good at was spelling. Up at the front of the classroom there was a poster covered with lots of small pieces of paper, and at the top Miss Wilson had written in big letters 'Our First Day With Ink'. From where she sat, Helen could pick out her own work, blotless and exact. Over by the window was the nature table. There was a bird's nest on it, and the broken shells of a blackbird's eggs that someone had found. There was a wasp's nest too, and then jam-jars with twigs in them, and a label glued on each to say what the twigs were: horse-chestnut, hips, haws, hazel, snow-berries. The fruits were all wrinkled because the nature table was beside a radiator. On the window-sills were pots of geraniums and busy Lizzies. At breaktime every day when the children were drinking their milk Miss Wilson had some tea. Between break and lunch she would leave the tea pot aside, and then as soon as the bell went for lunch and they'd finished saying the Angelus, she'd pour the cold tea into the flower pots, until it seeped out into the saucers.

At last! One of the bigger boys or girls was ringing a handbell down the corridor, and everybody in Helen's class got up from their desks. They packed their books into their bags and put their chairs upside-down on their desks. The board was wiped clean while Colette and Anthony brushed the floor, because it was their turn to do it. They all gabbled a quick prayer to their guardian angel to look after them when they were on the way home from school; then ran out to the cloakroom to change their shoes and put on their coats.

The next morning, when they were getting ready to go into Ballymena, Helen said to her mammy flat out, 'I don't like going to see Granny Kelly.' Their mammy, who was wiping Sally's face with a damp flannel, pretended to be shocked. 'That's a terrible thing to say, Helen.'

'Well, you don't like it, do you? You hardly ever come with us. It's always Daddy who takes us to see her. Why don't you come with us today?'

'Oh, I can't go to Ballymena,' she said, uncurling Sally's fists and wiping the palms. 'I have too much to do; I have to mind the house.' Sally was whinging because she didn't want to go either, she wanted to stay with Mammy.

In the car on the way there Helen sat in the front because she was the eldest, and as they drove along she tried her father with the same remark. 'I don't like visiting Granny Kelly.'

'Neither do I,' he said.

'Why?' she asked, and he thought for a moment before replying. 'Because she doesn't like me. Your granny was cross with me for marrying your mammy. Mammy had been to the college in Belfast and worked hard and got all the exams to be a teacher, like her daddy had been, and Granny Kelly wanted that more than anything else in the world. And then as soon as your mammy got out of the college she met me and wanted to get married.'

'Couldn't she have done both? Worked and still got married?'

'Then who would have looked after you when you came along?'

Helen thought about this. Aunt Lucy was still working in the cigarette factory, but then she had Granny Kate to look after the baby and mind the house until Johnny and Declan and Una got home from school. 'I don't suppose Granny Kelly could have come and lived with us and looked after us,' she said uncertainly.

'What do you think?' her daddy said, looking at her sideways. 'Would you have liked that?'

'Oh, I like things just as they are,' Helen said quickly, and her daddy laughed.

'So do I,' he said.

Helen often used to think how, if one of her grannies had died before she had known them, she would have been left with a very limited idea of what a granny was. If she had known only Granny Kelly, she would have thought that all grannies were sad and forbidding, that they dressed only in black and lived sunk in deep chairs in dank parlours. If she'd only had Granny Kate to go by, she'd have thought a granny was someone who liked big hats and bright clothes, who always had a book or a magazine propped behind the taps of the kitchen sink when she was peeling potatoes, who couldn't pass a pram without stopping to admire the baby in it, and who had a fat, juicy laugh, so loud you could hear it through thick walls and closed doors.

Granny Kelly lived in a grey-painted terraced house with huge bay windows, not far from the centre of Ballymena. It was Auntie Rosemary who opened the door and led them into the dim parlour, where Granny Kelly was sitting. Helen felt a pain in her tummy, the sort you got when the teacher asked you a question and you didn't know the answer, and you knew she was going to be cross, because you should have known. She sat down on the sofa between Kate and Sally. One reason they didn't like visiting Granny Kelly was that it was so boring. Usually their cousins were out when they called, and they weren't as much fun as Uncle Brian's family anyway. They had no garden, no dogs or cats, and the television was never turned on when they were there. Very occasionally Kate or Helen would be called upon to recite a poem they had learnt at school, or to play something on the tinny piano, but in general, all they had to do was sit for an hour like pins in paper and behave themselves. Sometimes as she talked to their father Granny Kelly would stare hard at one of the girls, as if she didn't know who you were, and she was trying to find out by looking at you hard, from your shoes to your hair-ribbons. Helen hated this, for by the time Granny Kelly turned her stare upon one of the others, Helen would feel guilty of all sorts of things she hadn't done. She'd feel her face go red, and she would want to say, 'It wasn't me,' even though nobody had accused her of anything.

Auntie Rosemary sat a few moments and then went off to the kitchen. No sooner had she gone out than Uncle Michael came in. 'Hello, Charlie, hello, girls. Emily didn't come with you? Ah well. How's Kate? How's Sally? Well, Helen, how many slaps did you get at school this week?'

'None,' she said sullenly.

'Helen's a good scholar,' her father said, smiling at her. Uncle Michael made the same silly joke every time she saw him. 'What are you going to be when you grow up?' he went on. Helen knew the answer to this, but she wasn't quite sure how you said the word.

'I'm going to be an e- . . . an e- . . . '

'An eejit? Sure you're that already,' he interrupted her, and burst out with laughter at his own joke. Even Granny gave a nasty little smile. The feeling in the pit of Helen's stomach was worse now, but she was angry, too.

'Someone who goes to Egypt,' she said, as coldly as she could, 'and looks for mummies.'

'Sure your mammy's at home in the house,' he said, pretending to be baffled, and giving Granny Kelly a wink. 'What do you want to go off to Egypt for?'

'Not mammies, *mummies*,' said Kate, who always stuck up for Helen. 'They're people that have been dead for thousands of years, and they're all wrapped up in bandages, and they have lovely jewellery and some of them have a thing on them like a false face only it's made out of solid gold. Isn't that right, Helen?'

'Yes,' said Helen faintly, sorry now she'd ever brought up the subject. She should have said she wanted to be a teacher, then they'd have left her alone.

'Helen's going to do great things altogether,' said her father, smiling proudly at her.

'Oh, she'll put all that nonsense out of her head as soon as she grows up,' Granny Kelly said. 'First man looks twice at her, be he selling blades on a street corner, she'll be off after him, and you'll hear no more talk of her great ideas, you mark my words.'

Nobody said anything for a moment then: their father looked stunned and Sally whimpered into the silence because she knew something was wrong. At the sound of the tea tray tinkling in the hall, Uncle Michael leapt up to open the door for Aunt Rosemary.

There was a mug for Sally in with the cups and saucers, because the last time they'd been there, she had spilt her tea in her lap. Kate helped her little sister, unfolding a paper napkin for her while the plates of tomato and cheese sandwiches circulated. Tea in Granny Kelly's house didn't count as real food, it was just another exercise to make sure you knew the rules, and that you kept them, too. You had to have a respectable number of sandwiches before you could have something sweet, and then you had to choose the most unappealing biscuit on the plate, unless urged to go for something nicer (which you almost never were). Helen dreaded being given no option but to eat a piece of Aunt Rosemary's seed cake ever since the day Kate had remarked that not only did it look like it had mouse shit in it, it tasted like it too. But her luck was in today, for when the plate came to them there was one pink wafer left, which Kate took, and some Rich Tea biscuits, which Helen was content enough to accept.

As the adults chatted, more warily now, Helen gazed around the room. Even though there was a fire burning in the grate, the parlour always felt cold, perhaps because there were so many glass things in it: a glass-topped table with a biscuit-coloured linen runner on it; a china cabinet containing ornaments and the tea sets people had given Uncle Michael and Auntie Rosemary when they had got married, and a glass vase, which never had flowers in it. Over the fire there hung a framed picture of Grandad Kelly, and even though he had died ever such a long time ago, when their mammy was herself a child, his presence hung over the family in a way Helen couldn't fully understand, because he was seldom spoken of. She couldn't help imagining he must have been a rather terrifying person, if only because he'd been married to Granny Kelly. Her idea of her other grandfather was completely different, perhaps because she could faintly remember him, or because Granny Kate was always talking about him, telling them funny stories and then the tears would stand in her eyes, even while she was laughing and saying things like 'God, but there wasn't an ounce of harm in Francis, so there wasn't!' She used to wonder how her mother had borne her father's death, because the very worst thing Helen could imagine was losing either of her parents. Once she'd asked her mother about it, very timidly, and she'd looked so sad when she said, 'Oh yes, Helen, it was terrible. It made all the difference to me, all the difference in the world.'

His teaching certificate, with an impressive red seal on it, hung in an alcove, and his books, which no one ever read now, were locked in a glass-fronted bookcase. He'd been the headmaster in a little school up near Ballycastle, and on the mantelpiece was the handbell he'd used to ring, to call the children back from the playground when it was time for lessons again. Helen didn't even like to look at the bell, because it reminded her of the uproar there'd been one day when Kate picked it up and rang it. First, there'd been the hard metal clang of the bell, shockingly loud in the dim room, then Granny Kelly's cold fury at such a piece of boldness, then Kate crying with shame and hurt at the scolding she got, then Helen crying because Kate cried and Sally starting to howl, and their father putting his head in his hands: oh, that was the most horrible thing to remember! She looked away quickly from the bell, back at the picture of Grandad Kelly which hung over the fire. He didn't look stern or forbidding in the picture, but puzzled, quizzical.

Once, when they were on holiday at Portrush, their daddy had driven them round the coast to see Grandad Kelly's school. Tucked away in a green fold of the hills, it was a white-washed building with a blue door and high windows. Beside the school was the teacher's cottage, where their mammy had lived when she was small, with her parents and Uncle Michael. It was a lovely place, Helen thought: there were sheep in the fields and drystone walls, and all along the roadside there were hedges of wild fuchsia, purple and dark red. The sea crashed in the distance, and the wind had been blowing.

It was strange to think of the brightness there'd been there when you were sitting now in a chilly, dim parlour. A small lamp was lit on a table beside Granny Kelly, and the only other light in the room was whatever managed to seep in through the long cream blinds which were drawn against the sky. Granny Kelly had to sit in the dark all the time because she had bad eyes, and suddenly Helen thought how horrible that must be for her. No wonder she was grumpy. If Helen was old and stiff and had to wear black clothes all the time and sit in the dark, she would probably be irritable too. That was what Granny Kate was always saying, that you could never really know what it was like to be another person, and because of that, it was wrong for you to judge them. Only God could judge, because only God could see into people's hearts.

But what a relief it was when their father looked at his watch and stood up! Then, their goodbyes made, they stepped into the street, and it was as if they'd been in the house for a week, rather than an hour or so. Even though it was a day in winter and it was starting to rain out of a cloudy sky, it still seemed bright and fresh to be out in the air again.

They got their wellingtons: black ones for Helen and Kate, red ones for Sally, their daddy and the shop assistant anxiously pressing the toes of each in turn to make sure that the fit was right. Kate would have liked to have red wellies too, but they didn't have them in her size. They did some other bits and pieces of shopping, and then he took them into a café and bought them sausage and chips and a bottle of Fanta each, while he had some more tea and a piece of apple pie, and smoked a cigarette. He looked much happier than he had done earlier.

'I hope I'm not like Granny Kelly when I get old,' Kate said, shaking the ketchup bottle over her chips.

'Oh, there'll be no fear of that,' their daddy said. 'You'll be like your Granny Kate, you're as like as two peas in a pod, so you are.'

Kate beamed. 'Helen'll be like Granny Kelly, then,' she said impishly.

'I will not!' Helen protested, but their daddy just smiled. 'Ah, Helen'll be her own woman, won't you, love?'

After that he bought them a comic each, and a quarter of sweets that were weighed out for them from glass jars: Clove

sweet moment
w/dad

Rock for Helen, Cherry Lips for Kate, Jelly Babies for Sally. He also bought a box of Milk Tray chocolates for their mammy.

Sally slept in the car on the way home, while Kate read her comic. Helen, who was in her usual place in the front seat, would have liked to have read hers too, but she thought it was more polite to talk to her daddy and keep him company. She liked the journey, anyway, especially the part where you came over the top of Roguery, and far below you could see Lough Neagh, and over to the right was Lough Beg, that their daddy called The Wee Lough, and in the distance were the mountains. When you came over this road at night, it looked like you were driving towards some huge city, because of all the lights, but during the day you could see that it was all just a scattering of small towns, villages and isolated farms.

She wondered if their mammy would be waiting for them, and as the car pulled up at the front of the house they could see her face look out anxiously from behind the parlour curtains.

Chapter Five

MONDAY

She rang David at his home rather than at the television studio, because if he was at work at this time of day it meant he wouldn't be able to see her this evening, so there was no point in contacting him there. She was relieved when she heard his voice on the other end of the line, brisk and distant as he said his number, and warming immediately when he realised who was calling him.

'Helen, how are you?'

'I'm fine,' she said, stiffly. It was a sort of code that had evolved between them, so that David would automatically realise that she wasn't alone, would probably guess, correctly, that Owen, the solicitor with whom Helen worked, was near by and couldn't but overhear her conversation. What David couldn't know was that Helen was particularly sensitive about this today because she'd blundered a few hours earlier, having had a loud, tactless row with her mother, losing her temper and shouting down the phone in such a way that Owen was bound to hear her, even though he was in the next room. She'd felt embarrassed and repentant as soon as she hung up, and as a result was perhaps overly cautious now.

'I wondered if you'd like to come over for an hour or so this evening.'

'Are you in poor form?' he asked.

'Oh, I've known better, I must say,' she replied, in even tones, frowning and doodling tight black grids with heavy pressure on the telephone pad.

He said he would love to come. 'Steve's off in London this week, so I'm here on my own anyway.'

'I can send out for a Chinese.' She heard him swearing on the other end of the line, and smiled. 'No, wait, I think there's a sort of a pie thing in the fridge. Or did I eat that? I can't remember.'

'I'll tell you this, I'm not eating it, even if it is still there. Leave the food to me.'

'I've got some really good wine.'
'You reckon?'
'It was a present.' Any other time, she would have told him that Cate had brought it over from London for her, but today she didn't want to mention her sister. 'It's Bordeaux.'
'What year?'
Helen laughed. 'How the hell do I know? It's out in the car, I can't remember. Anyway, we can drink it tonight. Oh, and about the food, best make it something simple, something that needs hardly any cooking, eh?'
'Don't worry. I've seen your kitchen.'
'See you sometime after seven, all right?'
'Seven's great. 'Bye.'
It was shortly after six-thirty when Helen pulled into the parking bay in front of her house. As was usual on a Monday she had luggage to take from the boot, having gone straight to work from her family home that morning. The car blipped when she locked it. Helen lived in a development of upmarket townhouses, just off the Ormeau Road. 'It's a sort of housing estate, to be honest about it,' she used to say, which always annoyed Owen, who lived in a similar place not far from Helen. She liked it, though, that her colleagues and friends lived near by: David and Steve were just a few streets away. She'd bought the house for financial motives, and the even more prosaic reason that she needed a place to live, but felt no emotional attachment to it whatsoever, nor did she ever want to. Even before she bought it she'd remarked to her mother that she thought it didn't have much character, and her mother had agreed: 'New houses never do.' But the horror of what had happened to their father had been compounded by it having taken place in Brian's house. She remembered then a dream she had had, years ago, when she was at university, of watching Brian's house burning down, and weeping because she would never be able to go there again. And now, even though the house was intact, it was lost to her. She grew to appreciate the very sterility of the place in Belfast: having moved in as soon as the builders moved out she was confident that it was, psychically, a blank.
She could have done more to make it more comfortable inside: she knew that. It was too sparsely furnished. 'There's nothing

actually wrong with it,' Cate had said, the last time she had been there, 'it's just that there's not enough of it.' She was right, Helen thought, the combination of clinical neatness in the main room with the chilly atmosphere always struck her particularly strongly after she had been home for the weekend. She knew she needed more pictures, more rugs, more *things*, it was just a question of wanting to have them, and of taking the time and trouble to go out and get them.

She took the bottles of wine out and set them on the table in the main room, then took her bags upstairs to change out of her work clothes. Anyone seeing her bedroom (and she took great care that no one ever did) would have been amazed by the contrast with the rest of the house. She pushed the door open, and had to push hard, against a pile of newspapers and political magazines which had toppled over and blocked the way. She picked her path carefully over a floor littered with unwashed coffee cups, compact discs, books and stray shoes, to the bed, where she upended her luggage, and shook out the contents; then rummaged for her sweatshirt, trainers and jeans. She changed into these, and then, in the wardrobe at the top of the stairs, where she carefully stored the sober clothes she kept for work, she hung up the suit she had been wearing. Most evenings, she would eat something quick in the kitchen and then come upstairs for the rest of the night. She had a television here, and a CD player, and an armchair she particularly liked: an old one her mother had given her when she bought the new suite for the parlour.

As she came back into the room, she picked up a CD of Bach cantatas, and put it into the machine. Music was her personal obsession. She shared with David a fondness for old movies; shared it literally in that they used to get together sometimes and watch *film noir* videos, although that happened a lot less often now ever since Steve had moved in with him. But music was something for herself alone, and it was something she needed. She sat now, lost in the pure, formal structures of the cantatas, looking up in annoyance when the doorbell suddenly rang and wondering who it could be, until she remembered David.

'Are you sure you're ready for this?' she said to him, standing by the closed kitchen door. David nodded.

'I've long since known that your idea of running a house is to go to Crazy Prices and buy a load of cheese and fruit and stuff, bring it home, stick it in the fridge, and then send out for pizzas every night. Then when the things in the fridge have rotted past all recognition, you put them in the bin and start all over again. I keep telling you, there's more to it than that.'

Helen smiled sadly. 'You're wrong. I've been cooking, you see, that's the problem.' She threw open the kitchen door, and even David's eyes widened at the sight of the overflowing bin, the sticky hob, the brimming sink, where a forest of saucepan handles projected from the greasy water. Helen pulled out the grill pan, as if that might be clean and would redeem her, but it was full of congealed fat. She pulled a face, and slotted the grill back into the cooker.

'See your house?' David said. 'It's like a wee palace, so it is.'

In the months immediately after her father's death, Helen had socialised frantically because she was afraid of being alone with her grief. Sympathetic friends and colleagues asked her round to dinner, or suggested going out for an evening's drinking, and she accepted every invitation on the spot, including one to a Christmas party at Owen's house. It was at this party that she met David, whom she recognised from television, but also from having seen him on occasion in restaurants or hotel bars around the city, and in the press gallery at the court. When they were introduced, she acknowledged him curtly. The evening was interrupted constantly by Owen's and his wife Mary's little son howling over the baby alarm system, until Mary finally admitted defeat and carried the child into the room where the party was going on. As soon as he had been deposited in his playpen, he stopped crying and became contentedly occupied with the toys which were there. David and Helen watched him pick up a red plastic cup and turn it over in his hands, gazing at it with total absorption, as though it were the most fascinating object imaginable. Suddenly the baby dropped the red cup and picked up a blue plastic brick. The red cup rolled away, forgotten, while the baby looked at the new object with the same consuming interest it had had for the cup a few moments earlier.

'Maybe he'll be a journalist when he grows up,' Helen said.
'What makes you say that?'
'He's got the right sort of attention span.'
'I take it you don't think much of journalists, then?'
'Most of the time I don't know how they live with themselves.'
'You know you're being unfair,' he said.
'Am I?' Helen replied, but she noticed he looked hurt, which was disconcerting, when she'd simply set out to annoy him. She didn't wait for him to reply, she shrugged and turned away.

When she went home that night, she lay awake for a long time, brooding upon how her father's murder had been treated by the media, a subject which fed in her a deep slow anger. There'd been the day after the funeral when she'd gone to McGovern's in Timinstown to buy some groceries, and there on the counter, on the front of one of the Northern Ireland newspapers, was a photograph of herself and Sally with their arms around each other weeping at the graveside. She'd felt sick, dizzy, furious all at once, she felt her face change colour. Mrs McGovern, embarrassed on her behalf, leant over and folded the paper to hide the photo. 'Wouldn't you think they'd know people had been through enough without doing things like that,' she said, and Helen had stared at her, unable to speak. Then Rosemary and Michael had called round to see them later that day, and Rosemary told them, rather shamefacedly, that while they were at the burial a young woman had come up to her and said, 'Poor Cate's taking it badly, isn't she?' Because of the familiar way she spoke, Rosemary assumed she must be a close friend of the sisters, and replied, 'Yes, but Helen's taking it worst of all, if you ask me.' She was shocked when, a short time later, she saw the woman writing in a notebook, and realised that she was a reporter, not a family friend. But worst of all had been the British tabloids, where the death was reported coldly and without sympathy, much being made of Brian's Sinn Fein membership, and the murder having taken place in his house. The inference was that he had only got what was coming to him. At their mother's insistence they'd made a formal complaint which was rejected. Helen had known it would be: her legal knowledge told her, after a close study of the texts, that they'd been damn clever: the tone was hostile, but no specific accusations were made, it was guilt by association. But they all took it to heart, especially their mother, a person for whom bitterness had hitherto been an unknown thing.

The morning after the party, Helen thanked Owen for having asked her along.

'Ah, give me a break, you had a lousy night, admit it. I saw you getting stuck into David McKenna. He's not a bad guy, Helen, believe me. He's had hard times himself.'

'You're breaking my heart,' Helen murmured.

'Listen to me: Mary's known him since they were children, they grew up in the same street.' Usually, Owen and Mary didn't like to talk about Mary's background. Helen knew that she'd started out in a tiny terraced house in a street off the lower Falls; knew too that it wasn't to be mentioned, so she was surprised at what Owen said. 'David's father was shot too, a man that never was in anything, and David was just a wee fella when it happened. His mother was left with five of them to rear. Nobody knows better than I do why you don't like journalists, and you're right, insofar as some of them are arseholes of the first order. But David's a decent guy. He's not the worst, not by a long chalk.'

Helen heard Owen out in silence. She thought about what he had said on and off during the day, and when they were closing up the office that evening, she asked for David's phone number.

'I owe you an apology,' she said, when she rang him that night.

'I know you do,' David replied. 'You owe me an explanation, too, and if you've any decency you'll buy me a drink.' She was grateful for his hard, dry tone, for she'd had a bellyful of people oozing sympathy at her by this stage; and when they did get together a few nights later in a city-centre pub, the tone was still sharp and unsentimental. They ordered two double Bushmills, for which Helen paid.

'I know what happened to your father,' he said bluntly. 'I saw the reports. Now I'm going to tell you about what happened to mine. He was an electrician, and he worked some of the time with another man, a friend of his, who was a carpenter. They were going to a job just outside the city, up in Hannahstown, one morning in winter, and they were ambushed. Their van was forced over to the side of the road, they were taken out, shot in the head and left there. Nobody was ever arrested or charged for it. My da's friend was in the IRA, a big shot, as it turned out. He had a huge paramilitary funeral. My father wasn't in the IRA or in anything else. He left five kids. I was the eldest; I was twelve. He was the same age that I am now, thirty-six. My mother was nearly demented. She told me later it wasn't just that she missed my father, it was more than the loneliness, although there was that. They'd got on great together; I don't ever remember them arguing or fighting. She told me she'd been terrified at the prospect of bringing up five children on her own, having to provide for us and get us educated and keep us out of trouble. Anyhow, that's another story in itself. The thing was, in the press reports of the case, my father got tarred with the same brush as your man, they made no distinction between them. As far as the papers were concerned, they were two terrorists, they got what they deserved, nobody was going to waste any sympathy on people like that. It really upset my father's brother, and it really upset me. I was only a child, but I knew that it wasn't true, and it wasn't fair. My uncle wanted to make some sort of complaint, but my mother told him to forget about it. "Who's going to care about the likes of us," she said, "that hasn't two cold pennies to rub together? Do you think the people that write things in the paper care what we think or feel? I have enough to be doing, left sitting with a houseful of children, without wasting my time making complaints that they'll only be laughing at behind my back." So I decided that when I grew up, I was going to be a journalist, that there was going to be at least one person who was telling the truth.' He laughed. 'Hell, I was only twelve, after all!'

'One thing I hadn't properly thought through until my father was killed was how hard it is for the emergency services. No matter what training they have, or how well suited they are to their jobs, it must grind them down, the things they have to face.'

'You're telling me,' David said. 'People don't know the half of it.'

It was a priest who had broken the news to Helen's mother and Sally. After Brian, he'd been the first person to arrive at the house. He was a curate, in his early twenties, who had only been ordained in the spring of that year; a banker's son who had grown up in a comfortable home in County Down, who had won a gold medal for Greek at university and spent a year in Rome. He was gentle and idealistic and kind-hearted, and he had never in his life seen anything like what he found in Brian's and Lucy's kitchen that night in late October. Sally told Helen afterwards how sorry they'd felt for him, his voice breaking as he tried to comfort them; his own serenity and peace clearly having been shattered by what he had seen.

'I suppose that's one thing I was lucky in from the start,' David went on, 'if you can call it lucky. I knew from the first that what was going on here wasn't exciting or glamorous. In fairness, I don't think any of the local reporters think that. They mostly grew up here, so they know the score. You get a lot of foreign journalists over here for a while when things get particularly bad, but as conflicts go, it's never been fashionable. Maybe in the sixties, early seventies, it was different, when there was a lot of street fighting, riots, but as far as the rest of the world, and the world media are concerned, it's too localised. The background isn't exotic enough, and anyway, it's never been a full-blown war. There's nothing to get gung-ho about in a body being found in a wet lane somewhere in, say, Tyrone, on a cold, bad night.' He admitted that you got cynical working there. When the number of people who had been killed was one off a round figure, you found yourself thinking about what you would say in a day or two, when the figure was reached. A photographer friend to whom he had said this remarked, 'Well, touch wood always that it won't be you.'

'But there's something about the whole nature of it,' Helen argued, 'about taking things and making stories about them, and that's all it amounts to: making up stories out of a few facts, and presenting them as though that interpretation was the absolute truth. That's what I can't stand.'

'But what do you want instead? Do you want nothing to be known? Would you really have preferred it if your father's death had been ignored? All news journalists are aware of the problems inherent in journalism, believe me. Trying to get the right balance, in cases like the one you're talking about, between reporting accurately and honestly on the one hand, and maintaining people's dignity, and not making them suffer any more on the other: that's a key issue in the whole undertaking, and everybody knows that.'

'I don't believe you,' she said. 'I think a lot of reporters couldn't care less. They have no empathy, no imagination. The medium is a blunt weapon in itself, that's the problem. It isn't fitted to dealing with complexity, it isn't comfortable with paradox or contradiction, and that's the heart of the problem, if you ask me.'

They had argued about this issue many times since that first night, and the most she would concede, even now, was that it was a necessary evil. 'It's like politics,' she said, 'in that it attracts people of dubious merit. If you've got any kind of decency or scruples, you wouldn't want to get involved in it in the first place, and to get on in either field, you need to have negative qualities, qualities that wouldn't be to your credit in any other capacity. But,' she granted, as he started to protest, 'there are exceptions. I will grant you that there are people in both journalism and politics who got involved from the best of motives, who are genuinely committed to being a force for change, a force for good, who weren't just interested in maintaining the status quo or feathering their own nests.' He'd told her that he'd never wanted to work for a newspaper in Northern Ireland, that it was just preaching to the converted, every side buying and reading the papers that expressed their own prejudices.

She wondered how he managed without being more cynical than he was as she followed his reports over the coming months. He lacked the complete coldness she'd noted in other journalists she knew, where professionalism was all, and it didn't matter if it was a killing or a Van Morrison concert they were covering, so long as it was a good story, smoothly presented.

One evening, about six months after they had first met, David rang and asked if he could come over to see her. He told her that something had happened and he didn't want to be by himself for the evening, nor with colleagues. She told him he was welcome; when he arrived she made coffee and let him tell her in his own good time what had happened.

'It was a story I had to cover this afternoon,' he said. 'I didn't think after all I've seen in the line of duty that anything could throw me again like this, so that's a shock, apart from anything else.'

'What was the story?' Helen said. She didn't look at him. As he continued to talk she wondered if he was going to start to cry.

'Your man they killed last night. Protestant, living in a mixed area, drives a taxi cab, gets a fare that forces him out of his own territory, gets his head blown off. Fucker in the office says this morning, "Well, place he lived, job he did, what else could he expect?" Christ, I tore into him for that! So this afternoon I had to go out to interview the widow. She wanted to talk to the media, wanted to appeal directly that there be no retaliation. She's sitting on a sofa in her house, with her three children and her mother, and every one of them done in from crying. The woman's as much bewildered as anything; keeps asking, "What am I going to do, left with three kids? How am I going to manage?" And I mean really asking, as if the cameraman or the guy doing the sound might be able to give her some sort of practical answer. My mother said exactly the same thing when my father was shot. It brought it all back.' He put his head in his hands for a moment, and they sat in silence. 'It was like seeing again what had happened to our family, only now as an adult, I can *really* see what it means. There's something about it that . . . that never stops or ends. Do you know what I mean?'

Helen did.

'When I came out of the house, I was shaking. I tried not to let the others see. I thought, I can't do this job any more. I can't go to another funeral, or talk to another widow, or to parents that have had a child killed, I just can't, Helen.'

Helen knew that he could, and she also knew that now was not the time to say it. She knew that by the next morning, he would regard this as weakness; that was why he had chosen to come to her. For she knew the same feeling of weary depression which came from working in a relentlessly negative atmosphere. From her work and her life she knew the fate of both the victims and the perpetrators, and both were dreadful.

The following morning, when she turned on the radio, she heard that a Catholic man had been killed, down in the Markets area. The UFF said it was in retaliation for the killing of the taxi driver.

Almost a year later, Helen said to David, 'Do you remember that man who was killed, the taxi driver? They've charged somebody with it, a young guy, Oliver Maguire.'

'So I heard.'

'We're defending him.'

Helen had once commented to Cate that what she liked least about being in her thirties was how it became harder to make friends. Even without their realising it, people's lives shut like flowers at dusk, became set in the cement of career, marriage, children, mortgage, pension funds and life insurance. When you were in your twenties, things were still undecided, but by the time people turned thirty, choices had been made; hopes and plans had either worked out or had not. People began to assess if those they knew had done as well as they expected them to; and admired their successes or shunned their failure accordingly. Similarly, they looked to others to console and support them in their fate; and this anxious assessment of peers was no less thorough for usually being unconscious. One thing was certain: it certainly took its toll of friendships. Helen found that her relations with people she'd known since university cooled and waned in accordance with these social laws which, she grew to realise, were as strict as the laws of physics.

With childhood friends, it was different. No matter what social differences there were, differences of class, career or income, there was the absence of some sort of obstruction, which was always there with others. She still felt at ease with her cousins, or people like Willy Larkin, with whom she'd gone to school, and whom she would sometimes meet when she was down home at the weekend. Perhaps it was simply that if you'd known people when they were children, you'd known them at their most vunerable, and you never forgot it.

As for David, the strange thing was that their friendship did have that same quality. Perhaps because his childhood had ended so abruptly it had a particular significance, and he had an uncanny facility for remembering and describing it so vividly that it filled in Helen's own slight knowledge of the city as it was in the nineteen sixties. She didn't reciprocate by telling him about her own childhood. She suspected that David wouldn't have been particularly interested, and that suited her, because she preferred to keep it private, to herself and her sisters.

The other significant thing which suggested a particular closeness between them was that they were able to fight with each other: they could trade insults without any danger of the friendship being spoiled. Helen criticised him for his vanity over his looks and clothes, a matter which went far beyond the mere need to be well turned out for his job. There was nothing he liked better than being recognised in public. The first time it happened when he was in Helen's company, she could scarcely believe that his naïve delight was for real: 'Look! Those people are staring at us and whispering to each other! They've recognised me, they know who I am. Don't stare, pretend we haven't noticed them.'

'They're probably saying what a clapped-out old wreck you are in the flesh, compared to how you look on television,' Helen said. She took him to task for his nervousness (and he conceded that he had a problem with this), so that she would physically wrench from his hands the paper napkin he was absent-mindedly shredding, or the flower he was taking apart. She in her turn would take things from him in the vein of 'There's a wee nun in you, a real wee prim prig of a nun, so there is,' or he would tell her she was a slob and needed someone to take her in hand and sort her out, only she was so damn grumpy that it was no wonder people weren't exactly queueing up for the job. 'Piss off,' she would say, and he'd reply, 'You see what I mean?'

While David was preparing the food, Helen wondered what, if anything, she would say to him about Cate. He was sure to ask why she had felt down in the afternoon, and there was no point in trying to fob him off with a lie, because David always knew at once when she wasn't telling the truth. Of course she would talk to him about it, perhaps even at some length, because they shared all their worries frankly, but it was too soon, she thought. It wasn't just that if she talked to him about it before she had had a chance to talk to Cate, she would be betraying her sister. It was also that she didn't know how Cate herself felt about things, that if she were simply to say, 'Cate's pregnant,' it would sound banal, and Helen wasn't at all sure that it was banal, and if it wasn't, then what was it? She wondered how Cate herself saw it, and suspected that she would be secretly delighted, even if she was, for a day or so, for form's sake, pretending to go along with her mother's view that Cate had been overtaken by calamity. Thinking of this reminded her of her mother, and she cringed to think of how she had spoken to her earlier that day. She went upstairs to her bedroom, and phoned home. Sally answered.

'I'm glad you called, I wanted to ring you later anyway.'

'I wanted to tell Mammy I'm sorry for shouting at her earlier.'

'I'll pass on the message, but to tell you the truth, it's the best thing you could have done. It worked like a charm,' Sally said coolly. 'I've banned Cate's situation as a subject of conversation for the rest of the night, and I'll make sure we all get a good night's sleep. What I wanted to ask you is would it be all right for Cate to go to Belfast tomorrow and stay the night with you?'

'Of course, no problem. Tell her to call at my office for a key, so that she can let herself in if she gets here before I get home from work.'

'Thanks a million, Helen. I just want Mammy to have a bit of time apart from Cate right now, to get used to the idea of what's happening, and I want to have time to talk to her by herself.'

'Are you sure that's wise?'

'Trust me, really, I know what I'm about. And listen, don't worry. Obviously there've been a lot of tears today, but it'll pass, everything'll be all right.'

Feeling much better from this than she would have expected, she went back to the living room, where David was finishing setting out plates of salads and cold meats. As she had expected, he was impressed with the wine.

'Cate gave it to me. She came home at the weekend. She's got problems at the moment, and we're all in a bit of a pother about it, but I'll tell you next time I see you.' He nodded, and didn't pursue the subject. 'How are things with Steve and yourself? You said he was off in London again.' David made a wry face and sighed.

'I don't know what to think, truly I don't. He's gone for a week. It's supposed to be for work, but I know that's just an excuse. I suppose I can only explain it by saying that things are exactly as they were in the past, only then it was a case of my going over there as often as I could to see him; and now it's a case of him going back as often as he can.'

Steve's introduction to Northern Ireland, and his eventual decision to live there, was something in which Helen had been implicated. Early on in their friendship, David told Helen he was involved with a man in London, whom he visited often because he was too afraid to come to Belfast. 'Keep asking,' Helen had said. 'He may change his mind in due course.' And finally, Steve did decide to risk a weekend trip.

But David wasn't as delighted by this as Helen had expected him to be. 'What if he hates it? Seeing soldiers all over the place; and the barracks all fortified and stuff; that's going to frighten the life out of him. And what if anything happens? I mean, what if a bomb goes off, or the car gets hijacked or something?'

'Look, this was your idea in the first place; you can't back out of it now,' Helen said. 'All you can do is plan it very carefully, and hope for the best.'

She offered to help him, so they got together and discussed at length the things it would be all right for Steve to see, and those from which he should absolutely be protected. Steve arrived the following Friday evening, and on Saturday morning Helen called round to David's house to be introduced.

'So how's it going?' Helen whispered when Steve was out of the room.

'Great, so far. No problems,' David whispered back. 'He didn't pay much heed to the checkpoint at the airport, and once we got on to the motorway, we just barrelled up to the city. My luck was in: you know what a marvellous evening it was yesterday. Belfast Lough was like glass, the sun was on the mountains, it couldn't have been better. Steve couldn't get over how beautiful it was, and that sort of made up for the city being so ugly when we got into it. He says it reminds him of Manchester, and fortunately, he likes Manchester. So far, so good. Let's just hope the weather holds.'

And the weather did hold, throughout the weekend. David rang Helen at work on Monday to say everything had gone according to plan. He'd taken Steve down to the Mournes on Saturday, and they'd had lunch in Newcastle. In Belfast, he'd put him in a snug at the Crown, with as much Guinness and as many oysters as he could manage.

'And nothing he saw freaked him out?'

'No, but he didn't realise how hard I was working to make sure he did see precious little. We saw a few jeeps of soldiers in the city centre, but he expected that. The thing is, he expected far more, far worse. No, I think we can say it's been an unqualified success.'

A few weeks later, David went over to London. On his return, he called to see Helen.

'I don't know how to tell you this,' he said, 'but I've been the victim of my own success. Steve wants to come and live here.'

'What should I say? Congratulations?'

'No!' he cried. 'This isn't what I wanted: not what I wanted at all. I just wanted him to feel good about coming over here from time to time.'

'He obviously liked Northern Ireland much more than you expected.'

David looked at her as if she had lost her mind. '*Liked*, Helen? How could he have liked it? He didn't even see it. Roscoffs, the Crown and the Mountains of Mourne: how can he decide on the strength of that?'

'Well then,' Helen said, after a moment's thought, 'you're just going to have to get him to come back and have another look, aren't you?' And she smiled.

A few weeks later, Steve returned. This time, when David collected him at the airport, he didn't drive into Belfast by the motorway, but went over the Divis mountain, through Turf Lodge and then down on to the Falls Road, pointing out the heavily fortified barracks and all the other things which, before, he would have been at pains to conceal. He parked outside the off-licence above which Helen had her office. 'Won't be a minute,' he said, locking Steve in the car. 'Don't go away.' An army foot patrol obligingly ambled past at that moment, and when David returned, Steve looked suitably anxious.

On the Saturday he took him back over to West Belfast, took him through the narrow web of streets, showed him the Republican murals on the gable walls around the lower Falls, then took him over to the Shankill and showed him the Loyalist murals.

The 'Peace Line', an ugly structure of corrugated iron and barbed wire, which separated the two communities, apparently shocked Steve more than anything else he saw. In Milltown Cemetery, David showed him the many IRA graves, and the Republican plot where Bobby Sands and some of the other hunger strikers were buried; and he pointed out how the gunman who attacked mourners at a funeral in 1987 would have been able to get into the lower part of the graveyard from the Loyalist 'Village'. The whole time David and Steve were in the cemetery, an army helicopter hovered directly overhead, and there was drizzling rain.

'It didn't work,' David told Helen a week later. 'He's still hellbent on coming to live here.' Steve was far from foolish. He said he'd been shocked and depressed by much he had seen, but he'd expected this: he knew the first visit had been utterly unrepresentative. 'Do you know what he said? "It strikes me that what's going on here is almost as much a class thing as a sectarian issue." Is that shrewd or what? And so he argued then that he wouldn't be exposed to the conflict very much, because he'd be safe in the part of town where I live.'

'So he hasn't even moved here yet and already he's trotting out the old line, "Where *I* live it's safe, but in such and such a place you could get shot at any moment"?'

David shrugged. 'Looks like it. He's fed up with London too. I suspect that's a really crucial point. He noticed the high standard of living here; saw how much money there is washing around in certain circles. He just couldn't believe the prices of property: you can get something really nice here for an absolute fraction of what you'd have to pay for something comparable anywhere in England, let alone London. He says he's sick of spending hours packed in the Tube going to his work every day; that London's filthy and dangerous now. No, Steve's decided that he wants out, and that he wants to come here.'

'Look on the bright side then: maybe he'll really like it here,' Helen said, but David shook his head.

'He'll get bored,' he said. 'It'll be all right for a while, and then he'll begin to miss London, no matter what he says. Believe me, I know him well. And get this: the chain of clothes shops he works for is opening a branch in Belfast and they need a manager to come over from England to set it up. Not surprisingly, people aren't exactly falling over themselves to apply, so he's in with a very good chance of getting the job.'

'Is it that you really don't want him to come over here?'

'No, it's just this: it won't work out. I know it won't work out.'

'And have you ever considered going to live in London?'

He stared at her with incomprehension. 'You are joking, aren't you? What about my work? What if . . . what if they packed me off to something like . . . like the fucking Lib. Dem. Party conference? Can you *imagine* it? Christ!'

And so Steve moved to Belfast and David was wrong only about the length of time it would take for the novelty to wear off. It was a good six months before Steve started to grumble, longer again before he started to make trips back to London.

'Is it anything in particular?' Helen asked now, over dinner, and David shook his head.

'It's just what I expected. I don't know what's going to happen now,' he said. 'Or maybe I do, and that's the problem.' Helen poured more wine into his glass. He was twisting the edge of a wicker tablemat out of shape, and he looked so miserable that, for once, she let him away with it.

'This is terrible,' he said. 'I thought the idea was that I came here to cheer you up. Tell you what, there's a documentary on TV tonight for the twenty-fifth anniversary of the start of the Troubles. We'll have a look at that; that'll lift our hearts.'

And the thing was, that it did: they watched with something between grief and hilarity the old black-and-white footage of marches and riots. The young women wore miniskirts and had long, straight hair; all the older women wore headscarfs.

'It all looks so old-fashioned, I just can't believe it,' Helen said. 'You just don't appreciate how things have changed until you see something like this.'

'But you can see too how it started,' David said. The people on the screen looked weary and put-upon: it would have been easy to believe that they were too cowed ever to be a threat, and they could imagine the shock it must have been when their patience broke.

'What do you think is the biggest difference between now and then?' Helen asked.

David replied unhesitatingly: 'We are. The educated Catholic middle class. I don't think anyone fully anticipated that, or thought through what it would mean, but it should have been easy to foresee.'

'People like that,' and she pointed at the screen, 'wouldn't have been able to believe that their children could come so far, so fast.'

'Some of their children,' he corrected her.

'I still remember it from school, how the nuns used to din it into us all the time: "Work hard, girls, because you have more to give society than you can perhaps realise. We need our Catholic doctors and nurses and university lecturers; our Catholic lawyers and civil servants." Did you get that line at your school?'

'Of course we did. There was far more along those lines than there was suggestion that we might go on for the Church. And it did make a difference, just as the IRA campaign has made more of a difference to changes in attitudes than most people are prepared to admit.'

It made Helen feel sad to look at the images on the screen. It had been like that, yet not like that: the pictures told only part of the story. She remembered the austerity, even though she hadn't been aware of it at the time, and she wondered how you ever got to the essence of things, of your time, your society, your self. It struck her as strange that out of her whole family, she, the only one whose life was supposedly dedicated to the administration of justice, was the only one who didn't believe in it as a spiritual fact, who perhaps didn't believe in it at all. Before the programme was over, she could no longer bear to watch it.

They put on a video, and finished the wine. David left around midnight, promising to give her a call towards the end of the week.

Chapter Six

As Sally grew up, she continued to be frail and weak, and much more hesitant than either of her sisters. The nosebleeds from which she suffered continued on and off, but the doctors said they could do nothing for her. They also said they thought it was nothing serious, and that she would probably grow out of it in a year or two. Granny Kate took a great interest in this, as she did in everything concerning her grandchildren. She got Charlie to drive her and Sally down to the monastery in Portglenone, to ask the monks to pray for her. Kate and Helen were left out of this trip, much to their annoyance. Sally came back, looking frightened and proud, holding a prayer book Granny had bought for her at the monastery. She had medals, blue ones, for her sisters, and they added them to the already laden chains which they wore around their necks. Then, sometime later, Granny heard of someone in Ardboe who had a cure for nosebleeds, so she told Emily and Charlie that Sally ought to be taken there. This time, Helen and Kate clamoured to be taken along, and were surprised when their father and Granny had no objections.

Granny had managed to get hold of the phone number of the woman who had the cure, and had rung to make sure that she would be there that evening, because, she said, there was no point in driving all that distance on a fool's errand. The woman also gave Granny exact instructions on how to reach her house; which turned out to be a nondescript little place with a tin roof, hidden at the end of a pot-holed lane. 'You stay here now in the car, like good children,' their daddy said to Helen and Kate, in a tone which they knew meant it was pointless to argue with him. He led Granny and Sally to the house, which swallowed them up.

The minutes trickled by like hours. They always did, when you were left to wait in the car. Kate fiddled with the door locks as she grumbled, 'I bet there's nothing wrong with Sally at all. I bet she's just discovered some way to make her nose bleed when it suits her, just to get attention. Have you ever noticed how it always happens when her class are doing sums, or when we're all just ready to go out to Mass or at some time like that? It never happens in Uncle Brian's house, when we're all watching the film on television on a Sunday afternoon, or at home when Mammy's made us French toast, and never, ever when we're at Granny Kelly's because Sally knows she'd go bananas if you started bleeding all over her sofa.' They watched a few scraggy hens pick around miserably near the door of the house. For five minutes they didn't speak, but sat in a silence as deep as the silence in a church. 'I bet we've been here for over an hour by now,' Kate said.

'I wonder what the woman's doing to Sally,' Helen said, with relish. They knew vaguely about cures. Granny Kate's brother was said to have had a cure for strains and sprains, which involved tying flax around the arm or leg that was hurt and then saying special prayers, but they'd heard about others that were more interesting, more dramatic: cures for sties involving thorns from a gooseberry bush, and a cure for shingles where two burning sticks from the fire were held in the form of a cross. Until Sally returned they passed the time inventing cures to which the woman might be submitting her, cures which involved cowpats, nettles, raw eggs and the like, laughing hysterically at the ideas they came up with.

Like the house in which she lived, the woman with the cure looked completely unremarkable: they saw her when Sally, Granny and their father were leaving, and she came to the door to see them off. Helen and Kate clamoured to know what they'd missed: 'What did she do to you, what did she say?'

'I'm not allowed to tell anybody,' Sally said smugly, 'or the cure won't work.'

'What did I tell you!' Kate cried.

But the evening wasn't as big a disappointment as it had looked like turning out to be, for their daddy stopped at a filling station to get petrol and when he went in to pay for it, he came out with crisps and chocolates crammed into a brown paper bag, which he handed into the back seat without the conditions or instructions their mother would have added to this gesture. He stripped the cellophane off a packet of Senior Service, and lit a cigarette, narrowing his eyes in a way Helen loved. She promised herself that she would start smoking just as soon as she was old enough, but she knew better than to say this to anyone. She liked the smell of the spent match, as he waved the flame out.

Then Granny Kate suggested that they go to see the Old Cross at Ardboe, because it was only just down the road, and it would be a pity to have come all this way and not seen it, especially with it being such a fine night. 'Have you ever been there before?' she asked the children.

'Aye, but we'd love to go again,' Kate said.

And so instead of heading straight for home, they drove for a short while down narrow roads with high hedges. Their daddy parked the car right beside the high cross, which was enclosed by railings. The surface of the stone was weathered, so that some of the biblical scenes carved on the cross had become indistinct. Their daddy pointed out and named Adam and Eve, the Marriage at Cana, the Last Judgement. It didn't matter that the pictures weren't perfectly clear, Helen thought: it was enough in itself that the cross was there; to think of it having stood there for all those hundreds of years amazed her almost as much as it amazed and delighted her father. He loved history, and he was always talking about it. Uncle Brian talked about history a lot too, but she would never have said that he loved it. There was a difference, although she wouldn't have known how to explain or define it. For her daddy, it was the fascination of thinking about people who had lived hundreds, even thousands, of years ago, where he lived now; there was something about the odd combination of closeness and distance that caught his imagination like nothing else. He'd taken them once to see the elk's head that had been found near Toome years earlier: a grey bony thing that frightened the life out of them, with its massive antlers and hollow eye sockets. 'Can you imagine a yoke like that wandering around here? Doesn't that beat all?' Helen would always remember the sob of excitement in his voice. 'Isn't the world a wonderful place!' Now and then in the newspaper there'd be a piece about a farmer somewhere who'd found something on his land: a Viking sword, or a pot of coins, or even a dug-out canoe from the Iron Age, and he'd always draw their attention to it, read it out to them. 'Would you like that to be you?' their mammy would say. 'I'd die happy, so I would,' he always replied.

They went through the gate into the graveyard which lay behind the cross. There was the ruin of a tiny church there, and the graveyard itself overlooked the wide expanse of the lough. It was a warm, sticky evening, and Granny Kate flapped her hand in front of her face to drive away the midges that hummed around her. 'Hasn't it got terrible heavy,' she complained. 'It wouldn't surprise me if we had thunder out of this.' The enormous sky was full of dark-blue clouds, and although it was late in the evening now, there was still a strong, odd light which lit up the trees and the black-and-white cattle that were grazing in a field below the graveyard. When they heard voices, the cattle slowly raised their heads, then plodded across the field to see what was happening.

Charlie dug into his jacket pocket, and pulled out a handful of loose change. He gave the children a penny each, to hammer into the tree at the far side of the graveyard. From a distance it looked quite ordinary, perhaps a bit stunted, but when you got closer you could see that its trunk was almost more metal than wood, for people had hammered coins, pins and nails into it. Their daddy helped them each to find a place for them to hammer in their penny. It wasn't difficult, for the wood of the tree was quite soft.

'Don't forget to make a wish,' Granny said.

'I'm going to wish that Sally's nose doesn't get better, so that we get plenty more nice outings like this,' Kate said.

'Why, you cheeky wee monkey,' Granny said, but she was laughing, for all that she tried to hide it.

When they were in the car on the way home, Kate bribed Sally with Rolos to try and coax her into telling what the cure had been, while Helen listened in to what the grown-ups were talking about.

'Brian asked me to be sure and ask you if you want to go with him to the march on Saturday,' Granny said.

'What march is that?'

'The civil rights march that's to be in Coalisland. I thought he told you about it already.'

'Aye, now you mention it, I think he did say something about it to me a while back. Is Peter going?'

'Are you joking me?'

Their daddy was quiet for a while, and then he said, 'Ach, I don't know. Do you think it'll do any good?'

'Well it won't do any harm,' Granny said. 'I'd have thought you'd have had a bit more go in you, Charlie. I'd be there myself if I was younger than I am now. When you think of what people have to put up with in this country, well, we have to make a start somewhere in telling them that we've had enough of that.'

'I suppose you're right,' he said. 'Tell Brian I'll go with him.'

But when the time came he didn't go, because one of the cattle fell sick. He was up all Friday night with it, and they had to call the vet twice. When Brian called to collect his brother on his way to Coalisland, Charlie just shook his head. 'March? I'd fall in a pile I'm that done. But I'll go with you another time, so I will.'

On the Sunday, when the sisters went over to Brian's house their cousins Johnny and Declan were full of the march. 'It was great. We all sat on the road and sang rebel songs. There was nothing the police could do to stop us. Get your daddy to bring you along the next time.'

The summer ended, school started again, and Sally's nose-bleeds began once more. Helen and Kate became embarrassed at being called out of class; dreaded the moment when some wee girl would come into the room and say, 'Please, Miss, Sally Quinn's not well again, and she needs one of her big sisters.'

'And so then you have to go to her class and she's lying on a rug in the bookstore, like an eejit,' Helen told their mother.

'I can't help it,' Sally wailed.

'She can, too,' Kate said, when their mother decided to keep Sally at home after her nose bled on a Monday and then again on the Tuesday. For the rest of that week, while Helen and Kate were being hurried through their breakfast, and packed off to school with a few cheese sandwiches, Sally would creep into her parents' warm, empty bed, where she snoozed and drowsed until the middle of the day. Then she got up and after lunch, would spend the rest of the afternoon playing with the kittens in the back yard, helping her mother to make pastry, or just doing some colouring in at the kitchen table. Her nose didn't bleed once during these days, and she was fine over the weekend, but when Helen and Kate were getting up for school on Monday morning, they could hear Sally's thin whine: 'I'm not well, Mammy.'

Still in her pyjamas, Kate stormed into the other room. 'If she's not going, Helen and me are staying at home too, because it's not fair.' Their mother stood up for Sally, but then their daddy weighed in, and said that all three of them would be going to school, and that there would be no more nonsense about it. Sally grizzled a bit, but she and her mammy knew that because he hardly ever got involved in matters like this, when he did, there was no turning him. Kate grinned as the three of them got into the car, including Sally with her satchel and her sandwiches. 'And if you don't feel well, don't be sending for Helen or for me, because we won't come.'

Sally was fine that day, and for weeks afterwards was, as Uncle Peter said, 'as healthy as a kipper'.

There was another march announced, this time it was to be in Derry. At home now, all the talk was about civil rights, and their father said that he wouldn't miss this march, 'no matter if every beast I have keels over the night before it'. The Apprentice Boys had called a march for the same day when the civil rights march was announced, and so they both had been declared illegal, which of course made it more important for everybody to be there. The children clamoured to be taken along too, but neither of their parents would hear of it.

'You're too small,' their father insisted. 'If there was any trouble and you got hurt, even the least little bit, even if you just got very badly frightened, I'd never forgive myself for it.'

'But Declan and Johnny are going.'

'Aye, that's as may be, but Una isn't going.' This didn't explain or excuse anything for Helen and Kate, it just made it seem worse.

'I can't wait until I'm grown up,' Helen said. 'I'm going to do exactly as I please!'

To make it up to them, Granny said she would take them out for the day: 'We'll go to the Holy Well.'

'How will we get there?'

'We'll walk.'

'But it's miles away! We'll never walk that!'

Granny laughed. 'Of course you will, you only think that it's far. Sure if you went on the march, you'd have to walk at least that, maybe far further.'

Kate looked doubtful: she thought she could see Granny smiling. 'I tell you what, I'll ask Peter to come and collect us, so you won't have to walk the whole way back home afterwards.'

The walk turned out to be more enjoyable than they had expected, and they dawdled along the roads, which rose and fell and twisted and turned; roads lined with hedges in their autumn colours, and bright with berries. The long thick grass in the ditches was wet when they stepped into it, to avoid the cars and tractors which occasionally passed them by. The people in the vehicles lifted their hands to the family, whether they knew them or not, and Granny Kate greeted them in return. A tractor passed them, driven by a young man with thick black hair.

'That's Willy Larkin's big brother, Tony,' Kate said. 'Willy says somebody saw a Mystery Man in the woods behind the school last week. He says he had a big dark coat on him, and a black hat, but where his face should have been, there was only a blank.'

'And did Willy himself see this man?' Granny asked, as Sally gripped her hand more tightly.

'No, somebody told him about it, and then he told me.'

'If people know he's there in the woods, how come he's such a mystery?'

'I don't know,' Kate said. She was disappointed that Granny was so dismissive of the idea of the Mystery Man: she'd enjoyed the fright of it, the thought of the dark, faceless figure.

'Sure if he had no face, wouldn't he be walking into things? How would he be able to see where he was going? How would he eat his dinner, if he didn't have a mouth?'

'Maybe it just was that you couldn't see his face, I don't know,' Kate replied, uncertain now.

Helen was only half-listening to this: she was still thinking about Tony Larkin, about something he'd done at the carnival during the last football tournament at the start of the summer; something which had upset her, particularly because she hadn't been able to understand why.

They always went to the carnival at least once when it was

on. Usually it was their daddy who took them, and he'd give them fistfuls of loose change to play the fruit machines or to pay the woman at the hoopla stall, who looked like an African queen, with wooden bands packed on her arms, from her wrist to above her elbow. They'd go on the swingboats, or the dodgem cars. Helen liked the noise of the place; it excited her: the sound of the big generator that ran the amusements, the screams and shouts of people, the raucous music. There were bright, gaudy lights, vans selling ice cream, minerals and chips, and a marquee, where there'd be a dance for the grown-ups, late in the evening. Usually there was nothing Helen liked better than the carnival, but on this particular evening she already felt a bit uneasy, because Uncle Peter was there, staggering about the place with the neck of a bottle sticking out of his coat pocket. She saw her daddy go over and talk earnestly to him at one point, as if he were trying to explain something difficult to him. She noticed how alike they looked. It was as if her daddy had two selves, and the good, sober one was trying to persuade the one who was always getting drunk to change his ways. Uncle Peter didn't want to listen: eventually she saw him push her father's arm aside, and then he walked unsteadily away. She went off then and played at the hoopla for a while with her sisters. Later, she saw Uncle Peter arguing with some young boys. They were teasing him and laughing at him, and Helen felt hurt and angry on his behalf, but there was nothing she could do to help him. She walked away. Sally and Kate got on the dodgem cars, and she was standing watching them when her daddy came up to her and drew her aside, so that she would be able to hear what he was saying above the loud music.

'I have to take Uncle Peter home,' he said, pressing a few coins into her hand. 'Look after the other two until I get back. Buy yourselves ice creams, or whatever you want. I'll be as quick as I can.' She turned and watched him go, watched him walk over to where Uncle Peter was sitting on the wet ground behind a van selling chips. He had his arms folded across his knees, and his head resting on his arms, as if he wanted to sleep. Helen watched her father gently help him to his feet, and then lead him away from the field where the carnival was taking place, out to the road where the cars were parked.

When Sally and Kate came off the dodgems, Helen was vague in her explanations as to where their father had gone. She bought them each an ice cream cone, and then she paid for her sisters to go on the waltzers. For a while she stood watching them spinning and screaming, then she turned to look at the swing-boats which were near by. Mostly it was children who played with these, but the couple in the swingboat at the end were Tony Larkin, and a fair-haired girl his own age, whose name Helen didn't know, but whom she vaguely recognised from seeing her at the chapel on Sundays. Tony had just left school, so that meant he was a grown-up.

He paid the man, who put the money in a leather pouch hanging around his neck, then set the boat going with a sudden, sharp tug of his hand. Tony and the girl pulled hard on the ropes to make the boat swing, then they both stood up, and by bending their knees and using the force of their bodies they made the boat swing faster and higher. Before long, Helen wasn't the only one who was aware of them: people stopped what they were doing and watched as the boat swung up to its highest possible point, so that it looked as if the couple might fall out. Then abruptly the boat dropped, and swung back in the opposite direction, again reaching the highest point. It seemed to stop for a few seconds at the top each time, and this pause gave the movement of the boat a slow, strange rhythm, in spite of the abrupt drops the boat made from each extremity of height. Even though the music was still playing, there was a kind of silence in the stillness which fell over the field, as people stopped what they were doing and stared, wondering how it would all end. The man who owned the swingboats tried to stop them, but the boat was going too high and too fast. He attempted once to lift the plank of wood which, held against the bottom of the boat, would usually have been enough to bring it to a standstill, but this time it was too dangerous: the plank was knocked from his hand, and the man had to wait until the couple slowed and stopped in their own time.

Tony helped the girl to climb out of the boat. Somebody laughed, somebody whistled, somebody near Helen said, 'The cheeky bitch.' The fair-haired girl, who was walking past at that moment, heard it too, and she went red but looked defiant, for all that, then Helen saw her turn her head urgently, to see where Tony was. Helen didn't understand why what she had just seen made her feel so strange, so confused. She only knew that she wanted her father, and when she suddenly saw him coming through the gate into the field again, she ran over at once, and buried her face in his jacket.

Even today, on the walk with her sisters and grandmother, she wished that her father was there with them. She never enjoyed outings like this half as much when he wasn't there. He loved and understood such places. Even last night he'd been telling them about how, when she was a child, Granny Kate had gone there on a pilgrimage with her mother, travelling by charabanc from Magherafelt, and how people had come from far and wide every year. 'Imagine them when you're there,' he'd said. He'd told them about the well, too, and how there were stones in it that were supposed to save you from drowning, and that when people had had to emigrate to America, they'd always wanted to take one of these stones with them. But it was Uncle Peter who had told her that the well was a pagan place, and that the Christians had then just taken it over, and pretended that it was theirs.

The well was enclosed, and over it hung a hazel tree, with rags and handkerchiefs tied to it. Helen remembered what Uncle Peter had said: the well had a strange atmosphere, not like the deep, still peace of an empty chapel, but powerful, defiant, somehow secretive. Granny Kate pulled out a bunch of clean cotton rags she had brought with her, and handed them one each. She told them to dip the rags in the water of the well and bless themselves with them, then tie them on to the bush. Granny helped Sally, and tapped her on the nose with the damp cloth before bending a branch of the tree down, so that Sally could tie on her rag.

'This is great gas,' Kate said, but Helen realised she felt foolish. She was only doing this strange thing because she had been told to do it, and she didn't understand how it could possibly do any good. Would God really cure Sally's nosebleeds because Our Lady asked Him to, and because Sally had asked Our Lady, and then tied a bit of wet rag on a bush? Granny made them all join their hands and say a prayer together, and then they all trooped away.

They walked by the water's edge while they waited for Uncle Peter to come and collect them. They were right down by the shore of Lough Neagh, and from this part you could see the huge expanse of water more clearly than from where they lived; you could see the shores in the distance. They looked out across at the Sperrins and Slieve Gallion, and they thought of their father, off at the march in Derry. Helen still wished that she had been allowed to go with him.

But when they got back to the house, they heard that the march hadn't gone off peacefully. There had been riots, and when their father and Brian didn't come home at the time they were expected, the children could see how worried their mother was, although she tried to hide it. The police had blocked the march and baton-charged the marchers. On television, they watched black-and-white pictures of crowds running, of people with blood on their faces and shirts; of men being pulled along the ground by the hair, or being beaten where they lay. They saw a man, one of the organisers, pleading for calm and reason, and before he could finish what he was saying, he was struck in the stomach with a baton. After that, Emily wasn't able to pretend any longer that she wasn't anxious. When at last they heard a car pull up outside, they all rushed out to meet him.

'There was no sense in what happened today,' he said, angry and shaken. 'They just hammered the living daylights out of people.' He said they were late home because Brian had been badly cut on the face, and they'd decided to take him to the hospital, in case the wound needed stitches. They'd had to wait for a long time there, because so many people had been brought in wounded, and then it had taken them a long time to get back to where the car was parked. He was glad that it had been on the television. 'I suppose it would have suited them better for all this to have been kept quiet.'

There were more civil rights marches organised in Belfast later that year, some organised by the students at the university, and although Charlie and Brian didn't go to them, all the talk at home now was about civil rights, and how things would have to change. The children couldn't understand all of what was being said. One phrase they heard people using over and over was, 'Live, oul' horse, and you'll get grass.'

Halloween came, and their daddy took them over to Brian's house, for them to celebrate it with their cousins, as they did every year. He laughed when he got into the car and looked over his shoulder to see three small witches sitting in the back seat. They were all wearing pointed paper hats with moons and stars printed on them: he'd bought them for the children himself, in McGovern's. All three were wearing the masks they'd made in art class at school. 'You'd put the heart across a body,' he said to them, as he started the engine.

They ran screaming around the bonfire Uncle Peter had built for them, and Helen felt both frightened and excited as she watched the firelight on the blackened faces of her sisters and cousins. They had fireworks too: Roman candles and Catherine wheels, sparklers and rockets. The coloured lights flowed briefly like magical liquids when Uncle Peter set the fireworks off, and the children covered their ears at the loud noise. Afterwards, you couldn't remember the fireworks exactly as they had been: there was something about the nature of them that made it impossible, until another one was lit. Later, they moved into the back scullery, where Aunt Lucy filled a zinc bath with water, and floated yellow apples in it for them to try to catch and pull out with their teeth. She put piles of flour on dinner plates, and a wrapped toffee on the top, again for them to pick up and claim, without using their fingers. 'Make as much mess as you want,' she said indulgently: and they did.

And then when they were bored with that, they went into the kitchen where Granny was sitting by the stove. She laughed when she saw them: 'Look at the cut of yis!' They had cups of strong, sweet tea, slices of buttered brack; there were bowls of monkey nuts, and oranges; and an apple pie Granny had made, with coins hidden in it.

'I always loved Halloween,' Granny said. 'I always remember there was a game I played, when I was older than you are, to find out who I was going to marry.' She told them of how, when she was sixteen, she'd sat before a mirror at night, combing her hair and eating an apple. 'The idea was, that at the very stroke of midnight, you'd see the face of the man you were to marry reflected in the mirror.'

'That would be so scary, Granny,' Una said. 'That would be just like seeing a ghost.'

'It would be worse if you did it and didn't see anybody,' Kate said. 'That would be a disappointment: you wouldn't know if it meant that you were never going to get married, or if it was just that the game wasn't working.'

'Oh, I saw something,' Granny said. She told them that a face had appeared: faintly at first, as if in a mist, but gradually it became clearer until it was as if she was looking at a flesh-and-blood person standing behind her, just at her very shoulder, leaning down and smiling at her in the mirror. 'You'd have sworn on all you held dear, that if you'd turned round, he'd have been standing there in the room with you: but of course, I didn't dare to turn.'

'I'd have died on the spot!' Una said. Helen noticed that Una's eyes were so wide by this stage that there was a clear white rim around the blue of her iris.

'I took a good, hard look at him though,' Granny went on. 'I wanted to be able to recognise him when I did meet him in later life. But it didn't work out as simply as that.'

They already knew the story of how Granny and Grandad had met: how she'd been working in a draper's shop in Magherafelt, and he'd come in one day, looking for a jacket. She'd told them this story so often that they all had a clear image in their minds of the dim shop, the high wooden counter, the smell of wool, the heavy ledger in which she had to record all the purchases. But it was hard to imagine Granny and Grandad as young people and looking as they did in the framed photographs in the parlour: Granny with her hair piled high on her head in an extravagant roll, Grandad a light-boned, timid-looking boy.

'There was a wee bell fixed to the back of the door, that rang so that if you were out in the back, you'd know a customer had come into the shop. I remember as well the first day Francis came in. He was looking for a tweed jacket, and I had been out in the store with just the very thing, when I heard the bell ring as he came in. But I knew if I sold him what he wanted, he might never come back to the shop again. So I brought in three jackets for him to try, that I knew fine well would drown him. God, I can see him yet, with the sleeves to the tips of his fingers. So I said that we'd be getting more in, and the best thing would be for him to come back the next day he was in town. "I always be here on a Wednesday," says he. So the next Wednesday morning, I made sure that all the jackets that were his size were well hidden, and told him they still hadn't arrived. I always remember he smiled when I said that. "I'll be back next week, then." So the next Wednesday morning, again I weeded out all the jackets in his size. Eleven o'clock, in comes Francis, and the pair of us go over to the rail, and start going through them. But hadn't I missed one! About the fifth jacket along, doesn't the label say exactly the size he'd been looking for. So he looks at it, then looks at me, then pushes the jacket along the rail, and we go through the rest of them. "Nothing," says he at the end of it. "It looks like I'm just going to have to keep coming in here every week. But that's no great hardship." And I knew then that I had him!' Granny Kate said.

'But this is the spooky part,' she went on. 'One night, a few years after we were married, I was sitting combing my hair in front of the big mirror that's in the back room of this house to this very day, when Francis came into the room and stood behind me. I looked at his reflection, and only then did I realise that it was him: the very same man I'd seen in the mirror at midnight, on Halloween, years earlier.' Una gave a little scream.

'You'll have these children up half the night with bad dreams,' Aunt Lucy said.

Granny Kate looked surprised. 'But it's a lovely story,' she said. 'I mean, it wasn't as if he was dead at the time: not that that would have scared me. I'd never have been frightened of Francis, living or dead. After he'd gone I used to think how lovely it would be to look up and see him standing there before me again, for I missed him sorely.' Aunt Lucy shoved a bowl of monkey nuts under Una's nose. 'Eat these,' she said, 'and put the ghosts out of your head.' But it wouldn't have been Halloween if Granny hadn't given you a good fright: it was as much a part of the celebrations as having brack to eat, or making your own false face.

For the pattern of their lives was as predictable as the seasons.

The regular round of necessity was broken by celebrations and feasts: Christmas, Easter, family birthdays. The scope of their lives was tiny but it was profound, and to them, it was immense. The physical bounds of their world were confined to little more than a few fields and houses, but they knew these places with the deep, unconscious knowledge that a bird or a fox might have for its habitat. The idea of home was something they lived so completely that they would have been at a loss to define it. But they would have known to be inadequate such phrases as: 'It's where you're from,' 'It's the place you live,' 'It's where your family are.'

And yet for all this they knew that their lives, so complete in themselves, were off centre in relation to the society beyond those few fields and houses. They recognised this most acutely every July, when they were often taken to the Antrim coast for the day, and as they went through Ballymena and Broughshane, they would see all the Union Jacks flying at the houses, and the red, white and blue bunting across the streets. They thought that the Orange arches which spanned the roads in the towns were ugly, and creepy, too, with their strange symbols: a ladder, a set square and compass, a five-pointed star. They knew that they weren't supposed to be able to understand what these things meant; and they knew, too, without having to be told that the motto painted on the arches: 'Welcome here, Brethren!' didn't include the Quinn family.

They would see photographs of the Orange marches in the newspapers, or they would see reports on television, but they never, in all their childhood, actually saw an Orange march taking place, for their parents always made a point of staying at home on that day, complaining bitterly that you were made a prisoner in your own home whether you liked it or not. It wasn't even so much that it would never have occurred to the children to ask to be taken along to see one: they just knew that it wasn't for them: they weren't particularly interested, and they knew that they weren't wanted there. For the most part, they didn't even think about it, for their lives were complete as they were.

In the weeks leading up to Christmas, there were two fixed events in their calendar: one was a visit to Miss Regan, the woman their mother had lived with when she was teaching in

Belfast. The other was a visit to Granny Kelly in Ballymena. On the first Saturday in December they set out, potatoes and turf in the boot, on the back window a tray of eggs and a Christmas cake their mother had baked. She had a Christmas present for Miss Regan too, a gift set of lily of the valley soap and talc, wrapped in paper printed with poinsettias. She never agonised over what she would buy her friend, as she did when she was trying to choose a gift for Granny Kelly.

There was always something embarrassing and exciting about the moment when they arrived. Miss Regan's tiny, cluttered parlour could barely contain the fuss, for Emily and Miss Regan would both keep talking at the same time, and they both cried a little bit, even though they pretended not to, and wiped the tears away almost before they had come. Even after all these years, Miss Regan still was amazed at the fact of Emily's life now, and the children, and how tall they'd grown since last she saw them, were a particular source of wonder.

After drinking three glasses of white lemonade, Helen had to go to the toilet, and as she stood washing her hands at the basin she looked out of the window across the rows and rows of chimney pots and slate roofs, slicked with rain, under a low grey sky. She wondered how her mother had lived there, when she thought of the fields, the wide sky and the light at home. She thought she would feel suffocated to live where all the houses were jammed together in rows, and opened out directly on to the street, without so much as a little square of grass in front of them. And yet how her mother had loved it, for she still spoke of the year when she had been a teacher as a special time, a time when she'd been happy. Helen tried to imagine her mother as a much younger woman, but when she tried to picture her as someone who wasn't her mother, she drew a blank: she found she didn't like the idea. She dried her hands on the towel, and hurried back downstairs again.

Her parents and Miss Regan were talking about politics and civil rights when she went back into the room. All the grown-ups she knew talked about little else these days: except for Uncle Peter. There was an air of defiant excitement about them when they spoke of these things, something she wasn't used to seeing in her family or her teacher or anyone she knew.

When their father had finished his tea, he took the children into the city centre, leaving Emily to spend some hours with her friend. He took them to see Santa in the Co-Op and did some shopping until such time as their mother came into the town and met up with them at a time and place they had arranged earlier. In Cornmarket, they saw a man wearing a thing like a large black-plastic bib, with 'What does it profit a man if he gains the whole world, but loses his soul?' printed on it in bold white letters. The man was shouting about God and Jesus and sin and salvation, and Kate made her mind up that she wanted to see one of the leaflets he was distributing to the passers-by. When her parents weren't looking, she took one. 'Here, Sally, put this in your pocket for me,' she said, stuffing it into Sally's anorak before her little sister could say anything. And it was there that their mother found it when she went to look for Sally's mittens a while later. 'What's this?' she said, smoothing out the folded sheet, and the children pressed round to see, as they hadn't had a chance to look at it so far.

The leaflet showed a crude drawing of an enormous bottle, to which many tiny figures, some on their knees and struggling, were bound by chains. 'Are you a slave to the evil of alcohol?' was printed under it, in heavy type, and then there was a text, sprinkled with quotations from the Bible. Sally looked from her mother to her father, her mouth slightly open, a furtive look on her face. Charlie started to laugh so much, that people around looked at them.

'Now I hope you'll pay heed to that, Sally,' he said, 'for your mammy and me have had enough of you reeling in night after night, taking the two sides of the road with you.' Sally, who didn't know what he was talking about, smiled cautiously, and looked even more guilty.

When they went to see Granny Kelly, a few days before Christmas, it was a different type of outing altogether. They had to get dressed up in their Sunday clothes, and as they waited for their father to get the car ready, Helen noticed how her mother, standing over by the window, was twisting the rings on her fingers, a sullen, unhappy look in her eyes. Their daddy came back into the house.

'Are you right?'

'I want to change my skirt,' she said, moving to the door.

He smiled and said wearily, 'Your skirt's grand, you look lovely in it. There's no need to change.'

'Ach, I don't know, I don't feel right in it.'

'Put on your green one, then.'

Perhaps their parents didn't realise that the children's sensibilities were delicately tuned to emotional falseness, and so they registered the contrast between this, the tense atmosphere in the car and the apparent delight displayed on their arrival in Ballymena. Granny Kelly herself, wreathed in smiles, came out to the door to welcome them, and led them into a parlour which looked warmer than usual, because of the glittering Christmas tree and the foil streamers. Uncle Michael, Aunt Rosemary and the cousins were there, and a casual observer might have been fooled. But the children noticed how their daddy and Uncle Michael both talked more loudly than usual, and that although their mother smiled and smiled, it never went beyond her mouth, never reached her eyes. When she laughed, it was forced and nervous, not the full, unbuttoned laughter they would hear at home. The children sat neatly on the sofa, sucking pink wafer biscuits and sipping weak tea, and noticing far more than the adults in the room would ever have believed.

After all the chit-chat died down the conversation turned, inevitably, to civil rights, and the marches which had been taking place during the autumn.

'Bloody head-cases, so they are,' Uncle Michael said.

'You think so?' This was the children's mother, and the tone of her voice had changed, but Uncle Michael either didn't notice, or didn't care. He gave a little laugh and shook his head as if it were all such nonsense it was hardly worth talking about.

'I mean, how do you think it's going to end? O'Neill has offered them a few odds and ends to keep them quiet, and of course that's got the other side's backs up. Do these People's Democracy crowd think the ones up in Stormont are going to turn round and say, "God, right enough, there is people in this country that have damn all and we're doing less than nothing to help them; we'd better start giving them jobs and houses and whatever else they want"?'

'So are people to just sit there like wee mice, and not even ask for what's their due?'

Uncle Michael shook his head again. 'It'll end in a bloodbath,' he said. 'The other side are going to resent the least thing that's given. They have the power, and they're not just going to let it be taken away from them. Mark my words: a bloodbath, and the people will have brought it upon themselves.'

'It's not a question of one side or the other,' their father began, and he said something about socialism, but their grandmother interrupted him.

'Communists, more like,' she said. 'It's the students I feel most angry about. Look at the chance they've been given. If they would sit in the universities and study and work hard, they'd have nothing to complain about, they'd get on in life, get jobs and money; but oh no, they have to be out about the country marching and protesting. The university should just close their doors on them, should boot them out and take in students who are prepared to stick to their books and work.'

'Well now, I'm afraid I can't agree with you at all there, Mrs Kelly,' their father said, and they knew this time that he wasn't going to allow himself to be interrupted or talked down. 'I was on the march in Derry in October, the one that was disrupted, and I met some of the students there, and I can tell you that I thought them admirable people. They're not involved in this for themselves. They're concerned about the people in this country who haven't had their chances, and who aren't going to be helped in any way unless somebody makes a stand and gets things moving, unless the people who do have something begin to speak out for those who have nothing.'

'It's up to every person to look out for himself,' Granny said, and Uncle Michael nodded at this. 'I hate to have to say it about my own people, but the Catholics in this country are a feckless, lazy bunch. Given them an opportunity, and they'll turn their backs on it and walk away.'

The children could see their parents were angered by this, but they didn't realise that it was because their father thought what she said was meant to be a slight against their mother; and their mother took it for a veiled insult against her husband's family.

'The next march there is,' their mother said, 'I'll be on it.'

Everyone in the room looked at her in surprise. 'And I'll take the children too.'

When they got into the car to go home, a short while later, Kate said, 'It's good to have that out of the way, isn't it? Now we can settle down and begin to enjoy Christmas.'

'Oh, Kate,' their mother said, and they thought she was going to laugh; but she started to cry instead.

But she kept her word. When the civil rights march from Belfast to Derry took place some two weeks later, it was Emily who insisted that the whole family go to cheer them on. They had to stand and wait for a long time in the raw air; and when at last the students did appear, led by a tired-looking man shouting into a loud hailer, the children felt a sharp mixture of fear and excitement, which was new to them, but which they were to experience many times in the coming years. Helen's father bent down and whispered in her ear, 'You're looking at history.' But Helen realised this without having to be told. That night she listened to her mother telling Granny Kate how the person leading the march had shouted 'One man' and everybody else had shouted 'One vote,' 'One family,' 'One house.' 'There was a policeman standing right at my elbow,' she said to Granny, 'and I didn't give two hoots, I just shouted back with the rest of them.' Helen remembered how her mother had looked, standing on the grass verge by the side of the road, with Sally clutching a fistful of her skirt as usual. Her face was red with the cold, but when she shouted the slogans, she'd lost her usual timidity and shyness. Helen knew to look at her how serious all this was: something important had changed.

Chapter Seven

TUESDAY

Just after Cate had left the house that morning to drive to Belfast, she'd met Brian on the road, walking towards her. She stopped the car and rolled down the window.

'I've a bit of news for you,' she said, and watched his smile fade with apprehension. 'I'm going to have a baby.'

'Christ Almighty!' Cate smiled foolishly in spite of herself, and drummed her fingers on the steering wheel, while Brian stood looking at her for some moments.

'Well,' he said eventually, 'as the old saying goes, these things happen in the best-regulated families. How's your mammy taking it?'

'Much as you'd expect.'

'These things sort themselves out in time,' he said, after another pause. 'I'll call up and see her later this morning.'

'Oh, I think I'd give her a wee while yet,' Cate said hastily. 'I'm clearing out myself for a night, to stay with Helen and give Mammy a chance to think it through.'

'It's as bad as that?'

'I suppose so,' Cate replied, suddenly miserable. Brian leaned towards her. 'Ach, daughter, this is the worst bit. I mind the time . . . I mind . . . ' He looked away. 'Your mammy'll come round to it. It's always a shock at first, so it is.'

'You're telling me.' He told her to look after herself. As she drove away she realised that she felt brighter for having spoken to him, without being able to explain to herself exactly why that should be.

For a moment she even wondered if she felt well enough to head off somewhere for the day; maybe to County Down, that would be good, ending up in Belfast just in time for Helen's arrival home from work. But she dismissed the idea in the very moment it came to her. She'd slept badly the night before; perhaps she'd need to take a nap for an hour or two in Helen's place this afternoon. On top of that, she still felt wretched with morning sickness. That at least was one of the benefits of having told her family what had happened: she would no longer have to go through the charade of having to pretend to be well when she felt terrible. God, but Sally was decent! She'd come tapping on Cate's bedroom door this morning with tea and toast. Having that before she got out of bed had been a good help, as opposed to coming downstairs on an empty stomach and trying not to gag when her mother asked her would she like some scrambled egg. She'd always been great, Sally, and Cate felt guilty now for having taken her so much for granted in the past. The way she'd handed over her car keys, too, without making a big deal about it.

But that was nothing new either. Often, when Cate was home for a week in the summer, she'd go out for the day with her mother and Sally in Sally's car. They always liked to go to such places as the Glens of Antrim or the Giant's Causeway, somewhere you could see magnificent scenery. They would have a picnic, or Cate would treat them to lunch in a hotel. But Sally realised (although she didn't pretend to understand) that Cate liked to go to other places too. 'The keys are there,' she would say, nodding towards where they hung, near the stove. 'Off you go, if you want.'

And off Cate did go, many times, driving for hours through the countryside alone, trying to fathom Northern Ireland in a way which wasn't, if you still lived there, necessary. Or advisable, she thought. Or possible, even.

Swatragh and Draperstown; Magherafelt and Toome; Plumbridge and Castledawson: her family couldn't understand her interest in these places. She drove through pinched villages where the edges of the footpaths were painted red, white and blue, where there were Orange Lodges and locked churches; through more prosperous towns with their memorials from the Great War and their baskets of lobelia and fuchsia hanging from brackets from the street lamps, with their Tidy Town awards on burnished plaques and their proper shopfronts. She drove through villages where unemployed men stood on street corners and dragged on cigarettes, or ambled up and down between the chip shop and the bookie's, past walls which bore Republican graffiti or incongruously glamorous advertisements on huge hoardings. She saw Planter towns that had had the heart bombed out of them; 'Business as Usual' signs pasted on the chipboard nailed over the broken windows of The Northern Bank and Williamson's Hardware. Now and then she would see a Mission tent, or a temporary road sign indicating the way to a 'Scripture Summer Camp'. She drove along narrow roads between shaggy wet hedges of hawthorn and beech. Once, somewhere in South Derry, she saw a field where a few pale cattle stood up to their knees in nettles and scutchgrass before a ruined building with 'INLA rule' painted on it in crude white letters. The cattle stared at her mildly as she passed by.

She saw signposts for places which had once held no particular significance but whose names were now tainted by the memory of things which had been done there: Claudy, Enniskillen, Ballykelly. She drove and drove and drove under grey skies and soft clouds. The towns and fields slipped past her until she felt that she was watching a film, and then she realised that if she had been asked to pick a single word to sum up her feelings towards Northern Ireland she would be at a complete loss, so much so that she didn't even know whether a negative or a positive word would have been more apt.

As she drove to Belfast this morning, she remembered how, during these summer drives, she would sometimes fantasise about moving back to the north to live there, particularly when she saw a house which took her fancy: always a magnificent stone house with ivy growing on it, maybe with a garden running down to a river, the whole thing surrounded by lime trees and oaks. She'd look at a high distant window and imagine herself standing there, looking out from another life. But it didn't amount to anything, this fantasy; she would do as much if she were on holiday in the Cotswolds or in Tuscany, and build a vague life for herself around some house or market or town half-glimpsed and as quickly forgotten, both the fact of the place and the thought it had stirred.

Once, during one of her summer drives, she had stopped to buy some petrol in a village in Fermanagh, and she'd been particularly taken with the place. It had been a bright morning and she remembered flowers and an air of quiet prosperity, neat shops, outside one of which bunches of carrots hung with their leafy tops intact. She thought that this looked like the kind of place to which so many of the people she knew in London would like to move, and it belied the idea many of them would have had of life in Northern Ireland. But later that day, while she was listening to the car radio, she heard a report which said that a man of twenty, an RUC reservist, had been shot dead while working in his father's vegetable shop in that same village. And although she didn't want to pass through the place again when she was driving home that evening, she had no choice. By then the weather had broken; and the plastic tape which the police had tied to lamp-posts to cordon off the area flapped and strained in the strong wind and rain. An army checkpoint had been set up and every car was being stopped and the whole thing was ghastly and depressing. She thought of the young man dead and felt ashamed of her own easy sentimentality earlier in the day.

But she was careful never to talk to her family, especially to her mother, about the idea of her moving back to the north, for she was afraid that it might be taken seriously.

Past Antrim, she turned on the car radio and listened to the news headlines. A man had been shot in his home in North Belfast during the night. A few more bleak items followed, and then the weather forecast, which said that it would be 'mild and fair', although Cate could already see dark clouds gathering. Once when she was home she'd remarked to Helen that she thought the forecasts were often inaccurate in Northern Ireland. 'It's probably deliberate,' Helen had replied. 'If they read out the average day's news here and then said at the end of it, "Oh, and by the way, it's going to bucket rain for the next twenty-four hours," it might be more than people could take.'

She switched off the radio again and slotted in a cassette, but as she approached Belfast and the traffic got heavier and more complicated she turned the music off too, the better to concentrate. Lorries thundered past on either side of her. 'Ulster still needs Jesus', it said in large letters on the side of a church. Far in the distance to her left she could see a cemetery and beyond that Belfast Lough. She drove on, down past the docks and the yellow gantries. She rather liked seeing this part of the city, although she never day-dreamed about living in Belfast. She drove over the Westlink to reach Helen's office, and it took all of her skill to negotiate her way. She'd driven this in the past, but had asked Sally to talk her through it again that morning before she left the house. She almost missed her turning and ended up on the road to Dublin. The part of the lower Falls where Helen had her office always reminded Cate more of her mother than of her sister, although it had changed a lot since the time she had lived and taught there. Cate was never comfortable in this part of town; she always felt nervous and conspicuous and was afraid that something would happen there. Knowing that this was a prejudice didn't help her greatly.

She hadn't been to Helen's office before, but had little difficulty finding it. A green door beside an off-licence ('Handy at the end of a long day,' Helen used to remark laconically) opened on to a narrow flight of stairs, once she had rung the bell and the buzzer had sounded. At the top of the stairs she turned right into a tiny room where a young man and a woman with a baby were sitting forlornly on a couple of worn-out chairs. The walls were covered in beauty board, and a spider plant was expiring in the corner. Cate could see now what Helen meant about the off licence. The offices in which Cate worked in London were actually quite functional and drab, given the glamorous image of the magazine; but this was something else. A door on the far side of the room opened and a man in his early forties came out. 'Now, Mr and Mrs . . .' he started to say, and then he noticed Cate. 'Oh, hello, Helen said you would be calling,' he said, and ushered her through to his office. 'I'll see you in a minute,' he threw over his shoulder as an afterthought to the waiting couple, and closed the door. The office was perhaps slightly bigger than the waiting room, but looked smaller because of the buff folders which were everywhere: two desks were piled high with them, they were heaped on the window-sill, piled on a chair, scattered across the floor. It was like something out of Dickens, Cate thought, and it shocked her to think of her sister spending her working life in such a place.

'Helen had to go down to the Crumlin Road to see someone this morning. She left this for you,' Owen said, opening a drawer and taking out a key, which he handed to her. Cate had only met Owen a couple of times before, but he was always very friendly towards her. 'More than he is to me,' Sally had once said grumpily. 'He wouldn't give me the light of day if he could help it. I'm just a wee primary school teacher; what is there to be gained by knowing the likes of me?'

'My wife Mary was showing me that interview you did with Robert De Niro last month,' Owen went on. 'Very impressive!'

'Oh, that,' Cate said. 'You know how it is, these things always sound much more exciting than they actually are. De Niro's notoriously difficult to interview.'

'Ah, go on out of that, don't try to tell me that meeting film stars is less glamorous than this,' and Cate, glancing around at the worn carpet, the dingy filing cabinets and the buff folders, took his point, and made no such denial. Owen followed her glance, and picked up a folder from the desk. 'Helen was reading a thing out to me the other day about what they call the paperless office, and saying "Why can't we have one of those?" We had a good laugh about it.'

Cate forced a smile. 'Be sure and thank Helen for me,' she said, 'and tell her I'll see her this evening. I won't take up any more of your time; I know you have people waiting.'

'They're well used to it,' Owen said, as he crossed to the door. 'If you're around later in the week, give us a ring. Mary would love to have you over for an evening.' Cate gave him one of her marvellous smiles, and fled. When she got into the car she realised that she felt miserable again. Everything around her looked bleak, and she couldn't find it in herself to rise above it. She wasn't usually like this, she thought, as she turned on the ignition.

Her spirits didn't lift when she pulled up outside Helen's house a short while later, with its stark garden adorned by a lone tree in a tub. It depressed her to think of her sister driving over every evening from that office, that horrible office, to this place, which was so wrong for her. Even Helen hadn't been able to stand up to social pressure, even she conformed. She wasn't like Owen who threw himself blindly and shamelessly into the quest for social approval like an otter leaping into a river; nor like Cate herself, whose very career and standing with her colleagues depended upon her ability to read the signs of the times more quickly and fluently than most, and to endorse them with enthusiasm. Helen should have stayed in Andersonstown, where she'd been living when she first started to work with Owen,

Cate thought. She'd liked it there, but the pressure to conform had been too much, even for an idealist like Helen. Cate let herself into the house and found no comfort in the bare hall and the chilly sitting room. She stood for a few moments trying to decide what changes were needed: a stronger, warmer colour for the walls, to begin with. The room was big, it could take it. Maybe some sort of urn over in that corner, or there needed to be more focus on the fireplace . . . This was a habit of Cate's, she couldn't help doing it, even in houses more successfully furnished than this. She did it to other women too, assessing their clothes, their hair, their make-up, professionally, but not unkindly, she liked to think.

As it was now, the most striking feature of the room was a large framed photograph of Helen and her father on the lawn at Queen's, Helen in her academic gown with her scroll in her hands. She and her father were smiling at each other in such a way that the picture would have appealed even to someone who had met neither of the people in it: the affection between them lifted it above the usual run of graduation photographs. Staring hard at Helen's image, Cate remembered the words her cousin Una had used when she collected Cate at the airport that night two years ago. 'Helen's just gone to pieces,' was how she'd put it, when Cate asked after her mother and sisters, and when Cate saw Helen, later that night and in the following days, the phrase had come back to her as being horrifyingly accurate.

Beside the graduation photograph, which sat on top of a bookcase, there was another, much smaller picture: a framed black-and-white snapshot showing the three sisters when they were children, sitting on the back step of the house, eating sliders. Cate, smiling, took it in her hands and sat down on the sofa to study it in detail. Charlie Quinn's daughters. Anyone could easily have recognised each of them from their adult selves, the similarity was almost comic.

The first year Cate had been in London, a colleague had remarked to her in mid December that she would be spending Christmas with her parents, and that her sister would be there too.

'Not that it matters much to me,' the woman added, 'we're not very close to each other.'

'When did you last hear from her?' Cate had asked, and the woman had frowned and thought for a moment.

'I don't think we've been in touch at all since a New Year's Eve party last year, now I come to think of it.' Cate was so amazed by this she hadn't known what to say. It was just around this time that she'd changed the spelling of her name, and the family didn't like it: Helen was being particularly prickly and difficult, but no matter how awkward it was between them the idea of their not being in touch for a whole year, and it being such a matter-of-fact thing, struck her as impossible. She could see that the other woman had noticed her reaction, even though Cate still made no comment.

'It's no big deal, you know,' her colleague said. 'We have nothing in common with each other.'

But this only mystified Cate further. What did she have 'in common' with Sally and Helen, except that they were sisters? Surely that was the whole point of family. It was to change strangers into friends that you needed some kind of shared interests, beliefs or aspirations, but with your sisters, what you had 'in common' was each other. Looking back on this now, years later, she was even a bit ashamed to realise how much she'd taken her own family for granted, how unremarkable she'd found the tremendous warmth and love in which she had grown up. She'd always known that childhood was important, and to catch a glimpse into the unhappiness of other people's lives had shocked and unsettled her.

She replaced the photograph on top of the bookcase and went into the kitchen, little knowing that Helen had cleaned it since the weekend, and that what she found so untidy was a significant improvement on what had gone before. Out of the few things available there, she prepared something for herself to eat. There was some bread and cream crackers, but the bread was hard, and the crackers were soft; so she had a cup of instant soup and an apple. She washed up her cup and spoon afterwards, and cleaned around the stove and sink too, thinking vaguely that this might make Helen even a little bit more kindly disposed to her: Cate knew that she needed all the help she could muster.

When she had finished in the kitchen, she made herself a pot of tea and took it back into the other room, where she settled down on the sofa to read. An hour or so later, having tired of her book, she rummaged through Helen's video collection, and decided to watch *The Third Man*. When it was over, she had something more to eat. Had it not been for the rain which was now steadily falling, she would have gone for a walk; but instead she sat down on the sofa again, and picked up her book. Immediately, an irresistible sleepiness came over her. She took off her shoes, put a cushion under her head, and within moments she was in a deep sleep, from which she was awoken some hours later by the sound of the phone ringing.

'It's me.' When Cate's family called each other up on the phone, they never identified themselves by any other means than this phrase, and the recipient of the call was never confused or baffled, for even a moment, as to which member of the family was speaking to them. 'Oh, hello, Helen.'

'Are you all right?'

'Yes, fine, great,' Cate lied, for she had been hauled out of a dream about the man whose child she was expecting, and felt disoriented now to be listening all of a sudden to Helen talking about what time she expected to be home. She would stop off and get pizzas to save them having to cook and would that be all right, and did she want a Four Seasons or a Pepperoni, and Cate was saying yes, yes, whatever you want, whatever you think best. And then suddenly the conversation was over, and she was sitting there holding a buzzing receiver, and trying not to cry.

The dream had been horrible. She had never dreamt about him before, she even thought about him far less often than she would ever have believed likely in such circumstances. She had, however, dreamt frequently about the child, and that wasn't pleasant either: always the same, of going into a nursery and seeing a cot at the far side of the room, with the child sitting in it, in a straight-backed, rather adult posture. When Cate approached it, the child would turn and look at her in a somewhat sceptical way, which always made Cate feel glad that it was too small to be able to talk, because it looked as if it would have plenty to say if it could.

In this new dream, the child's father had looked pretty sceptical too. They were sitting together in a restaurant to which they had often gone, but which she would never have considered for a moment as a suitable venue for breaking the news to him. But it appeared that that was what she had just done, and he was reacting as she had feared he might, without ever really thinking that he would. In her dream he was surpassing her worst imaginings, denouncing her loudly, so that everyone could hear. The whole place fell silent, the sound of conversation and the clatter of cutlery dying away, and although people pretended not to listen she knew that everyone was agog. How could they fail to hear his loud accusations of selfishness and deceit, and what would they make of her own failure to argue against this? She couldn't find a word to say in her own defence, although as soon as she awoke, it was all she could do not to start blurting out excuses and explanations to her sister.

Not that she'd needed to explain herself, up until yesterday, for in reality he had been kind to her, and had offered her all the help and support she wanted, which was none; she only intended to go on with her life without him, and she wondered afterwards why she had told him at all, why she had risked trouble. The only reason that she could dredge up was that it wouldn't have been either fair or decent to keep him ignorant of the situation, and that had been of enormous importance to her, to be able to tell herself that she was acting with fairness, and decency. But now, in the aftermath of her dream, she was no longer so sure about this.

There were two clear points which Cate could not reconcile. One was that she would never admit she had deliberately set out to get pregnant; she'd have sworn that by all she held dear. The other was that when she received the results of her pregnancy test, she'd felt a rush of pure delight. And she'd never have admitted that to anyone, either.

What had happened? Was it just because of the age she had reached? She didn't think so; nor did she like to. She didn't like to make a connection between this and her father's death, but everything was different now because of that. Even while her life had appeared to go on much as before, to her it was utterly changed, in ways she would never have expected. Her initial reactions had surprised her. The grief and anger she felt she could understand, but she couldn't explain why, on returning to

London, she'd flung herself back into life there as if her own life depended on it. One of the first things she did after the funeral was to arrange to have her apartment redecorated in pale colours which gave a greater sense of light and space. She sometimes bought more flowers than she had vases for; she became seriously interested in food and invited people round to dinner more often than ever before. She bought herself some new clothes which, even by her own extravagant standards, were outrageously expensive. But when she was with her friends she could sometimes see that they weren't at ease with her the way she was, that there was something about all this which didn't add up. So sometimes she went alone at nights amongst strangers, and she watched the crowds surge in the West End, she craved noise and brightness and colour.

And yet, for all of that, her life had gone sour. The grief was always there. It was as if for years she'd been walking on a tightrope, but had been so skilled and gifted that she hadn't even known she was doing it. Now she had suddenly swayed, had looked down and seen that she might well fall, and fall a long, long way. Worse, people wouldn't care, it would be little more than a curious spectacle to them; and some people would be quite happy even to shake the rope.

There'd been a coolness and reserve with some of her colleagues after the funeral, and it was something more than the English being less comfortable with the bereaved than the Irish were. What they were thinking only dawned on her slowly, and it was so horrible that she shrank away, afraid of having to confront it until she was forced to do so; and of course it wasn't long before that happened.

One day, about three weeks after she returned to work, a journalist who had often done freelance work for the magazine in the past had called in to discuss a supplement which had been commissioned in Cate's absence. As she looked through the initial work he'd brought along she remarked, 'I'm sorry I wasn't in on this from the start, but I was in Ireland,' and she didn't know why she added, 'My father died.'

'Yes, I know,' the man replied. 'I read about it in the papers.'

Cate lifted her head from the material she had been glancing through and stared hard at the man, but he stared back coldly at her, and did not speak. 'He thinks my father was a terrorist,' she said to herself. 'He thinks that he brought his fate upon himself; that he deserves the death he got.'

Afterwards, she couldn't remember how she'd brought the exchange between them to a close. She remembered sitting at her desk leafing through the pages he'd left with her, not seeing them, and wondering if your heart could literally turn to iron in your chest, for she felt like that was what was happening to her. She didn't think she could contain her anger, she surprised herself at how calmly she was able to say to a colleague who came into the room, 'We'll go through with this project because it was commissioned when I was away, but I don't want to use him again in future. The quality of his work has gone down; we need fresh talent for the magazine.' But when her colleague protested (as well she might have done, Cate knew, for there was absolutely nothing wrong with the man's work), it was then that her temper broke.

'Did you hear me?' she said, banging the desk with her fist. 'I'm in charge of this department. What I say goes, and I say that he won't work for us again. Is that clear? Is it?'

She could see how the other woman was shaking with fright as she left the room after this unexpected outburst and Cate's own hands were trembling as, sitting alone now, she covered her eyes. She knew that she was in the wrong. Later, she might apologise to the other woman, but she wouldn't go back on her word about the journalist. So she was being unfair: well, life was unfair and if he didn't know that, it was time he found out. Yet even as she recognised and nursed her own meanness of spirit, she was appalled by it. Her anger this afternoon came from the same source that had caused Sally, gentle, good-hearted Sally, to say words Cate could never have imagined coming from her: 'I hate those people, and I hope somebody kills them.'

When she left the office at the end of that day, she felt inexplicably weary. Usually, she would unthinkingly join the rushing river of commuters which had shocked and disturbed her when she had first arrived in London, but which was so much a part of the city that it now seemed barely worthy of mention. Having become a part of that phenomenon herself, she had been mildly surprised at the strength of Sally's reaction when she visited her:

'When they say "rush hour" here, they really do mean it, don't they?'

But on this particular evening, Cate felt as though she had just arrived in the city, and was unable to cope with it. On Hungerford Bridge, people jostled her and impatiently pushed her out of the way. The tracks sparked blue as a packed train pulled slowly out of Charing Cross. She could see the faces and bodies of people pressed up against the glass of the windows, like bottled fruit. The rumbling weight and proximity of the passing train unnerved her. Abruptly, Cate pulled herself out of the flood of people, into one of the recessed areas of the bridge, where she leaned against the railings and looked down at the green water sliding past. Then she raised her eyes to take in the huge, glittering city: the festoons of white lights swaying along the South Bank, the dark winter sky, the dome of St Paul's and the lit, clustered buildings all around it: the whole unstoppable engine of the city itself.

In her apartment, there was a vase of stiff, thornless yellow roses. Before leaving for work that morning she had gently inclined one of the flowers towards her, and stared into the heart of it, into the dense arcs of pure colour. Had there ever been another such rose? Yes indeed: she remembered the fat, soft yellow roses her grandmother had grown, and which still grew: Brian would bring them to Cate's mother in slack bouquets, the stems sheathed in tinfoil. The roses would grow and fade and grow again; the tree would force out leaves and then buds and then roses, no matter who lived or died, no matter who saw the blossom, or cared for its existence. And the city before her, she now realised, was as fragile as the roses, constantly renewing itself, but a finite thing, an illusion. And although she could not remember making any conscious decision there, later, when she thought about why she wanted to have children she would always remember that evening when she stood upon the bridge; and how, on returning to her apartment she found upon the table scattered yellow petals. The only explanation she would ever be able to give was this: 'I wanted something real.'

She turned and looked at the clock. In no time at all now, Helen would be back.

Chapter Eight

Now all the newspapers from London and Dublin, as well as those from Belfast, were full of articles about what was happening in Northern Ireland. On television, there were reports of marches which ended in violence; of bomb attacks on water and power installations; and endless political wrangling. The children knew all this was important because of the attention given to it not just by their parents, but by almost all the adults they knew; who spent hours talking about what was happening, what might happen, and what ought to happen. The sisters quickly learnt not to interrupt any of these discussions, nor to make a noise while the news was on the radio or television; but they were still too young to understand fully what was happening. There was tremendous delight and excitement at home when Bernadette Devlin was elected to Westminster; but Helen's, Kate's and Sally's lives were still more completely focused on such matters as a spelling test at school, or a trip to the dentist's, or the prospect of an outing to the cinema in Magherafelt or Ballymena. They discovered in April that year that their cat Tigger was going to have kittens, and they happily watched her swell over the weeks until she was like a furry torpedo waddling around the back yard. They petted her and prepared a new bed for her; pleaded with their mother for the cat to be given extra food and milk; speculated on how many kittens she might have, and what names they would give to them.

But then Lord O'Neill, the Prime Minister of Northern Ireland, resigned on the very day Tigger produced her brood, 'and bloody well spoiled everything', as Kate said that night. She'd rushed into the house to announce the news about the cat, only to be hushed by her parents, who were staring at each other with incredulity and anger as they listened to a well-bred voice speaking on the radio.

'He was the best of a bad lot,' their father said at the end of the broadcast, 'and if that's what he thinks of us, you can just imagine how the rest of them see us. What is it, sweetheart?'

'Tigger had her babies,' Kate said, 'six of them,' and she didn't know why her mother laughed ironically at this, nor why she said, 'That's three more than I had!'

Things degenerated quickly over the following months, and came to a crisis that summer. For a time, the reports they saw on television were still at odds with the world around them. They watched images of policemen in Derry, in full riot gear, battle against people throwing stones and petrol bombs. Derry was little more than an hour away by car, but it wasn't a city they ever visited, unlike their cousins: Aunt Lucy had a sister there, and Johnny, Declan and Una used to be taken to see her. They watched the black-and-white pictures while their parents fretted, and then they stepped out of the house again into the light of an August evening, where the swallows swooped and dipped in jagged flight around the back yard; where cattle ambled through the long grass; and where the honeysuckle bloomed by the green gate.

But then the rioting spread to Belfast, and trouble broke into their world. On a television news report they recognised the street where their mother's friend Miss Regan lived, whose house they visited every Christmas. At the end of the street was a burnt-out car, and the reporter said that many people in that part of the city had been forced to flee their homes. Their father urged their mother to phone Miss Regan and tell her she could come to stay with them if she wanted, until things calmed down, and when she couldn't get any response, they worried until late that afternoon, when Miss Regan rang them. She told them she had gone to stay with her sister in Newry, 'although who knows if I'll ever be able to go back to my own house,' she said, 'or if I'll have a house to go back to. It's like a war, Emily.'

Emily tried to comfort her by saying what a good thing it was that the British government had decided to send troops to Northern Ireland. The people who lived in the areas where the trouble took place over the summer were relieved and thought that they would be protected now from further harm. Emily and Charlie also thought it was a good thing, but Uncle Brian disagreed. 'It would have been better if our own had been able to look after us,' he said. 'Dublin has let us down badly. Lynch'll live to regret his empty promises.'

'But if the Irish army were to get involved, we'll have all-out civil war,' his brother protested, and Brian shrugged.

'It looks like we're going to have it anyway,' he said.

The British troops were first in Derry, then Belfast, and then all over the north. It was strange at first to see their heavily armoured vehicles on the quiet country roads. Helicopters would land in the fields near the house, their blades beating flat the grass and startling the cattle where they grazed. 'I suppose we'll get used to it,' Charlie said, to which Brian replied, 'Well, you shouldn't. They ought not to be here, and don't you forget it.'

Brian was not alone in his growing militancy. By the end of the year, the attitude of most of the people they knew towards the soldiers had soured considerably. Charlie wouldn't be drawn on this, and protested mildly that they'd done him no harm. His contact with the army was mostly confined to brief exchanges at security checkpoints, until the day the military actually came to call on them at home.

They were all at table in the kitchen one Saturday in the middle of the day, when Kate, who was facing the window, suddenly said, 'Daddy, there's a soldier in the back yard; no, more than one, look!' At that moment, someone knocked on the back door. 'You all stay here,' their father said, as he went to answer it. They sat, hushed, trying to hear what was being said, and when their father came back into the room, there were two soldiers with him.

'These men want to ask us a few questions,' he said to Emily.

'We'll go into the front room, then,' she said, seeing the soldiers glance at the remains of the meal on the table.

The room into which they all now went was dark, formal and seldom used. Emily and the children perched stiffly on the armchairs and sofa, Charlie stood with his back to the cold hearth, and the younger of the two soldiers, who was carrying a long gun, moved over towards the china cabinet. Through the small, deep windows, they could see the shadow of another soldier standing by the front door, and yet another was hunkered down beside the tree. Taking out a notebook and pen the soldier who was obviously in charge explained politely that their regiment, which he named, was new to the area, and they needed to have some information on people living locally. He said that their help and co-operation would be appreciated.

'I'll start with you, Sir, if I may. Your name?'

'Charles Quinn.'

'Can you spell that for me, please?'

The soldier went on to ask his middle names, his occupation and date of birth. 'And now you, Madam.'

'Emily Mary Quinn.'

'Maiden name?'

She looked surprised at this, but she answered.

'Date of birth?'

She flashed a glance at the children, then looked at her fingernails and mumbled something.

'I'm sorry, Madam?' She repeated what she had said, loud enough to be audible this time, but in sullen tones.

'And now these young ladies,' he said, smiling at the sisters. They saw their parents look at each other, puzzled and slightly alarmed. Their father shrugged and coughed. 'Well, that's Helen,' he said before Helen herself could speak, 'and she was born on the tenth of January 1959.' When the soldier had full details of everyone in the house, down to and including Sally, he asked if anyone else lived with them, or stayed in the house frequently. He wanted to know how many outbuildings there were on the farm, and whether or not they had a dog.

'I suppose you want to know the dog's name too,' Sally said, and the soldier, looking up sharply from his notebook, stared hard at her. 'He – he's called Brandy,' she said, in a voice barely above a whisper.

'Is he now?' the soldier said, smiling. 'And is he a good dog?' Sally nodded.

'I have a dog at home in England,' he said, pleasantly, as he put away his notebook and pen. 'He's called Muffin. He's a Labrador.'

'I don't know what Brandy is,' Charlie said. 'I think he's a bit of everything,' and he and the soldier pretended to laugh. Then the soldier thanked them, and Charlie showed the two men to the door.

And as soon as it was over, they could hardly believe it had happened. They watched from the window as the soldiers walked away out from the shadow of the house and into the bright sun, fanning midges from their faces. As soon as they were out of sight it was as if they had imagined this strange thing, that two soldiers, one in full battle dress and with a gun, the other with an accent they could barely understand, had come into their front room and asked them all sorts of odd, personal questions, and then gone away again.

'In under Christ, what was all that in aid of?' Emily said when Charlie came back into the room.

'Damned if I know,' he replied. 'Did you notice the one over by the china cabinet, the face of him? He was no more than a child; I'm sure his ma isn't getting a wink of sleep with him over here. I'm glad I was civil to them,' he went on, digging into his pocket for his cigarettes and matches. 'There's no harm in being civil.'

It was a phrase he repeated that evening to his brother, on whom the soldier had also called.

'You should have told them hell roast all,' Brian insisted. 'You're too bloody soft, Charlie, that's your trouble. Believe you me, they can find out all they want to know about you without ever asking you, or you telling them anything.'

'I think Brian's right,' Emily said. 'What call have they to be asking the likes of me, in my own house, what age I am and what my name was before I was married?'

'It was the bit about the dog got me,' Charlie said. 'What odds is it to them if I have a dog?' Brian rolled his eyes.

'They want to know that,' he said, 'so that when they're snooping around your five outbuildings in the middle of the night, they'll know what the likelihood is of there being a dog about that'll sink its teeth in their arses. Christ, Charlie, did you come down in the last shower, or what?'

'Well, I'm sure there's plenty of them no more want to be here than we want to have them here,' he said.

About a week after that, Kate and her father were in McGovern's shop when a soldier came in, wanting to buy cigarettes.

'I'm afraid I can't serve you,' Mrs McGovern said.

'Any reason for that?'

'You know as well as I do,' she replied. The man shrugged, and left the shop again.

'I'm sorry about that, Charlie, but what am I to do?' she said, lifting down a jar of Clove Rock and starting to weigh it out. 'I don't want to antagonise the army, but by the same token, there's men in this country and if they thought I was serving soldiers they wouldn't leave me with one stone on top of the other of either house or shop.'

'You needn't be apologising to me,' he said, 'I know the way you're fixed.'

'It's not fair of them to come and ask me, so it's not,' she went on. 'They know fine well the sort of area this is, and they're only doing it to see what I say.'

In due course the soldiers stopped coming to the houses to ask for information, and they stopped attempting to buy things in the local shops. Stories began to circulate about young men: friends of friends, or the sons of people they knew; driving home from dances late at night and being stopped at checkpoints and beaten up for no apparent reason. In broad daylight Charlie would be stopped at a road block a few hundred yards from his house, and asked his name and occupation. They would look at his driving licence and make him open the boot of the car. They would ask him where he was coming from: 'That grey house there, beyond the tree,'; and where he was going: 'Up to the shop, to buy a newspaper.' When he came back, less than five minutes later, the same soldier would stop him and, poker faced, ask him exactly the same questions again, as if he had never seen him before, and would again make him open the boot of the car. When this happened to him time and again, even Charlie's legendary patience broke, and he began to feel sullen and resentful towards the security forces.

That spring, Granny Kate fell and broke her arm. She made light of it; and the whole family was amused when she appeared at Mass on Sunday with the arm tied up in a sling made from a silk scarf which toned in perfectly with the suit she was wearing. 'Just because I've hurt myself doesn't mean I have to stop being elegant, does it?' she said. School ended for the summer, and they enjoyed the laziness of long, empty days; while always aware that things were still getting worse in the society around them.

Then, one morning in August, so early that they were all still in bed, the telephone rang. It woke Helen and she crept to the door of the bedroom to hear what was being said. It was evidently Granny Kate, and she was upset about something, because their father kept trying to calm and soothe her. 'I'll be over now, as soon as ever I can,' Helen heard him say. Then she stood very still as he came up the stairs again and passed the door behind which she was standing. She strained her ears to hear what he said to their mother when he went back to the bedroom.

'That was Mammy. The soldiers came this morning and took away Peter and Brian. They're all in a state about it; I said I'd go over to them immediately.'

'Can I come too?' Helen was at the door of her parents' room now. 'Please?' Her father started to protest, but for once it was Emily who argued in her favour. 'Take her with you. If the soldiers stop you on the road, there might be less of a chance of them giving you trouble if you have Helen there.'

'You're more optimistic than I am, if you think that,' he replied, but he told Helen to go and get dressed as fast as she could.

It was still dark when they left the house, with the faintest tinge of light on the eastern horizon. When they arrived at Brian's and Lucy's place, her father called out, 'It's only me,' when he knocked on the door. Lucy let them in through the back scullery and into the kitchen. The place was in uproar. All of the children were out of bed, and all of them were crying. Lucy was red eyed too. Only Granny Kate, tightly wrapped in a pale-blue dressing gown, seemed to have retained any sense of calm, and that was tempered with anger.

'We heard a banging at the front door, that woke every one of us up. Brian was going to answer it; and he was halfway down the stairs when he heard them shouting that it was the army. "What'll I do?" says he, but at that minute the army kicked the door in. They saw him on the stairs and they came up after him, grabbed him by the hair and said, "Are you Brian Quinn?" Brian says, "Aye," and they tell him he has three minutes to get dressed; that they're taking him away. Then Peter comes out of his room, he hears this, and says, "What's all this, what are youse doing to my brother?" So the soldier that was in charge just nods at Peter and says, "We'll take you too." And they half-pushed the two of them down the stairs, and threw them in the back of a big army truck that was waiting outside. I asked them where they were taking them, and why, and they wouldn't tell me.'

'What shape was Peter in?'

'He's been well this past couple of weeks; he was sleeping here in the house. But the both of them were afraid.'

'Jesus, this is desperate.'

'I was scared they'd have taken you, too. I was that glad when I rang you up, and you answered.'

Helen's father suddenly turned to Lucy. 'Would you ever make us all a cup of tea, love? Look at Declan there, his teeth's chattering, look at Una. Away into the scullery there, and help your mammy.'

Lucy and her children went out of the room, and under cover of the sound of the running tap, as the kettle was filled, and the clatter of crockery, Helen's father said to Granny softly, urgently, 'Do you know have we anything to fear with Brian?' Her eyes fixed on the door to the scullery, she shook her head vehemently. 'Are you sure, Mammy?' he urged in a low voice. 'Are you sure he's in nothing, that there's no stuff about the place?'

'I'm certain,' she said, also speaking very quietly. 'I was afraid something like this might happen. I was afraid of more than that, I was scared that if there was things about the place the children might come across them, or the army, and I could never live here if anybody was hurt or killed about the place. So I got Brian on his own about three weeks ago. I asked him straight out, was he in the IRA, and he said no; and I asked him was he keeping guns or stuff safe for anybody, and he said no again. I told him that if he ever did, it would be the end of all, and I warned him that if he ever did anything that got Peter into trouble, or that got anybody hurt, I'd leave this house and go and live somewhere else. And he told me I could put my mind at rest on that score.'

'So why did they lift him?'

His mother shrugged. 'Why did they lift Peter?' she said, as Declan came into the room carrying a tray with cups and saucers on it.

Later that morning, when they heard that people had been interned all over the north, and they learnt the names of some of their other neighbours who had been taken away, their father no longer puzzled as to why his brothers had been included; rather, it seemed odd that they hadn't come for him, too. As well as local known Republican sympathisers like Brian, and Willy Larkin's father, they'd taken people like Mrs McGovern's two brothers, one of whom was involved in the civil rights movement, and one of whom had no political involvement whatsoever; although Mrs McGovern remarked grimly, 'That might change, after all this.'

Charlie spent the rest of that day trying to find out where Peter and Brian had been taken. Mrs McGovern rang late in the afternoon to say that she now knew her brothers were in an army barracks up near Derry, and that maybe all the men from one particular area were being taken to the same place. The following day they discovered she had been correct in this guess; following a nervous night, in which Charlie had feared that they would come for him too, but saw no way to avoid it.

They were released in the early evening of the second day, and when Lucy rang to tell Charlie that they were home, he immediately drove over to see them, and again took Helen with him.

What they found on their arrival, though, confounded Helen's expectations. She knew that they would be glad to be home, and a relieved, even happy, atmosphere was what she expected to find, instead of the electric anger of the family at the brothers ever having been taken away, and at the rough treatment they had received. It was hard to believe that they had only been gone for two days, for they looked so utterly different; weary and unshaven, as though they had undertaken a long journey. Brian also had a cut just under his right eye. He told them the soldiers had interrogated him for hours, wanting to know the names of people who were in the IRA, and of people he knew who had guns and explosives. They'd bullied and threatened him, and when he said he didn't know any such names, he'd been hit in the face. His fury and the violence of his language as he described what had happened frightened Helen.

She withdrew to the sofa at the far side of the room, where

Peter was sitting. Brian's dog, Spike, was sitting at his feet, with its head lolling against Peter's knees. He had his left hand on the dog, stroking and ruffling the hair on its neck; and in his right hand he held a tumbler of neat whiskey, from which he was steadily drinking. He barely spoke, just nodded or said 'Aye,' when Brian asked for confirmation of some point he was making. As he raised the glass to his mouth, Helen noticed the frayed cuff of his shirt, and suddenly she made the connection between Peter and what Brian was saying. She saw Peter being dragged out of an army jeep, being sworn at and kicked, she saw soldiers scream abuse in his face, saw them twist his arms up behind his back until he cried out. He drained his glass as though it had contained water, and quietly asked Declan to bring him over the bottle from the table. Helen felt a terrible anger now too, an anger she would never forget.

But no sooner were they all back at school, and trying to settle down for the autumn, than something else happened, which broke into their lives and upset them. One night, in late September, Tony Larkin, the eldest brother of Helen's school friend Willy Larkin, died planting a bomb at an electricity pylon over near Magherafelt. 'A pylon,' their father said bitterly when he heard the news. 'A fucking electricity pylon,' and that startled them, for he almost never used language like that. 'Where did he think that was going to get any of us? Did he think that was going to free Ireland?' Tony was nineteen. Lucy rang them early in the morning to tell them what had happened, Mrs McGovern having phoned her. Everyone wanted to save everyone else the shock of hearing it for the first time on the radio. But even forewarned, there was something unsettling about watching the television that evening, and hearing a name so familiar pronounced in so distant and public a way. The newsreader struggled with the pronunciation of the name of the place where Tony had died. All that day they had heard people talk in hushed, grieved tones about what had happened, and it was odd now to hear the same story told blankly and without emotion.

Helen remembered how much Willy had looked up to Tony; how he had boasted about him. 'Our Tony's not afraid of anything, so he's not.' Once Tony had killed a fox. He gave the skin to Willy, who brought it into school to show everybody; and that was what Helen remembered now, the rank smell of the red pelt, and Willy stroking the fur with his hands and saying, 'There's nobody in the country as brave as our Tony.' When Helen closed her eyes, she saw the desolate field where foxes lived, and where Tony died; a field bound by dense hedges of hawthorn and sloe. She and Kate had heard the bomb explode. Just as they drifted off to sleep the night before, there'd been a long rumble in the distance. They'd both known at once that it wasn't thunder, and not just because the weather earlier that evening hadn't promised thunder. Already they had learnt to distinguish between that noise and the flat, sullen trailing sound a bomb made. 'I wonder where that is,' Kate had said, and then they'd fallen asleep.

That night, their parents went to the wake, and when they came home the children could see that their mother had been crying. A strange atmosphere hung over everyone and everything at the time of Tony's death, a hushed and grieved air, and there was a distance between people, as though no matter how much they talked, they remained deeply isolated from each other. The children noticed this at home, at school, where they said prayers for Tony, and for his family; and it was most apparent in the church on the day of Tony's funeral, which they attended at their father's insistence. They were shocked when they saw Willy and his family, for they looked as if they were living in some other dimension; and the children thought that if they had tried to speak or to communicate with them in any way, the family wouldn't have been able to connect. Mrs Larkin looked as if she were locked into some terrible dream, from which she didn't have the energy to struggle to awaken. She looked as if she had been crying for two solid days; and when Kate said this to Emily later that day her mother replied, 'You're probably right in that.' They had never before seen so many people packed into the small church, and by the end of the funeral, Kate thought she might faint from the heat and the stuffy air, and the heavy smell of incense as the coffin was carried out. As soon as they were outside the doors of the church, a tricolour was put over the coffin, and a beret and black gloves placed upon it. Brian told them afterwards that he'd heard that Father Black had forbidden them to put the flag on the coffin while it was still inside the church building. Six men and women emerged from the crowd. They were dressed all in black, with black berets and dark glasses, and they walked three on either side of the cortège from the door of the church to the graveside. Amongst them Helen recognised the fair-haired girl whom she'd seen with Tony at the carnival, and on other occasions; and in spite of the dark glasses, you could see that she'd been crying too. Father Black said the last prayers of the ceremony as the coffin was lowered into the ground, and the people standing near by heard Mrs Larkin say, 'Tony, Tony, how am I ever going to live without you?'

And then something happened to break the air of dignified sadness which had marked the day up until then. The men and women in black produced guns, and when someone gave orders in Irish, they raised their arms and fired a volley of shots over the open grave. Many of the mourners applauded loudly; some of the men even whistled and cheered. Their Uncle Brian was one of the men who clapped hardest of all, but their father didn't join in.

When they got into the car to go home, they sat in silence for a moment, and then he said to them, 'Never forget what you saw today; and never let anybody try to tell you that it was anything other than a life wasted, and lives destroyed.'

Chapter Nine

WEDNESDAY

She'd always been fond of flowers and plants, but after Charlie was killed it became an obsession; the only thing in which she could become completely absorbed, often the only thing that made any sense to her. She grew sweet pea on a trellis and in a shaded part of the garden she grew red tulips clouded in forget-me-not. Under the windows she grew night-scented stock, and from the hearts of the white-and-purple stars the rich scent reeked at dusk. At Easter the house would be golden with the daffodils she put everywhere in vases and jugs and jars, their trumpets blasting the dim air; and no matter how many she cut more remained, heaving and sinking in thick waves of yellow and green on the deep bank where they grew. Every autumn she grew hyacinths in water. As the days grew shorter she watched the white roots creep down and the green shoots push up and then in the dull light of the year's end, the extraordinary flowers would burst out, and drench the rooms with their perfume. She made a garden of her husband's grave. She didn't know how to pray for him, so she cultivated roses on the earth that sheltered his body, and said to him in her heart, 'This is for you, Charlie.' Her daughters teased her about her mania, but she only smiled. She knew they understood. It made her able to bear time, because it hooked her into the circle of the seasons, and time would otherwise have been a horrible straight line, a straight, merciless journey at speed towards death. Instead of which, she had pulled Charlie back into the circle and back into her life, in a way which she wordlessly comprehended, and which offered to her the nearest approximation she would ever have to comfort or consolation.

She was sitting in the conservatory her daughters had had made for her on her sixtieth birthday. She'd been there yesterday morning trying to come to terms with Cate's news when Sally came to talk to her, and she'd insisted that they go to the kitchen, in case there should be hard words spoken that would poison the air and then she wouldn't be able to sit amongst the flowers ever again without being assailed by unpleasant memories. The flowers were important because things meant nothing to her, they never had, not since she was a small child. She wasn't sentimental about any *thing*. Not long after she was married, the Foreign Missions made an appeal for women to donate their wedding dresses to be sent for women in Africa to use. She'd gone straight home from church and got hers ready to be dispatched, but Charlie had done all in his power to talk her out of it, and they reached a compromise of sorts when she said she'd give the dress, but keep the veil and the tiara of paste stones she'd worn with it.

After he died, they'd found in his wardrobe a cache of memorabilia she hadn't known existed: a programme from a dinner dance they'd been to in Halls Hotel in Antrim in 1962, one of Cate's copy books from when she was in primary four, Christmas and birthday cards the girls had made for him when they were little, and a solemn letter Helen had written him when she was ten and Charlie had been in hospital with gallstones, telling him not to worry about the cattle 'because Uncle Peter and I are looking after them until you are well again'. Once they'd looked at them, she'd wanted to throw all these things away, but the girls were upset at the very idea. She couldn't see any point in keeping them, so the sisters had amicably divided the material amongst themselves.

Yes, she'd kept the tiara to placate Charlie, but it never meant anything to her. She let the children use it to play at dressing up as princesses, and in due course it became battered, the veil was faded and torn. Cate had come across it one day when she was about sixteen, and pounced on it. 'Oh Mammy, will you lend me this to wear when I get married?' she asked, cramming it on to her head; and they had all laughed to see it, even Charlie, because she had looked so funny, with her bright face under the broken crown of false stones.

It was a disappointment to her that none of the three had married. When they were growing up she'd always taken it for granted that they would: well, maybe not Sally, but probably Helen, and certainly Cate. It wasn't likely that it would happen now. People said times had changed, but Cate would find that they hadn't changed that much, people would still look down on her because she had a baby on her own. It was still a rare man who would take another man's child on board; and then if they didn't get on together, that would be the first thing he would cast up to her.

'I never wanted you to go to London!' she'd cried to Cate on Monday. 'I knew it would end in trouble.' Both Sally and Cate had stared at her mystified. 'I think you're missing the point, Mammy,' Sally had replied. But the point was, that Emily had always felt afraid when she thought of Cate's life in England. There was no logic to this, when she reasoned it out, for Cate was, and had always been, open to the point of transparency. If she had something to hide, would she have urged her mother so frequently to go and visit her? The invitations were never accepted, but Sally and Helen went to stay with Cate, and they, together with Michael and Rosemary, encountered only the kindness, luxury and generosity that were the essence of Cate. But once, when she was home for a holiday, Emily had gone into Cate's room and suddenly she understood what it was that troubled her. She looked at the big black Filofax on the dressing table, the glass dish full of rings and gold chains, the neat row of marvellous shoes over by the window: the sophistication of Cate's possessions made Emily see her not just as a daughter, but as a woman; a woman leading a woman's life in a vast, anonymous city, and she realised that it was the thought of that that had unconsciously frightened her.

And then there was Helen. Unlike Cate, she was completely dismissive of the idea of marriage, so much so that Emily found it hurtful. She remembered how at Young Michael's wedding (and what a deal of coaxing there'd been to get Helen to go to it!) Rosemary had said, half as a joke, 'And what about you, Helen, when are you going to give us a big day?' Certainly it was tactless, and Helen had a right to be annoyed, but her icy dismissal of the whole idea was so complete, so final, that Emily had been shocked and saddened by it. She couldn't understand why Helen would feel this way, given that she'd grown up in a house where there was a happy marriage. It wasn't as if Helen had seen her and Charlie fighting all the time, or Charlie drinking the stars out of the sky, the way some men did. She would have liked to ask Helen, but she was too afraid. She didn't like to admit that she was intimidated by her own daughter, but it was true. Sometimes when Cate came home she would feel a little strange with her at first, because she was beautiful. She looked like one of the models in that magazine she worked for, but her personality broke through the gloss almost at once. Within ten minutes of coming into the house she would have kicked off her shoes, she'd be looking in the cake tin, she'd be letting the cats into the kitchen to play with them, she'd be driving you mad and making you laugh the way she did when she was ten. But Helen was different, and always had been.

Cate had given her more worry than Helen and Sally put together, and look at the pickle she'd landed herself in now, and at her age, too. When Cate was a teenager Emily's biggest fear had been that Cate might get pregnant. She remembered lying in bed at night listening to the sound of the rain and the wind, Charlie snoring away beside her, but she wouldn't close an eye until she heard some old car rattle up to the house, and then the back door would open, and the longer the interval was between the car pulling up and the door opening the more anxious she would be. Then she would hear Cate tiptoe up the stairs, home from the dance that, more often than not, she'd argued about with Emily until she'd been granted grudging permission to attend it. She hadn't liked some of the boys Cate had gone about with in those days, they were a bit wild, and she worried even more about the ones she didn't know. Then once, in the middle of an argument she'd lost her temper and said, 'What if you get into trouble and have a baby, what then? That'll be your life ruined; and all your education lost.'

'My education?' Cate said. 'What about me? What about the baby? Is that the only thing that matters in life, education? And anyway, how can you say that to me? Everybody's always making me out to be far worse than I am.' She was crying by this stage, and Emily ended up apologising to her, but there was a coolness between them for a long time after that. Cate had felt deeply insulted and hurt by what her mother had said.

They'd never had any trouble with Helen going out to dances, because she'd never looked to go, she'd only ever attended to her school books. Emily had never seen anybody who studied as hard as Helen, and now she thought that perhaps she and Charlie should have tried to persuade her to go out more, although at the time she had been glad. She used to say that if the three of them had been like Cate she would have been at her wits' end with them. Oh it was all very well that Helen had a good job and money and a house, she'd made it to the top of the tree, but the price had been too high. She'd always been deeply serious, even when she was a child, yet Emily had never thought she would grow up to be so cold and formidable. Once, when they were all at the convent, Sister Benedict had said to Emily, 'Helen is, if anything, too much of a paragon. Kate is an imp, but she is also one of the most likeable girls in this school. And Sally does what she's told.'

She had never wanted daughters anyway: did they know that? Of course she'd never told them, but she read somewhere that children could pick up and understand far more than you would ever imagine in a house, even when they were tiny. She'd felt guilty at her own disappointment when Helen had been born, healthy and safe but not the son for whom she had longed. Charlie didn't care, in fact he'd been delighted. He said he didn't understand all the fuss about having boys. 'It's not as if we're royalty,' he'd said, 'and by the time she's grown up, women will be less put down than they are now.' All the Quinns had been delighted with Helen, because Charlie had had no sisters, and Brian's and Lucy's first child had been a boy too, so a girl was a great novelty in the family. Maybe that was why Helen and Cate had been closer to Charlie, right from the start. Helen was always so self-possessed, unlike Cate, who from day one had yowled and cried freely for whatever she needed or wanted, who had learnt how to charm people from before she could walk. 'She has me wound round her wee finger,' Charlie used to say, as if nothing could give him greater contentment.

And then when Emily was pregnant for the third time she'd been afraid that if it was another girl, she wouldn't be able to love it at all. The irony was, that she ended up closer to Sally than to either of the others. All the nurses in the hospital had remarked how much the new baby resembled Emily; and then she'd been weak and frail right from the start, so that she needed her mother in a way that perhaps Helen and Cate had not. Was it that she had known then that Sally would be her last child, and that the idea of a son was just a dream to be forgotten? From the very beginning they'd clung to each other, literally clung, Sally holding her skirt, holding her hand, always sitting beside her and pressing up close, as if she wanted to be absorbed back into Emily, as if she wanted to become her. And then the terrible days when she started school. Helen had gone off calmly when her time had come, and Cate, bored at home without her elder sister, had clamoured to be allowed to go too. But Sally had screamed and clutched the bannisters every morning for the first six weeks. It was Charlie who'd prised her fingers away and carried her, roaring, with her fists flailing, to the car where Helen and Cate were waiting, bemused and mildly entertained by the spectacle their little sister offered. Emily herself had lain on her bed and wept as the car drove off. The house was empty, and silent without the children; she'd hated it, and she kept Sally home on the slightest pretext, for the merest sniffle or ache.

Even now Sally was still slighter and frailer than her sisters, but there was a strength in her that Emily, who had thought she knew her youngest daughter to the depths of her soul, hadn't realised existed. She'd seen it first when Charlie was killed, not so much in the immediate aftermath, but in the weeks and months that followed, when other people thought she was probably beginning to 'get over' what had happened (as if she ever could!). Sally had known instinctively what she needed then, she'd known the times when Emily was truly helpless with grief, and then she'd cooked for her and looked after her. But she'd also known the times when Emily needed firmness, needed to be pushed. Then Sally would ask her mother to make scones or to let down the hem on a skirt for her, or insist on some other domestic chore that was exactly the distraction Emily needed. Sometimes Sally listened to her far into the night as she talked about Charlie, Charlie, Charlie. Sometimes she told her sharply that there was no point in wallowing in grief, ordered her to talk about something else; and all this tenderness and sharpness was administered with an exact, even eerie, knowledge of what sort of treatment Emily needed at any given moment.

But although she knew this side of Sally existed, Emily had been taken aback by her assertiveness on Monday, when Cate told them she was going to have a baby, issuing commands, packing Cate off to Belfast the next day and then going to work on Emily to win her round. It was the first major disagreement she'd had with Sally in her life. Even in the smallest things they were usually in accord, agreeing so easily on such matters as what colour to decorate the spare bedroom, so that any dissent was only initial, was like the hesitancy you might have in your own mind between the leaf green and the shell pink. It wasn't like two people discussing something, it was like one mind thinking aloud, debating with itself until it reached a decision as to what it liked best.

Emily had slept badly on Monday night, not because she was lying awake thinking about Cate, but because she found herself thinking about her own life and the course it had taken, thinking about her childhood in particular with an attention to detail she rarely allowed herself.

She couldn't remember her father's face properly, and that had always troubled her, puzzled her too, because she could remember other aspects of him so clearly: the tweed waistcoat that smelt of tobacco when you pressed your face into it, the bloodstone ring, the clip of his fountain pen in the breast pocket of his jacket. Images unfolded in her mind like flowers. She was sitting on his knee by the hearth and he showed her pictures in the embers of the fire: a man walking along a road, a cat washing itself, a house in a forest. She was sitting in class in the white school where he was headmaster. They had put their heads on their folded arms to rest, and she could hear the soothing drone of children in the next room reciting their tables: 'Two ones are two, two twos are four, two threes are six, two fours are eight . . .' and the sound was like a warm rug wrapped around her. After it rained, there was a rich smell of earth and vegetation. Her father took her to the beach, and they walked along the pale sand. They collected shells in a tin bucket, and he told her that all the seas were one sea, that one ocean merged imperceptibly into the next. The sea at the top of the world was cold, there were polar bears there, and icebergs; but the ocean in the tropics was warm and blue and there was coral there, and marvellous coloured fish. And then, later, she came to understand that time was like the ocean, in that all the things that had happened in the past were linked in an extraordinarily simple way. History was no more than the effect of one day following another, one day following another, spooling back from the present to a time when women wore odd hooped skirts and bonnets that hid their faces, back to a time when men killed each other with swords and thought the world was flat, back to a time when people lived in caves.

And then one morning her mother came to her bed and shook her out of her sleep; shook her out of the warm, happy dream that had been her life up until that moment, and told her that her daddy was dead, her daddy had gone to Heaven. She never saw him again.

Later that morning, she and Michael were driven through a landscape locked in a drizzling mist to stay in Ballymena with their mother's sister. They spent three days there, finding it impossible to play, as they were commanded to, in the high, dusty rooms where the light was grey and the only books available were heavy and huge, with close dark type and no pictures. Michael cried for his parents, cried for boredom, cried for fear; and Emily made desultory, big-sisterly attempts to comfort him, telling him that they'd soon be going home.

But when they were taken back to be with their mother, she was busy packing. 'It's not our house,' she explained briefly. 'We have to make way for the new teacher who'll be taking over your daddy's job.' Until she saw their mother efficiently breaking it up into its component parts, she hadn't thought of their home as being made of a series of independent objects. She'd thought that the dresser and the long pale table could exist only in relation to each other as a part of their kitchen, and it unsettled her to see her mother coolly decide to sell the one, and take the other with them when they left. There wouldn't be room in their aunt's house for all their things, and their mother expected them to understand this and to co-operate, not to be sentimental and selfish; so there was a tremendous fight over Emily's bucket of shells, a fight that began with a request, moved to coaxing, insistence, tears, shrieks, and ended with a full-blown tantrum, Emily kicking the bucket to the far side of the room and screaming that if she couldn't have the shells, she didn't want anything ever again.

In the years that followed, this rage would occasionally make itself felt. Her spirit was broken by the time she was twelve, but spirits, whether those of a child or a society, never break cleanly, and the people who didn't understand this were shocked when the dull, quiet girl, so eager to please, suddenly displayed a violent temper. They thought these two sides of her were at odds; couldn't understand that the malevolence was the logical corollary to the obsequiousness. One day followed another, and the image of the man she'd loved, who'd made his handkerchief into a mouse to make her laugh, who'd walked with her on the beach, and explained things to her, was replaced with a myth, a distant figure frowning in a picture frame, whom she could honour only by becoming a teacher, like him, and all her memories became like dreams.

'Nobody asked me if I wanted to be a teacher,' she would say to her daughters, years later. 'I was put to it. It would never have crossed Mammy's mind to ask me if I might have preferred to do something else. But I was lucky, I liked it more than I expected I would.'

She remembered how Cate had remarked once that it was only when you lived away from Northern Ireland that you realised, on returning, how deeply divided a society it was, and how strange the effect of that could be. As an example, she'd cited the time when Sally had absent-mindedly answered a hairdresser's stock question 'Where are you going for your holidays this summer?' with the word 'Italy', and how she'd seen the woman's face change colour in the mirror. She continued to snip in silence for a few moments more, then said, 'Will you be staying in the Vatican?'

'Actually, no,' Sally replied. 'I'm going to Rimini.'

The whole family had fallen about and laughed till they wept when Sally told them this; and thinking of it helped Emily to understand the point Cate was making. But when she was growing up, it had seemed completely natural that she should go to the local convent school, and after that to a Catholic teacher training college, and on leaving, teach in a Catholic school. Even though her daughters were old enough to remember Northern Ireland before the Troubles started in the late sixties, they'd only been children then, and couldn't have been aware of just how difficult it had been for Catholics at that time. Emily herself, as a young adult in the fifties, had only vaguely understood it. She remembered sitting in the garden of her aunt's house in Ballymena on a warm summer evening, listening to the sound of a flute band practising in the distant streets for the Twelfth celebrations. She listened idly first, just thinking how tinny it was, what poor music, but then she began to think about why they were playing, and as the flutes gave way to the harsh clatter of the big drums, she realised that those people hated her, *hated* her, and would give her and her family no quarter. And she felt not just the mild fear that was so habitual that she took it for granted, but also a bitter anger. Her mother had come into the garden at that moment and Emily had said furiously, 'Why do we have to listen to that? Why do we have to put up with it?' and her mother had looked at her with incomprehension. It was, until the time she met Charlie and Brian, her moment of greatest political awareness, but she wouldn't have been able then to define it thus.

At that time 'politics' meant Stormont, meant a Protestant government for a Protestant people, so if you happened to be a Catholic, the message was clear. You just worked as hard as possible within the tiny scope that was allowed to you, and that in itself was so time consuming and difficult that few, and certainly not Emily, had the insight or the necessary energy to begin even to think of how things ought to be, or might be, changed. Education was the only hope, it was like a rope that you struggled to cling to, in the hope of pulling yourself up to a position less disadvantaged than the one in which you started out. Keep your head down, look to your own, and don't expect too much in any case: nobody ever said those words explicitly to her, but then nobody needed to, because the world around her wordlessly insisted on this every single day of her life.

She felt ashamed now of her lack of awareness; but then it was only fair to remember that her sense of personal dispossession had been so intense that it perhaps would have been asking too much of her when she was a young girl to unravel the strands of her own unhappiness, to identify and name each cause in turn. Sometimes she remembered what her father had told her about time and the ocean; and the sense of dislocation from her life with him was so great that she couldn't believe nothing separated her from the past but that simple chain of one day following another, one day following another. The loss of her father, which brought with it the end of her childhood, left in her life a terrible wound which nothing could heal until the moment she walked through the door of a Belfast primary school as a trainee teacher. Lying in bed now, over forty years later, the names and faces of the children came back to her: Martin and Bernadette and Mary and Henry and Joe, with their open faces and harsh accents, their freckles and their scabby knees, their short trousers and cotton dresses: they were lovely children. They gave her more than they ever knew, for they gave her not a path back into her childhood, because that couldn't be done, but a way of building on the happiness of those early years in a way she would never have thought possible.

Ballymena was a quiet country market town, and although Emily hadn't enjoyed growing up there, she'd become used to its air of Presbyterian rectitude, its rain and Sunday silences. She hadn't expected to like Belfast, because on the occasional visits she'd made there it had seemed to her a loud, grimy, ugly place. When she went there to attend the teacher training college she found that even if these impressions were accurate, they were irrelevant. It might be an ugly city but it had a beautiful position, tucked between the mountains and the sea. The rows and rows of terraced red-brick houses, with the mills, the yellow gantries of the shipyards, the spires of the churches, and the bare slopes of the Black Mountain together gave the city its atmosphere. The air was smoky, and when she woke in the morning, she could hear the clang and rumble of trolley buses going up and down the Falls Road. She didn't tell her mother, but she decided that when she was qualified, she would do her best to find a job in Belfast, rather than go back to Ballymena as was expected of her.

She blossomed at the training college, and made friends there, which she hadn't done in Ballymena because she'd been made to feel that her aunt was doing a great favour in allowing them to live in her house, and that to start bringing other little girls in would be pushing her hospitality to its limits. In her first term she made friends with a woman called Agnes Bell, whose father owned a pub near Randalstown. Angular Aggie, they called her, because she stayed skinny no matter how much she ate. 'Amn't I a fierce rickle of bones?' she used to say plaintively, nipping at the flesh on her legs and arms. For all that, she loved clothes, and they'd often gone shopping together in the city centre. Because her father was so well off, Agnes could afford wonderful suits and dresses out of places like The Bank Buildings and Robinson and Cleaver's which were far beyond Emily's reach, even after she was qualified and earning a good wage.

She quarrelled with her mother over her first pay packet, something she never forgot and for which she never forgave her mother because it spoiled the long-awaited delight of having her own money that she had earned for herself. Michael was still at school, and she accepted that she would have to contribute substantially, but her mother thought that what she offered wasn't enough. More than that, she said that if Emily had any sense of gratitude for everything that had been done for her, and the education she had been given, she would hand over her pay packet unopened every Friday night, and let her mother decide how much should go to the family, and how much Emily should be given for, as her mother put it, 'her own amusement'. The 'amusement' included lodging in Miss Regan's tiny red-brick house near Clonard, and Emily's mother did regard that as a luxury which could have been done without if Emily had had the decency to look for a job in Ballymena, so that she could live at home again. 'No chance,' Emily had said to Agnes, and the two of them had danced round the room when they both got jobs in the same school in the lower Falls, where Emily had done her teaching practice. She'd needed good clothes too, nothing as classy as the things Agnes wore, but more and better than her mother realised, because it was important for teachers to be well turned out then. Everyone expected it, even the children, and you wouldn't have been respected if you were scruffy.

Her daughters thought that the life she'd lived then had been a terrible hardship, although it hadn't seemed so bad to her. 'How did you stand it at all?' they used to ask, but she'd actually enjoyed much of it, and she enjoyed telling her daughters about her life at that time. She described to them the frugal room she'd had in Miss Regan's house, Miss Regan who couldn't cook, whose fried eggs were always burnt on the bottom and raw on the top, whose sausages always split in the pan, whose steak suet pudding defied description. They used to go to Clonard Women's Confraternity together once a week ('Talk about high living!' Helen said). Sometimes to treat Miss Regan and to spare herself Emily would tell her not to cook a dinner and they had fish and chips instead, which Emily paid for. Even now, after all those years, Emily remembered how much she had enjoyed those evenings, and if ever anyone passed her on the street eating chips the smell of the vinegar and the fried potatoes brought back to her how much it had meant to her to sit in the minuscule parlour; and the fire in the hearth, Miss Regan's huge, kind eyes, the sound of the buses and the sound of the rain, the street lights dappling against the pulled blinds. She didn't try too hard to explain to the girls why she'd felt so contented then, because she'd have had to explain how cold her own home life had been, and even though she knew they knew about that, she would have felt disloyal. Sitting in the parlour in Belfast there'd been a cosiness, an easiness, that she had never felt in her own family home.

Emily still wasn't convinced that teaching was an easier job now than then. 'It was a real profession in my day,' she used to say to Sally, 'you were well regarded and society backed you up.' The children then would never have turned the word on you; Emily could scarcely believe some of the stories she heard now, of even very small children swearing and shouting at their teachers.

The conditions had been hard, though, there was no denying that: forty children to a class was nothing unusual. Sometimes you had had to share a classroom with another teacher, and then the lessons had to be carefully co-ordinated, so that one group wouldn't unduly disturb the other. Sally was shocked when Emily said she hadn't even had a chair, there hadn't been the space for it: there had just been a teacher's table pushed up hard against the wall. It meant that she'd been on her feet from the first bell of the day to the last. Often at the end of the week it was as much as she could do to drag herself into the city centre on a Friday afternoon and take the bus to Ballymena. Like most of the passengers, she usually fell asleep as they drove through the countryside. No wonder she'd been so reluctant to hand her wages straight over to her mother!

Sometimes it made her sad that the children she taught had such a tough future ahead of them. Emily might regret their lack of ambition, but at other times she would think it a blessing that they didn't have high aspirations that would only be frustrated. When she asked them what they wanted to do when they grew up most of the boys said, 'I want to drive a horse for Wordie, Miss,' meaning Wordie Cowan, the brewer. The girls didn't even have the prospect of the linen mills where their mothers worked, for by the nineteen fifties, even these were being closed down. On the buses Emily shrank from sitting beside the mill workers for fear that the long white threads that clung to their clothes would attach themselves to her own coat or dress. She felt guilty, though, about drawing back from these weary women, whose own mothers brought the women's children to school every day, and placed them in Emily's care. As far as the unemployed fathers were concerned, the big shipyards and the other heavy industries of Belfast might as well have been on the moon for all the chance they or their sons had of getting a job there, because they were Catholics. Only the most gifted, the most determined and the most hard working had even the slimmest chance of making out well in the world: and yet education was their hope.

During the course of the first autumn term, Agnes's brother Paul started to take an interest in her. He'd drive up to Belfast in his father's black Zephyr, and take her to the cinema, or dancing in the Floral Hall on the rare weekends she stayed in Belfast. She realised afterwards that she hadn't really been interested in him, he was as skinny as Agnes herself, and it was the attention he paid her that was flattering. She told her mother and aunt about him, not even thinking why: she'd have been shocked if anyone said she was boasting, but that was exactly what it was. She only realised how foolish she'd been when she proudly showed them the crystal necklace he gave her that Christmas. She remembered how her mother had held it up against the light, admiring its sparkle, and suddenly her aunt said, 'He must mean business, Emily.' She had a cold, strange feeling in the pit of her stomach. 'Oh, I don't know about that,' she said, reaching out her hands for the beads which felt to her now like morsels of ice. 'He has plenty of money, I'm sure as far as he's concerned it's just an ordinary wee Christmas present,' which somehow didn't add up with the triumph with which she'd first shown them the necklace some moments earlier. Her mother and aunt smiled, and her aunt said, 'Oh, go away on out of that!' Emily put the beads back in their box.

So when she started going out with Charlie a couple of months later, she didn't let on to her family. Funnily enough, she met him through Agnes too. Agnes had an uncle who was a priest on the Missions in Nigeria, and when he was at home for a holiday, Agnes's family held a big barn dance to raise money for him to take back to his parish.

All through their married life, Charlie would tease her because she couldn't remember the exact moment they met. But Agnes had dragged her around the dance that night presenting her to so many of her friends from home, that the moment when she said, 'Emily, this is Charlie Quinn,' became lost immediately in a blur of similar introductions. What Emily did remember was the end of the night, when she was saying goodbye to Charlie. 'The next time you're up in Belfast, come and see me,' she said. 'I'd like that. Agnes knows where I am.' He'd looked surprised, as well he might have done, for it must have looked terribly forward. But she was willing to risk having him think badly of her if that was necessary, if the alternative was not seeing him again because she'd stood too much on her dignity. At some point in the evening, after that initial introduction, they'd ended up together again, sitting on a bale of straw, drinking Coca-Cola, and talking. It made her realise how little she cared for Paul. What had mattered was not Paul himself, but that her mother would be impressed with the gifts he gave her, that Miss Regan would notice and admire the fine car in which he came to collect Emily, what mattered were the lunches, the dances, the trips to the cinema, but Paul himself didn't matter at all.

When Charlie did come to Belfast and started taking her out, it was Charlie himself Miss Regan commented on, not his possessions. 'He's a lovely big fella, Emily,' she said over their usual breakfast of burnt toast and gluey porridge the morning after she met him. Agnes proved to be a good friend, too, telling

Emily not to worry about Paul. 'I've told him already he's out of the picture.' Later in the spring she asked Emily if she'd mentioned Charlie to her family.

Emily said that she hadn't. 'Well, I would, if I were you, because they're going to get a right shock when you tell them you're getting married, and it turns out to be to some person they've never heard tell of.' Emily didn't reply, but she took the advice offered. Her mother didn't seem to notice, though, particularly when she found out how small and poor a farm he had. Emily insisted on this point, and her mother, she realised a long time afterwards, misunderstood this, took it as an indication that she wasn't, couldn't be, serious about him. Oh, she'd thought her own mother so cold in comparison with Charlie's mother when she met her, and there couldn't have been a clearer display of the difference than when they decided to get married: Emily's mother's anger and tears; Charlie's mother's tears and delight. 'Of course they're delighted,' Emily's mother said, 'they have all to gain and nothing to lose from this. What will you do about your career? I can't believe you're just going to throw it away like this.'

The worst thing was, her mother had a point here, something which Emily herself had thought about without resolving the problem. At the end of her first year's teaching, they took the children on a trip to Groomsport in County Down for the day. The only photographs she had from her time as a teacher were some pictures one of the other teachers took with a Box Brownie on that day, and every so often she would take them out and look at them. The children had been so excited: it was such a big treat then to go to the sea. The night before, Charlie had asked her to marry him, and she'd said yes. Sitting on the beach, she realised that she'd always thought that someday she probably would get married, but not for a long time. If she went to live in the country, she would have to give up her job in Belfast, but if she was married, it would be hard, maybe impossible, for her to find another job there. It wasn't seen as right for women to go on working when they were married, they were supposed to stay at home and look after their own children. It was so unfair that she couldn't have both, she thought, as she watched the children run and scream on the beach. Even Agnes, when she asked her later, wasn't able to offer her much comfort: they both remembered from the training college stories they heard about women who went for job interviews and who put their engagement rings in their pockets before they went in. But they always got found out, they never got the jobs, and were called deceitful and sly for having tried to hide their intentions.

A week after Emily told her mother she was engaged, her mother sent her a letter cut out from *The Irish News*. Emily had seen letters like this before, but coming in the post to her, with no accompanying note from her mother, it had seemed like a poison-pen letter directed to her personally, and the words burned into her mind:

> Sir,
>
> One notes with sorrow the growing number of girls who, on marrying, selfishly retain their jobs in our Catholic schools, thereby denying employment to unmarried girls who need teaching posts, and, more importantly, to men, many of whom may have wives and children of their own to support. To see such a lack of understanding of their own Christian vocation as wives and mothers makes one wonder if closer attention needs to be paid to the type of girl who is selected to be trained as teachers. Are girls so ignorant of the role God has ordained for them the sort of people to whom we should be entrusting the care of our children?
>
> Yours, etc.,
> Patrick Gallagher

She'd responded by tearing the cutting to shreds, and posting it back to her mother, again without a covering letter. Things went from bad to worse after that. Emily became increasingly bloody-minded: she would admit that now. So she couldn't have both her husband and her job. So be it: she chose to marry. So her expensive education would be wasted: was that not the fault of society, for not letting her use it? Why blame Emily? She made her mother admit without difficulty that it was to give it up for so little that was shocking to her. If Emily had decided to marry Paul, who would inherit his father's pub and house, that would have been a different matter. Education used as bait to get a good catch was, evidently, not a waste of years of study in the way marrying someone with no money was.

'She'll come round to me in time,' Charlie said, with endearing optimism. She never did.

And Sally knew her mother so well that it was just this point she had worked round to yesterday when she argued Cate's case. Poor Cate this, it had been, poor Cate that: to begin, her main concern had been to urge compassion. Cate must surely feel bad about what had happened, Sally argued. So what were they, her family, to do? Force her to feel more miserable still? What end would that serve, but to drive her away. Cate only had her family now. This man, whoever he was, had evidently walked away from the situation: were they to reject her too?

'And don't forget,' she'd said more than once, 'it's a baby we're talking about, your grandchild, my niece.'

'I never wanted a grandchild in these circumstances,' she'd said, and was surprised at the vehemence with which Sally had rounded on her.

'And do you think Cate wanted this? I'm sure Cate would have wanted to get married before she had children, but it hasn't worked out that way, and no one needs reminding of the pity of that less than Cate.'

Sally was right. You couldn't always choose what happened in life, but you *were* free to decide whether or not you thought something was worthy of regrets. 'If you regret things that don't merit it, you give them more power, more dignity than they deserve,' she thought. Sally had pressed on, though, pushing the issue to consequences that Emily might have allowed her mind to flit around, but which it was unbearable to hear spoken aloud. Once she knew the baby was on the way, what could Cate have done about it? Plenty. It would have been easy for Cate to have had an abortion in London, Sally said bluntly, and none of us would have been any the wiser. Is that what you really would have liked? she asked, as Emily howled and wept. No not that, never that. Well then, Sally said. But by having the baby, would she, Cate, be setting up a circle which, she, Emily, would be forever forcing her to square?

It was just this dilemma that Sally was asking Emily to spare Cate. Emily had thought that once she'd married Charlie, her mother would bow to the inevitable and accept him; but she didn't, and there was nothing Emily could do to change this. If her mother had decided not to accept that Emily had made a good marriage, that was her choice. After a few years, Emily had stopped trying to win her round: she seldom went to visit her: it was always Charlie who took the children to Ballymena to visit their grandmother, insisting that he would never be the cause of a total breakdown in communication between Emily and her family. 'Life's too short,' he kept saying. 'She won't always be there, and then you'll feel bad about it.'

'I feel bad about it already,' Emily had always replied to him. Believing that she was right and her mother was wrong was no proof against guilt. 'It was like walking around for thirty years with a nail in the sole of your shoe,' she used to tell Sally.

A few years after her mother died, which happened when the girls were still at school, Emily dreamt one night that she was with her family on a raft which was drifting down a river. Only Emily was awake: her daughters, husband, brother and mother were all curled up sleeping, and as she watched them, she was aware of all the things about them which she didn't like, which annoyed her. Her mother's rejection of Charlie. Helen's untidiness, her sarcasm. Cate, in the dream, was wearing her school uniform. Her nails and lips were crimson, and Emily thought bitterly about the rows they had had about make-up and dances and clothes. She looked at Charlie and remembered how angry she'd been when she found out that he'd been giving money to Peter, money they could well have been doing with for their daughters. Long-forgotten incidents, some serious, some trivial, crowded in on her as she stared at her sleeping family with vexation and resentment.

Suddenly, she became aware of the distant roar of water: aware of what it meant too. The raft was headed for a waterfall. They were all going to drown, and the raft drifted on inexorably. There was nothing she could do to avert disaster.

How different everything looked in the light of this knowledge! It was laughably foolish to get upset about Cate's lipstick. Charlie's largesse to his brother became a virtue rather than a flaw, but most significant of all, her attitude to her mother was transformed by the spirit of compassion and forgiveness she felt now towards her doomed family. She couldn't change the fact of things but she could change how she saw them, and in that way she could determine the effect they had on her. This knowledge was the nearest she ever came to a reconciliation with her mother, but she found she couldn't talk to anyone about what she had learnt, not even to Charlie. All she could do was try to tell her daughters that it was important to know what mattered in life and what didn't, and that often it was the things you wouldn't have expected that mattered the most, and that a great deal didn't matter at all.

She passed her hands over her eyes. It all seemed so long ago, because now everything was different. Against the dream of the raft she had to set another dream, one which had troubled her, night after night, which gave her no peace.

She was standing in Lucy's kitchen, and at her feet was a long thing over which someone had thrown a check table cloth. There were two feet sticking out at one end, wearing a pair of boots she'd helped Charlie to choose in a shop in Antrim. The other end of the cloth was dark and wet; there was a stench of blood and excrement. At the far side of the room, a young man was cowering: eighteen, nineteen years old at the most, a skinny, shivering boy in jeans and a tee-shirt, with ugly tattoos on his forearms. His face was red and distorted because he was crying. 'Please, Missus,' he kept saying to Emily, 'please, Missus, I'm sorry for what I did, I'm sorry, so I am, please, Missus . . . ' She stood staring at him until he was crying so hard that he could no longer make himself understood. Then Emily spoke, quietly, distinctly.

'I will never forgive you,' she said.

Oh she couldn't tell even her own daughters what it was like to wake from a dream like that and know it was the truth, to know that your heart had been forced shut. To be a woman in her late sixties, to have prayed to God every day of her life, and to be left so that she could feel no compassion, no mercy, only bitterness and hate, was a kind of horror she had never imagined.

She had confided only in Father Johnston, the young curate who had anointed Charlie, and she'd talked to him, oddly enough, because she believed he wouldn't be able to understand. He came to see her frequently after the killing. They sat facing each other across the kitchen table. Sometimes there would be long silences in which neither of them spoke. She turned away from him, looked out of the window at the winter sky, the bare trees, the grey waters of the lough.

'The world's empty to me without my husband,' she said to this young man, who'd probably never known what it was to take a girl in his arms and kiss her, much less share his life with someone for almost forty years. 'I can't forgive them for what they did, Father. I'll tell you more than that: I don't want to be able to forgive them either.'

'Mrs Quinn,' the curate said, and the tone of his voice made her turn towards him again. 'I saw what they did to your husband. If somebody did that to my father, I wouldn't be able to forgive them either. I think the best I could manage would be to pray that someday I might be able to want to forgive them.' They sat in silence again for some moments. 'I hope you don't mind that I come to see you so often,' he said, and Emily had realised then that it was as much to console himself as to console her that he came to her house. 'I go to see the other Mrs Quinn too, but that's different, being there . . . ' His voice trailed away, and he dropped his eyes, embarrassed, realising he had said too much. Brian had told her that he had heard the priest being sick out in the yard after what he'd seen in the house.

'You're always welcome here, Father,' Emily said. He smiled timidly at her, and she thought of how she had longed for a son. She called him 'Father' but she thought of him as a child.

He'd have been little more than a baby when the Troubles started, for it was twenty-five years ago now. When she was at school, she'd read about the Thirty Years War, and she remembered asking the teacher how there could have been such a thing. 'Did they fight battles every single day for the whole of the thirty years, Miss, or did they stop for a rest every year or so?' The teacher had said that she didn't know.

Not long before Cate came home, Sally had taken Emily into Ballymena to do some shopping. They went into the Skandia to have their lunch, and at a nearby table they saw Mrs Larkin. Emily said hello to her, and they exchanged a few words; but during their meal, she found that she couldn't help looking over at Mrs Larkin. A wee woman in a grey coat, you'd never have picked her out in a crowd, you'd never have been able to guess all she'd been through: how she stayed closed in her bedroom for months after Tony died; how she wouldn't utter a word, as if she had been struck dumb; how she'd been in and out of the mental hospital for years after that, until gradually she began to speak a little, to live again a little. At Charlie's wake she'd gripped Emily's hand and said, 'If people tell you you'll get over it, Mrs Quinn, don't believe them, because it isn't true.' There'd been well over three thousand people killed since the start of the Troubles, and every single one of them had parents or husbands and wives and children whose lives had been wrecked. It would be written about in the paper for two days, but as soon as the funeral was over it was as if that was the end, when it was really only the beginning.

Look at Lucy: poor Lucy, who had always been so relaxed, so easygoing. She'd been on tranquillisers and sleeping tablets for months after she saw Charlie being killed. They'd had a big security light installed in the yard, that switched itself on when anybody came near the house; and bolts and double locks fitted on the doors. It was like Fort Knox when you went over to see Brian and Lucy now, you could hear the keys rattling as they let you in; and still Lucy was living on her nerves.

Nobody could fathom the suffering the Troubles had brought people, and all the terrible things that had happened. When Sally came in a moment later with a cup of tea and some biscuits for Emily, it somehow confirmed this: Sally going over to the window and saying wasn't that a lovely chaffinch on the tree there; asking Emily if she was warm enough; admiring the Dutch fern Helen had bought for her a couple of weeks ago: this affectionate ordinariness was the dearest thing in life for Emily, and that was what had been destroyed: Charlie should have been there with them.

Sally turned away from the plants and sat down opposite her mother. 'Well, have you had a reasonable afternoon? Did you have a good think about things?'

'Ah, my mind's been all over the place. I was thinking about your daddy.'

'And about Cate?'

'I thought about all of you.'

Sally paused. 'And Cate?' she persisted gently.

It was some moments before Emily spoke. 'What I know, Sally, is this,' she said at last. 'The next time Cate comes home from England for a holiday, she won't be on her own. She'll have a wee baby with her. And I can make the pair of them welcome, or I can always be reminding Cate, even without saying anything directly to her, how bad a show it is for the child to have no father. And I could go on doing that until the child itself is old enough to know what's going on. But where would that get any of us? It's what your daddy was always saying, life's too short for that sort of thing. And yet it is a bad show, Sally, what's happened. I won't be able to feel the way I ought to or indeed want to for a while yet. And you and Cate are going to have to bear with me on that. I know what's required of me, but it'll take time. Cate will have to be told that.'

Sally smiled. 'This is as much as I ever expected you to be able to say at this stage; in fact I think it's great you're already this far forward. You're right, too, Cate will have to have this explained to her.'

They heard the sound of a car pulling up outside the house. 'That'll be her now. Stay there, I'll let her in, and I'll send her in to you, and you can tell her about it yourself, right now.'

Chapter Ten

They still went over to see Brian's and Lucy's family every Sunday afternoon. On one such day together with their cousins, they went out for a walk by the shore of the lough, and when they came back, they could hear voices raised in anger as they approached the house. On going into the kitchen, they found all three brothers locked in dispute.

'I'm not trying to make out it wasn't a bad business,' Brian was saying, 'for it was.'

' "Bad business"?' Peter shouted. 'For Christ's sake, it was a massacre!'

Even before he said this the children had guessed what the adults were arguing about; even when they had been down by the shore they knew that their parents would be talking about the bombings in Belfast, because for the past two days, no one had spoken about anything else. That Friday, twenty-two bombs had exploded in the city centre in the space of an hour and a quarter. Nine people were killed, although at first it had been thought that the toll was eleven: the dead had been so badly dismembered that the emergency services had had difficulty in knowing how many bodies they had actually found. Apart from the bombs, the IRA had made many hoax warnings that day, so that the city had been thrown into complete confusion, and people tried desperately to escape, only to find their way blocked every way they turned. Six of the people who died had been taking shelter in a bus station, having been warned away from a place near by.

'Don't you even begin to try to explain or justify what happened,' Charlie said, but Brian pressed on, loudly saying it was the fault of the British army, for having deliberately not passed on all the warnings in time.

'And if it had been one of your family killed, if it had been Lucy, or Declan, are you telling me you would still be talking the way you are?' Peter said.

'You have to see it in context,' Brian replied. 'This is a war, and in a war these things happen,' but he was again howled down by his brothers, neither of whom would make any direct connection between this and certain other things which had happened in the past. The children remembered the grief and anger of their parents six months earlier, when thirteen people had been shot dead in Derry. Their family, like almost all the families they knew, had hung a black flag from the window of their house; and the schools which the children attended had been closed for a day, as a mark of respect. 'That was wrong and this is wrong,' Charlie said now; 'the one doesn't make the other right.'

In the middle of the following night, Helen, who was a light sleeper, heard her father go past the door of her bedroom, and down the stairs. She waited and when, after what seemed to her like a long period of time, he hadn't returned, she crept out of her bed and tiptoed down to join him.

The whole house was still in darkness, and she groped her way along the hall until she stood at the open door of the kitchen. She could see the glow of his cigarette at the far side of the room, but even without that, she knew she would have been able to sense his presence there. 'Daddy,' she said, softly so as not to frighten him. He called her over to him and she went, the tiles of the floor stone cold under her slipperless feet, and when she reached him he wrapped his arms around her and hugged her tight. His stubble was rough against her face, but she didn't care, and she drank in the smell of him, which was tinged with cigarette smoke. 'What if . . . ?' he said eventually, and he embraced her harder. 'What if . . . ?' but he couldn't finish what he was trying to say, and she realised that he was crying. She knew now, all in a rush, what he was thinking; and there, in the darkness, it was as if she had already lost him, as if his loved body had already been violently destroyed. They clung to each other like people who had been saved from a shipwreck, or a burning building; but it was no use, the disaster had already happened. All over the country, people were living out the nightmare which she now dreaded more than anything else. Who was she to think she deserved to be spared? He took her back up to her room and tucked the blankets tightly around her in the bed;

he stroked her face and told her he loved her, he told her to sleep. But she gained a dark knowledge that night which would never leave her.

Everybody was afraid now. People were being abducted and killed; sometimes shot, sometimes beaten to death or mutilated with knives. Bombs exploded, often without warning, killing or maiming anyone who had the misfortune to be near by. A parked, empty car, even on a deserted country road, was now a thing to be feared. Sammy who drove the travelling shop, and the man who sold hardware out of a van, had both long since stopped calling at their house. Charlie accepted this because it wasn't a personal slight: as Protestants they no longer felt safe driving around a Catholic area at night. They no longer called with anyone the Quinns knew; but Charlie took to heart Wesley Campbell's refusal to do business with him any longer.

Wesley was a painter and decorator from Castledawson. Over the years he had done work for the family, many times, and they had always been happy with him, because he worked quickly and neatly, and charged a fair price for his labours. More than that, they had enjoyed his company. Every day he would have lunch with them, and during the meal he would keep them amused with droll stories about his mother, who lived with him and his wife. He used to compliment Emily on her baking; and all told, he was a friendly, kind-hearted man. So when Charlie rang him up and asked him when he would be free to come to paper two rooms for them, he was upset to find him evasive. 'I have a terrible amount of work on hand these days; I can't make any promises. I'll get in touch with you in a month or two, maybe.'

Charlie paid no heed to the 'maybe', and rang him up again later that year. This time it was Wesley's wife who answered the phone, and she left him in no doubt whatsoever that Wesley wasn't available to work for him, nor would he be at any time in the future. This curt dismissal left Charlie in a gloomy mood for days. 'Me and Wesley got on great together,' he kept saying. 'Why is he doing this to me? Sure he knows it makes no odds to me what church he goes to on a Sunday. If he never put his foot across the threshold of a church that would be his business. Maybe I'll ring him up again and tell him.'

'You'll do nothing of the sort,' Emily said quickly. 'Leave the man alone. He's probably too frightened to come to a Catholic house now, and you'll only embarrass him if you force the point.'

'Maybe you're right,' he said, and then, after a long pause he added, 'That's the terrible thing, Emily, you're probably right. Wesley afraid to come to my house. That shows you the pass we've come to in this country.'

His unhappiness about this episode was only compounded when he admitted defeat and hired a local man, who turned out to be a sloppy worker, and charged Charlie a fortune.

That September, Kate joined Helen at the grammar school, and did so with a bad grace. It wasn't so much that she wanted to stay at primary school; but she was appalled by the green uniform which she would have to wear every day for the next seven years. 'It's like being in jail, so it is,' she grumbled, and she complained too, once term started, that the teachers were praising Helen to her all the time. They said she would have to be a hard worker, and exceptionally well behaved, if she wanted to be considered as good a student as her sister. 'They might at least wait until they see what I'm like before they start making comparisons, and giving me such a hard time.'

Towards the end of that year, Granny Kelly died. It was Charlie who took the call from Michael and broke the news to Emily. The children, who were in the next room, heard her screaming 'No! No!' and rushed in to see what was wrong. They found their father trying to restrain their mother, who was howling and weeping. 'Why are you so upset?' Sally asked innocently when she heard the news. 'I thought you didn't like Granny Kelly at all,' and this only made their mother cry all the more.

The funeral was a dreary affair, conducted in Ballymena under lashing rain. Uncle Michael was wearing a beautifully cut overcoat; Aunt Rosemary was in fur, and having some difficulty in hiding her relief at Granny Kelly's demise. 'We looked shabby beside them,' Kate said that night, 'and they knew it, too. Mammy was the only person who cared a straw that Granny was dead.' Emily mourned her mother for months afterwards. She would sit looking out of the window, or would stare at the fire for hours, not saying or doing anything, not reading or knitting or doing crossword puzzles the way she would have done in the past. Sometimes, after the girls had gone to bed, they would hear their parents talking together far into the night, in the downstairs rooms. Occasionally, they would catch some of what was being said; and once Helen heard her father say, 'There is nothing you can do about the past. All you can do is make sure you don't make the same mistake again; don't ever alienate the girls so that they grow up to resent you. Stop thinking about your mammy, and start thinking about Kate.'

They hadn't been happy with the way Kate was settling into the convent, and the report they received at the end of that year only confused them further. She had consistently high marks, but the comments of her teachers were, in some cases, not so flattering.

'Are you really bold in class, Kate?'

'No, Daddy!'

'Well, your Geography teacher seems to think you are.'

'Oh she would,' Kate said, dismissively, 'she's just a bore and she only likes bores. Do you know what she teaches us, Daddy? About stones. Can you imagine? She has all these lumps of stone on the window-sill and she expects us to learn their names and how they were formed. Can you imagine anything more dull in the whole world? Anyway, what about Mr Higgins, I bet he says nice things about me.'

'What does he teach you?'

'Maths.'

'He says you're a delight to teach.' Kate grinned at this.

'See?' she said.

'I always thought you found Maths boring,' her father said, looking at her over the top of the report card.

'I do, it's even worse than Geography,' she replied, 'but Mr Higgins is lovely.'

There was more trouble the following autumn. After school, Kate often went into some of the shops in town, while waiting for her bus home. One day she went into a newsagent's to look at the magazines, and got so caught up in her reading that she almost missed her bus. She raced out of the shop and jumped on; and was so busy laughing and chattering with her friends that it was only when the bus came to her stop, three quarters of an hour later, that she realised she didn't have her school bag with her. Charlie rang the police station immediately, but the damage had been done. 'Major security alert, Kate,' he said, hanging up the receiver. 'They have the town centre closed off and the army's getting ready to blow up your school bag.'

Kate looked horrified, and then she began to smile. 'You're pulling my leg, aren't you?' But her father didn't smile back. 'Afraid not.'

He drove her back to the town to collect the bag, and 'face the music', as he put it. They had to go to the police barracks, and an RUC man gave Kate a tremendous telling-off. 'If I had my way, wee girls like you would be locked up in a cell for the night, to show you how serious this is, and then you wouldn't be so quick as to leave your property lying around you in future.'

'It was a simple enough mistake to make,' Charlie said, as Kate began to snivel, and the RUC man then turned on him. 'Well it is,' Charlie persisted. 'All the child did was to forget her school bag. That it caused such problems is more of a reflection on the sort of country we live in, rather than on her.' The policeman contented himself with a few remarks about irresponsible parents, and let them go.

Afterwards they sat in the car, and Charlie let Kate bawl her fill. He pulled out a clean white cotton handkerchief and passed it to her; she blew her nose loudly and raised a blotched face to him. 'I hate it here, now,' she said, through her tears. 'It's horrible. People are getting killed all the time, there's bombs and everything. Everybody's frightened or sad. When I grow up, I'm going to go away and live somewhere else.' She sniffed and added, as an afterthought, 'and it's always raining here, too.'

'Did you buy the magazine you were looking at in the shop?' he asked her, and she shook her head. He took a fistful of change from his pocket and thrust it at her. 'Away and get it now, and I'll wait here; only when you get back to the house, make sure and hide it under your coat so your mammy won't see it.'

Chapter Eleven

THURSDAY

Although the school the sisters had attended as small children and where Sally now taught was less than a mile from their home, it was a mile in the direction of nothing in particular. As a result, Cate had not had occassion even to pass it for many years, and she had not been inside the building since her time as a pupil there. But when Sally talked about her job, Cate would always say how much she would like to see the school again sometime, and on the day after she came back from having stayed with Helen, Sally suggested that they borrow a set of keys from the school caretaker, and satisfy Cate's nostalgia.

But as they drove there, Sally was annoyed with Cate, and for a foolish reason: Cate was in a good mood. Given that Sally's motive in suggesting the visit had had precisely that end – to distract Cate and to cheer her up – Sally could see that there was no logic to her own reaction. In spite of that, she couldn't help feeling resentful. Because she lived away from home, Cate had been spared the pain and emotional labour of helping their mother through her bereavement. And now here was Cate, home with a fresh dose of trouble, and again it fell to Sally to ease the burden: to placate their mother, to plead Cate's case, to defuse, as far as she could, all tension and anger, and prevent rows. She glanced at Cate, who was sitting beside her. Sally knew she would never be able to broach the subject. The long years of trying to please everyone had taken their toll. Concealing her true feelings if she knew they might cause pain or displeasure to those around her and saying the things she thought people wanted to hear had become so natural to her that she now found it impossible to do otherwise. As if to prove the point, Cate suddenly said, 'I'll never forget how good you've been to me this week, never,' and Sally found herself replying automatically, 'Oh, don't mention it. That's what sisters are for.'

They pulled up in front of the school gates and Sally said,

'Now you have to promise me that you won't go on about how small everything looks.'

But Cate promised nothing of the sort, and even before they went inside she was exclaiming about how the wall around the playground must have been lowered, because she could see over it so easily now, and she couldn't believe that the only reason for this was that she had grown so tall. As Sally struggled with the keys Cate went over to the window and, cupping her hands against the glass, she peered in.

'Oh, this is strange,' she cried, 'this is giving me goosebumps, it looks exactly the same as I remember it. God, I think I even remember that wall chart, the one with the rainbow on it. Do you think that's possible?'

'I doubt it,' Sally said drily, as she finally managed to open the door. 'We may not be great about updating the visual aids, but we're not *that* bad either!'

'It even smells the same,' Cate said, as she stepped inside.

'And the tiles, I remember the tiles now, but if you'd asked me the colour of the floor, I wouldn't have been able to tell you. It must feel so odd to you, to be working here.'

'Not in the least,' Sally said. 'I'm used to being here. It would feel far stranger if they closed the place, which they talk about doing often enough. I hardly ever think about the past. Maybe that's something I missed out on by not going away.'

They were standing in the hallway beside a row of low hooks, above each of which was a piece of paper with a name written on it. 'I had a tartan shoe-bag, yours was dark green with white spots, and Helen's was a sort of floral print. I think Granny made them for us. Why do I remember that? Why do some of those things stay in your mind so clearly and others don't?' Cate bent down and read the names of some of the children from the paper labels.

'Patrick Larkin. Is that Willy Larkin's son?'

'You wouldn't need to ask that if you saw him,' Sally said, 'for I don't think I ever saw a child that looked as like his da. You'd maybe ask me if we kept the same kids stashed away for twenty years, never mind the wall charts. Come in here, and I'll show you the room where I teach. I don't really like it when it looks like this,' she went on, nodding at the rows of tables on top of which were stacked all the chairs. 'You don't really get the full picture without the children. It looks bare, too, without the plants and the goldfish.'

'What do you do with them over the summer?'

'Mammy looks after the plants, and one of the children takes the fish home: we draw lots to see who it'll be. By September, it's usually the same story: the fish is dead, and the plants are so big that they won't fit on the window-sills any more. The wee fella who was minding the goldfish last year swore the one he brought back was the one he'd taken home but if it was, it had had a traumatic couple of months, for it had shrunk by a good two inches.'

Cate laughed. She was wandering around the room now looking at everything: the trays of wax crayons and the crates of wooden bricks; the paintings of skewed mothers and fathers lolling outside vivid, pointed houses with trees like lollipops; the list of words for colours written up in the colours themselves. Sally was glad that she hadn't said anything resentful, for it would only have caused bad feeling. Moreover, it might have given the impression that she wasn't pleased Cate was going to have a baby, and that wasn't the case at all. It was the circumstances of the pregnancy that caused problems for their mother, and therefore problems for the family. As far as Sally herself was concerned, the only thing that mattered was that Cate felt good about it, and she strongly suspected that she was hiding her delight for the time being: as Sally was herself. She truly was thrilled that there would be a baby in the family, and she felt sure that their mother would in time come round to the idea too. It was just getting her to that point that was delicate, and that was the key issue at the moment. Looking at Cate now, Sally noticed that she was wiping her eyes, and she decided it would be best not to ignore this.

'Ah, don't go getting all broody on me. Wait a few years and you'll see all this in a different light. You'll have more than your fair share of Play Doh pressed into your carpets and Lego down the back of your sofa, believe you me. You'll be longing for a bit of intelligent adult conversation, never mind a bit of peace and quiet.' Fortunately, Sally had hit the right note with her lightly teasing tone. Too mocking, and Cate would have dissolved into floods of tears; too soft and sentimental, and she would have done exactly the same. As it was, she laughed again, wiped her eyes again, and there were no more tears.

She turned to look at Sally, who was perched now on her teacher's chair, her hands sunk deep in her pockets. She was still so small, Sally, with her fine bones and her delicate face, and the way she wore her straight, toffee-coloured hair pulled back and tied in a ribbon emphasised her childlike appearance. But there was something about her that undercut this impression: something about her brow, the set of her mouth, that made her look like a child who had seen more than she ought to have done, a child who knew too much. Cate had never noticed this in her before, and she wondered when the change had come about. Sometimes she realised that she probably didn't know Sally as well as she knew Helen. She had assumed that her younger sister had a less complex personality than was actually the case, and Cate had therefore wrongly taken for granted what Sally's thoughts and feelings on certain matters would be. She was ashamed of this, looking at Sally now, who was sitting with her legs crossed, swinging her right shoe loosely from her toes.

'Do you ever regret that you stayed at home, Sally? That you never went away?'

The shoe fell to the floor, clattering loudly on the boards.

'I used to,' she said, 'a long time ago; and then it passed and I was glad to be here, and now, well, now it's different again. It's funny. All I ever wanted to do when I was growing up was to be a teacher and get a job here.' She paused, and pursed her lips. She didn't know how to explain to Cate that perhaps that wasn't the truth. Maybe she had only become a teacher to please her mother, and to be like her. She shrugged. 'Anyway, I left college and they offered me this post. The very day I started working, I felt trapped. I wanted out.'

'I never knew that,' Cate said.

'You never asked me, did you? In any case, I kept it well hidden. I gave Mammy a hint of it one night, said something to her about wasn't there a proverb about anyone being able to have whatever they wanted in this world, on condition that it wouldn't bring them the happiness they expected. She picked up at once what I was getting at: "You're not trying to tell me

. . ." she said, and I could see there was anger there, that I'd never be able to explain it to her. So I backed off at once, told her I was happy, I was grand, and that was an end to it. But I still felt restless for a good few years after that. And then I got used to it. You can get used to anything, can't you? That's what people say. Maybe it's true.'

'But why didn't you go?' Cate said. 'I know Mammy and Daddy wouldn't have minded in the long run.'

'Are you really sure of that? I'm not convinced that you're right. Who knows? Anyway, I knew that if I went away, I'd never be able to come back. I wouldn't have been *allowed* back, for one thing. This was a permanent post, and I discreetly looked into the possibility of my getting leave, maybe just for a year, but no. And I always knew that I would want to come back, so I had a straight choice: go away and stay away, or stay put. So here I am.'

'How could you be so sure that you would want to come back? Maybe you'd have enjoyed life more elsewhere, and wanted to stay away?'

Sally laughed. 'I was afraid of that. I was afraid that I would make strong links in some other place, but not strong enough, so that I'd feel discontented wherever I was. When I was over visiting you in those days, I used to think how great it would be to live there, but there was another side too. I felt loyal to home. I hated it when people said horrible things about Northern Ireland. Once, when I was in London I met a man, and he asked me where I was from. When I told him he said, "Oh well, you can't help that," and his friend laughed. I was so angry. I thought if I lived there, that was the sort of thing I'd have to put up with, and I wasn't prepared to stand for it. But it passed, anyway, and I did settle down at home.' She paused. 'It was all right, until Daddy died.' She took a deep breath. 'Now, I want out again. If it wasn't for Mammy, I'd leave tomorrow. I can't stand being in Northern Ireland. All that guff about it being a great wee place, and the people being so friendly. I feel ashamed for having gone along with all that; other people were being killed the way Daddy was, and I was one of the ones saying, "There's more to Northern Ireland than shooting and bombing." Anyway, I hinted to Mammy again, very gently, that I'd like to go away, but she wouldn't hear tell of it. She needs me now. And maybe I need her too.'

Sally was aware of the tremendous emotional dependency expressed in these final understated remarks. It was as much as she would admit to Cate; and Cate would expect no more. They rarely spoke of how their mother had taken possession of Sally so quickly and so completely. She would, of course, have denied it, but the last thing their mother ever wanted for Sally was for her to be autonomous and independent. It suited her perfectly to have her youngest daughter as a companion, whose will and whose nature she had formed to fit with her own needs. So completely had this been achieved that when Sally felt she lacked privacy in her life, or that her mother was selfish in her behaviour towards her, these thoughts were immediately joined by a searing guilt for allowing herself to entertain such ideas.

'But it's not just Mammy,' she quickly added. 'I remember being on holiday in Italy once, and loving it there until I saw this two-day-old English newspaper in a kiosk, with a report on the front page about a car bomb having exploded in Belfast. All at once, I wanted to be there. I felt guilty for not being at home, not that it would have made the slightest bit of difference. I mean, apart from the odd holiday I've been here right through the Troubles, and it hasn't made a blind bit of difference to anything. There hasn't been so much as a shot less fired because of me, but it would have made a difference if I hadn't been here, it would have made a difference to *me*. I can't explain it any better than that.'

'Don't worry,' Cate said, 'I know what you mean.' She remembered many such moments similar to the one Sally had described. One in particular had always remained vivid in her mind. It had been an evening in winter, and she had been working in the kitchen, slicing up beef in thin strips to make a stir-fry. The news was on the radio, and she'd only been half-listening to it, until they started to report on a man who had been found shot in South Armagh the previous night. They were interviewing the local priest who had been called out to anoint the man's body where it lay, in a secluded lane. Cate stopped chopping and put the knife down, as she listened to the soft, hesitant voice describing the rain and wind of the dark night, the long wet grass in which the body lay, how he had gone afterwards to break the news to the man's widow; and his soft voice, his sorrow, were compulsive and terrible. It entered Cate's mind like some gentle, awful thing from a dream, seeping from the radio into the bright, warm kitchen where she stood, looking now in revulsion at the cut, heaped meat on the bloodstained wooden board. She didn't know why, but she wanted then to be home.

'I often think,' Sally said, 'about that remark, "If you're not part of the solution, you're part of the problem." I don't know if I believe that.'

'Are you still in the SDLP?' Cate asked, and Sally laughed out loud.

'Oh that makes all the difference in the world, doesn't it? Sally Quinn's got her wee SDLP card, so we can all rest easy in our beds, we can all sit back and wait for peace to break out. Yes, I'm still a member, for what that's worth. I only ever joined because Mark, the headmaster in this school, asked me to, and it would have been embarrassing to refuse. I suppose I'm not being quite honest in saying that. I do support their principles, with a few reservations; but they're as good as you're going to get. And I know that there are lots of people who support Sinn Fein in a similar vein. The parents of a lot of the children in this school, for example. The SDLP's too middle class for them to feel comfortable with it, they don't feel it can truly speak for them. Lots of them would have much stronger Republican sentiments than I do, but that doesn't mean that they're completely comfortable with everything Sinn Fein says or does. They know at least that the root of all the trouble here is a political problem, and I give them credit for that. It's more than some of the politicians in this country will admit.'

Cate was standing at the back wall of the classroom now. 'Sally,' she said, 'do you blame Brian for what happened to Daddy?'

'No,' Sally said immediately; and then after a moment, 'Well, maybe sometimes, yes.' And then: 'Ach, I don't know. Does it matter?'

'I'd have thought so.'

'To Brian?'

'No, to you. I'd have thought it would be important to you to know exactly what you felt about something like that.'

Sally narrowed her eyes and looked at her sister. 'Can I remind you of something, Cate? In this society it's the people who aren't confused, it's the people who know exactly what they think and feel about things who are the most dangerous. As regards Brian, I might blame him more if it wasn't that he blames himself so much. He talks to me about it from time to time. I asked him not to mention it to Mammy any more, because it only upsets her. Less than a month ago he was still on at the same old thing, "If only I'd got back to the house a few minutes earlier." But I said to him, what odds would it have made? They'd just have killed the two of them, and Lucy would be left today the same as Mammy, and where would that have got any of us? It's a waste of emotional energy, but he can't seem to stop it. And he'd had his doubts for a long time before Daddy was killed. I remember years ago you'd have heard him talking about a thing being an "act of war". If you said about the IRA having done something he'd have answered you at once about things the British army had done, or the British government. And he still is a Republican, he always will be; it's too deep with him for that ever to change. But there are things he can't stomach now, things he won't defend. Cate, he saw what they did, and Lucy did, too. You saw for yourself last night the effect it's had.'

On Wednesday evening, Sally and Cate had gone with their mother to visit Brian. It was a smaller event than Brian had hoped for at the start of the week: they didn't have time to invite Una over, for it was Sally who had called and suggested they go that very evening, partly as a way of distracting both Cate and her mother from Cate's news.

Cate had thought she understood what had happened to Brian's house, and that was why she had refused to go there since the killing. She was afraid of what she might imagine lying on the uneven red tiles where, as children, they'd crouched at Halloween to crack nuts with a hammer. Finally, she'd let herself be persuaded by Sally's and Brian's pleading: 'It's different now.'

But it was the difference that was the problem; the room so utterly changed that only the familiar view from the window of hedges and sky proved that it was indeed the place Cate remembered. She'd stared around at the sterility, the newness of everything: the stripped pine units, the vinyl flooring, the high-backed chairs where Brian and Lucy sat looking ill at ease, no longer completely at home in their own kitchen.

'I suppose it needed done anyway,' Lucy said, and Brian mumbled, 'Ach, it was grand the way it was, but what can you do?'

What indeed? The changes meant that Cate didn't imagine her father lying murdered on the floor, as she had feared, but it also meant that she couldn't imagine the nut-cracking either. She had always thought of her childhood not principally in terms of time, but as a place to which she could always return. Now that was over. What was the word Lucy had used two years ago? 'Desecrated'. That was it. 'The place is desecrated.'

Sally was still talking. 'It's the likes of Aunt Rosemary who annoy me far more than Brian,' she insisted. 'She isn't even trying to understand what's happening here, and at some deep level, I don't think she really cares, so long as her nice cosy middle-class life goes on the same as it's always done. She thinks things are better in Northern Ireland than they were twenty-five years ago, because now there's a Marks and Spencer's in Ballymena.' Cate laughed. 'I'm not joking,' Sally said. 'I don't think she'd even want peace here if it meant a significant change in the material quality of her life. "If people would just stay out of trouble, if they would only get themselves jobs and work and not even think about politics,"' Sally mimicked. 'She's the last person I know who'll still say, "One side's as bad as another." Christ, what a country.' She looked around the room and laughed. 'I'd better watch what I say, I'm usually on my best behaviour in here.'

'Anyway,' she went on, 'you never told me how you got on with Helen the other day. I didn't like to ask in front of Mammy.'

Cate covered her eyes with her hands. 'God, it was dire!' she said. The image was still fixed in her mind of Helen's arrival home. She had rung the bell, because Cate had the keys; and the way she'd leapt up, alarmed at its soft chime, meant Cate couldn't deny to herself how anxious she was about the encounter. But even dire things had their funny side, and when she did open the door the sight of Helen standing there in a navy Alexon suit and cream blouse, a briefcase in one hand and two boxed pizzas held gingerly aloft in the other, did to some extent take the sting out of the moment.

'What did she say to you?' Sally asked.

'Not much,' Cate replied. 'That was the problem.' She'd strongly suspected that Helen was thinking things which, if she uttered them, would be so hurtful that Cate would never be able to forgive or forget them, that their relationship would be damaged beyond repair. 'Only a member of your own family really knows how to hurt you,' someone had once remarked to her, and she remembered how strong an impression this had made on her; a truth she had never before recognised. Oh Helen could have broken her that evening, could have made her weep, made her hate herself; but she didn't and Cate couldn't understand why. Helen remained inscrutable, and when Cate blurted out something about knowing it was an embarrassment to the family, and mentioned Rosemary, a smile had actually flickered around Helen's lips. 'Don't you worry about Auntie Rosemary,' she said. 'If there's any trouble, you leave Auntie Rosemary to me.'

She asked about the father of Cate's child, and bizarrely, Cate thought, one of the first things she wanted to know was whether or not she had any photographs of him.

'I think so,' Cate said, which strictly wasn't the truth, for she knew that she did. Back in London she had a small album which contained photos she'd taken at a picnic they'd made on Hampstead Heath one day in winter. It had been her idea; he'd thought it foolish at first but she'd won him round, choosing a day which was cold but with a bright sun and hard, clear skies. She'd brought hot wine in a flask and she'd pestered him all afternoon, taking photographs; once or twice asking passers-by to take pictures of them together. He'd got into the swing of it all quickly. They'd eaten the fruit and bread she'd brought with her and he said it was great, that winter picnics were as good an idea as winter holidays. But she remembered how, when she was unpacking the picnic basket alone that evening in her kitchen, she'd caught herself thinking, yes, it had been good, it had been fun, it would have been worth doing even if . . . if what? She pulled herself up short. He was just a man she liked, that was all, there was nothing behind it; why shouldn't she go to a park and drink wine and laugh and take photographs with someone she liked?

'Yes,' she said, 'I think I have some photos somewhere,' and she knew that someday she would show her child those photos of a man laughing on a park bench, a man raising his glass to the camera, a man looking out from behind a tree; and she would say, 'That is your father.' And that would be all she would have to show. The child would gaze at the pictures, would drink them in with its eyes, would engage in the impossible task of trying to know this man. And the child would ask passionately the questions which Helen had asked, with seeming dispassion: what is his name? Where is he from? What does he do? Helen left pauses between the questions, and showed no reaction to the answers. How did they meet? Did he know Cate was pregnant? What about the legal side of things, did she need any help with that? Would they keep up contact after the child was born? As the questions became more sensitive Helen's manner of asking became more gentle, so that Cate felt she could evade them if she wished, that were she simply to shrug and refuse to answer Helen would pass on without comment or surprise. She couldn't help fearing that all this was just a trick, even a professional trick from her legal work, a way of softening Cate up and making her relax so that her harsh accusations, when she did finally unleash them, would have a more devastating effect. But when, after a very long pause, Helen finally drew the conversation to a close it was in sorrow and not in anger.

'Imagine,' she said, in a voice so low Cate could scarcely hear her. 'Imagine never having had a father.'

As Cate now explained to Sally, this was all somehow infinitely worse than the row she had been expecting.

'I worry about Helen,' Sally said. 'Her work's getting in on her at the moment, if you ask me; but you know what she's like, you daren't say a word. As far as you're concerned, though, I wouldn't take too much notice. She'll come round in due course, Mammy too. As for me, I'm delighted already.'

'I know you love children,' Cate replied; and Sally didn't know how to respond to this remark. To say how much she felt the family needed something like this would have been to point up how haunted and threatened she had felt herself to be over the past two years. She glanced around the classroom uneasily, not liking to remember a strange incident which had taken place there about six months earlier. The children had been sitting at their tables one morning drawing pictures with thick crayons, and Sally had been going from one to another, admiring their work and helping them when necessary. Straightening up from one child's desk, she saw a van stop at the school gates. The man in it, whom she didn't recognise, got out and ran across the playground towards the door of the school. Something closed in her heart. 'This is it,' she thought.

'Put your crayons down,' she said to the children. 'Fold your arms, put your head on your arms and close your eyes.' It was a wholly inadequate response, she realised, but even afterwards, she couldn't think of what she should have done instead. She stood there looking at the door, waiting for the man to burst in. But nothing happened, and nothing happened; the children fidgeted and some of them peeped through their eyelids and they shifted uneasily on their low chairs, because they could sense Sally's anxiety. And then suddenly through the window she saw the man again, running away from the school now, through the steady rain . . . the rain!

Sally started to laugh, a shrill, edgy laugh with no mirth in it. All the children sat up now, and opened their eyes. 'Stand up,' she said to them. 'We're going to sing a song.' She started them off, her own voice quavering and unsteady, 'Head and shoulders, knees and toes, knees and toes,' and the children joined in. Their off-key mewing voices calmed her as they did the actions, pointing to the parts of their body in turn as they named them: 'Ears and eyes and teeth and nose.' And then they stopped singing, and the bell rang for break; she let them out of the classroom and locked the door behind them, and she sat down at her desk, put her head on her folded arms and wept uncontrollably.

She cried because she might not have been wrong. Over the past twenty-odd years, all kinds of people had been killed or maimed. Many of them might have thought that the tasks in which they were engaged would have nullified their risk of danger, but they would have been wrong. Bricklayers and binmen on their tea break had been shot. They'd killed a man driving a school bus full of children; opened fire on supporters at a football match; and shot people sitting in a bookie's watching horse racing on television. Men lying in bed asleep beside their wives or girlfriends had been woken up and murdered. At each new variation, Sally had shared in the shock of those around her. To kill the members of a showband! How could anyone go into a church and start shooting at the congregation? And yet each event seemed to be no preparation, no warning for the next. Until someone attacked mourners at a funeral, and threw hand grenades at them, it seemed impossible that this should ever happen. So no one had ever gone into a primary school in Northern Ireland and opened fire on a gaggle of five-year-olds and their female teacher: what did that prove? Nothing, Sally thought. Just because a thing hasn't happened doesn't mean that it never will.

It would have upset her too much to try to explain all of this to Cate; possibly it would have upset Cate too, and there was no point in that. Sally looked at her sister, who was standing at the window. Cate also wanted to explain something to Sally, but didn't know how to go about it without revealing more than she wished. She was afraid that underneath it all even Sally disapproved of her having a baby without her being married, without her being in a long-term relationship, in fact without now being in any relationship at all. She found it slightly alarming that Sally's attitudes could have become so tolerant, so liberal, without Cate having been aware of it. She'd always taken it for granted that her family thought it was only a matter of time before she, Cate, met someone with whom she would want to spend the rest of her life. Cate, too, had expected that for many years, and had been increasingly dismayed as, time and again, things fell apart. Worst of all, she couldn't understand why. It wasn't that she was attracted to men who were violent or cruel and with whom a relationship was inevitably doomed. No matter how good things were, there was always a nagging voice in the back of her mind saying that it wasn't good enough. No matter how much she loved someone, she would inevitably find herself lying awake in the middle of the night, unable to avoid the thought that something was missing. Enlightenment, when it finally came, was abrupt and painful.

She'd been having lunch in a restaurant with a man whom she'd been seeing for about six months, chatting to him about Sally, from whom she'd had a letter that morning, when suddenly the man interrupted her. 'Cate, I can't tell you how sick I am of hearing you go on and on about your bloody family. Do you ever think of anything else?'

Cate stared him hard in the face, then apologised with icy formality. 'Don't worry, you won't have to listen to me going on about my bloody family in future, I can promise you that.' He knew what he'd said had been thoughtless and he retracted it at once, but the damage had been done, and more than he could realise. Unwittingly, he'd gone straight to the root of the problem, like the doctor who asks, mildly, 'Does it hurt if I touch you here?' whereupon the patient shrieks and all but passes out. It wasn't just that the man had slighted her family: Cate was shocked to realise that the point he made was valid.

Was it possible to have too happy a childhood, to be loved too much? She had asked herself that one day, when she was travelling on the Underground and noticed a little girl with her mother. The child, aged about eight, was snuggled up close to the side of a woman whom she closely resembled and who continually stroked the child's face with her fingertips, occasionally bending over to plant a kiss in front of the polka-dotted Alice band which spanned the small head. The little girl's legs were curled up in such a way that her feet stuck out into the aisle, and once or twice the woman said, 'Sit up straight, my treasure, you're going to make people's coats dirty with your shoes when they walk past.' But although the child twitched her feet in vague response to this, she didn't move. Instead she glanced around the carriage languidly, as though the people on whom her glance fell were barely worthy of her attention. Cate had stared at her, wondering how the child would adapt when she grew up, and was forced out of this bubble of maternal affection. What future love could ever match it? She would have to learn that others were indifferent to her, even that they disliked her, and would she grow to resent her mother for not having prepared her for this; for having given her so much that nothing could ever again be enough?

At the time, Cate had merely observed all this, making no connection between herself and the smug child. But when the man had pointed out how obsessed she was with her family, she'd remembered that day on the train, and although she'd tried to deny any connection in her mind, it didn't work. She'd not, perhaps, been as spoiled or indulged as she imagined the other child to be, but the end result was the same. If it wasn't true, why was she here now, why was she standing with Sally in the classroom where they'd been pupils so many years ago? Why, in London, was she always not just noticing, but actually looking for things which had in them something of the intensity, the wildness she remembered from those days? In the food hall of a large department store, she'd seen glass jars packed with tiny, brown-flecked eggs in fluid, as though memory itself could be preserved, like lavender, like fruit. Certain quaint flowers: lupins, stock and snapdragons; or dim, chill rooms with mirrors and heavy furniture, could have the same effect. Even when the associations weren't particularly pleasant, she appreciated them for the access they gave her to her own past. Best of all was the sky itself; the sky at which she now gazed through the classroom window, a watery lemon light splitting heavy, dark clouds.

'When all this is over,' she said to Sally, 'they'll probably want to make a memorial. I hope they do something original. They should build it around the sky.'

'What do you mean?'

'I mean incorporate the sky into the design of it . . . whatever it is.' Cate's voice trailed away, and she continued to stare out of the window. She imagined a room, a perfectly square room. Three of its walls, unbroken by windows, would be covered by neat rows of names, over three thousand of them; and the fourth wall would be nothing but window. The whole structure would be built where the horizon was low, and the sky huge. It would be a place which afforded dignity to memory, where you could bring your anger, as well as your grief.

'And what,' Sally said, 'makes you think it's going to end?'

Cate turned to face her. 'There are articles in the papers from time to time which suggest that there's far more going on behind the scenes than we're being told, and that things could suddenly change. I think Helen thinks the same.'

Sally shook her head. 'I wish I could believe it. Living here, you see too much to expect anything to change quickly. I'll believe it's going to end when it ends. Didn't you hear the news this morning, about that man being shot?' Cate nodded. They sat in silence for a few moments. 'I hope I'm wrong,' Sally said again. She picked up the keys to the school. 'Come and I'll show you the other rooms, and then we can go home.'

Chapter Twelve

Helen, Sally and Kate arrived home from school at half-past four. This evening, as always, the first thing they did was to change out of their school uniforms, and put on jumpers and jeans. When they came downstairs again, their mother had a dinner of pork chops, mashed potatoes and peas ready for them. By the time this was finished, it was almost half-past five. Together with their parents, they watched the local news on television, and then at six, the international news from the BBC. Helen only watched the first quarter of an hour of this: by six-fifteen she was at her desk, preparing to start her homework.

Because their mother set such store by education, each of the three sisters had a proper place to study, unlike some of their friends at school, who had to do their homework at the kitchen table, or in a living room where the television was always on. Helen had a desk in her bedroom; Kate had a table in the bedroom she shared with Sally, and Sally did her homework in the parlour. When Helen went off to university in Belfast the following year, Sally would do her homework where Helen now worked.

Helen's desk was beside a window which looked out on the back of the house; and in the spring and autumn it was a great distraction to her. She could see the field behind the house and the lough in the distance, and what she could see beyond that depended on the weather: sometimes the houses on the far shore would stand out, vivid and white; sometimes mist and rain would lock everything in greyness, and the shore, even the lough itself, would be obscured. Often when she should have been working her mind would wander, and she would day-dream, gazing out at the sky, or at the cattle walking slowly through the field. It was a strange and, Helen realised, an unfair thing that she was always treated as the paragon of the Quinn family, for Kate was every bit as bright as her elder sister. She was that rare thing: a studious rebel, and her powers of concentration were far superior to Helen's. Kate worked with her back to the window and a lamp on her desk. She completed her homework in half the time it took Helen, and spent the rest of the evening watching television, leafing through the fashion magazines she bought with her pocket money; or locked in the bathroom conditioning her hair, or giving herself face-packs. With Helen it was pure will, and no matter how much she did, she never felt that it was enough. She was a straight A student: but then so was Kate.

From six-fifteen until seven-fifteen this evening, she worked on an essay about first-person narrative in *Great Expectations*. From seven-fifteen until eight o'clock, she read a chapter of *La maison de Claudine*, looking up in her dictionary the French words she didn't understand, and copying them into her vocabulary notebook. At eight o'clock, she went down to the kitchen and made a cup of tea. She took it back up to her room, switched on the radio, and twiddled with the dial until she found some music she liked. As she sat listening to it, she let her mind wander around the day's events. She realised how tired she was, but she still had her History homework to do.

This afternoon, she had had to go and see the headmistress, Sister Benedict, in her office, to discuss the choices she had made on her UCCA form. All the girls in her year had to do this, and lots of them dreaded it because the nun could be harsh, scolding them for vanity in applying to do subjects for which they had no hope of being accepted. Sometimes people would be castigated for the exact opposite, for not being sufficiently ambitious, for not fulfilling their potential.

'Maybe she'll try to coax you into being a nun,' Kate had said to Helen on the bus to school that morning, and Helen had snorted with laughter at the idea of it. 'You never know,' Kate said. 'I don't think anyone's ever going to waste their time trying to persuade me. The thought of it! Living in a big house with a pack of other women and all of them dressed exactly the same as me, and no men allowed. No chance!'

Helen had been working in the library when one of her classmates came and said that Sister Benedict wanted to see her. To reach the headmistress's office required Helen to walk almost the full length of the school, along wood-panelled corridors, past coloured-plaster statues on plinths, with posies of flowers before them, past closed doors from behind which came the sound of singing, or chanted verbs, or the solitary voice of a teacher explaining something to her class. Once, when Granny Kate had visited the school, she had remarked, 'You'd nearly think a place like this ought to be more untidy than it is, with a couple of hundred girls in it, five days a week.' Helen agreed, as she noted the neat cloakrooms, the posters pinned up along the corridors, the carefully tended plants on the window-sills. There was a smell of warm apple pie coming from the Domestic Science kitchens. That was probably Kate's class: she'd had with her on the bus this morning the old Kimberly biscuit tin in which she carried her apron and the covered dish in which she would bring home the fruits of her labours. Kate had insisted on doing Domestic Science O level, because she wanted to study Needlework. She had had a difficult time persuading Sister Benedict to allow her to do this. Far from encouraging home-making skills in her pupils, the nun regarded it as a course of study suitable only for those who weren't bright enough to do an extra science subject. She'd wanted Kate to do Physics. But whatever Kate's skill was at Needlework, she was a hopeless cook. God, the thing she'd brought home last week! Kate had claimed it was a steamed suet pudding. Helen had seen her down at the back of the bus, trying to get some of the boys from the Academy to taste it, as a dare.

Sister Benedict's office, when Helen went into it, was noticeably warmer than the corridor outside. It was a classic autumn day in Northern Ireland. Beyond the window, leaves were streaming down from the trees in a strong wind, and heavy rain poured down the glass. Sister Benedict, who had been staring at this, turned when Helen came into the room. The nun was wearing a thick black cardigan over her habit. She had spent over twenty years in Africa, and had never been able to get used to the Irish climate again. Every child in the school knew of this foible. 'Isn't it terribly cold, girls?' she would say when she passed them in the corridor, tapping the radiators to make sure they were switched on. She used to complain about draughts, and was at loggerheads with the vice principal, Sister Philomena, who was forever opening doors and windows, and who was as obsessed with fresh air as Sister Benedict was with warmth. But then, the two nuns were frequently at odds over many things, and the temperature of the school was one of their least significant points of difference.

Although it was Sister Benedict who, as principal, finally assessed and signed the university application forms, it was Sister Philomena, the form teacher of the final-year class, who helped the girls to fill in the forms correctly. A few years ago, she had poured scorn on the pupils who put 'British' in the space where they were to put their nationality, and instructed them to change it to 'Irish'. This had not gone down at all well in the home of one girl, whose father was a policeman. He made a special visit to the school to express his displeasure to Sister Benedict, who had, in turn, so rumour had it, given Sister Philomena a ferocious lecture about what she had done. Ever since then, when they came to the section of the form dealing with nationality, Sister Philomena told the girls to ask their parents what they should put there; and ever since then, the pupils had been divided in their allegiance, admiring and supporting either one nun or the other.

In their free time, the girls would sometimes argue about this. Although the school was completely Catholic, there were still sharp divisions of political opinion within it. Girls like Brian's and Lucy's daughter Una liked Sister Philomena. Because she had grown up in Derry, they said, she understood how Catholics were discriminated against in Northern Ireland; unlike Sister Benedict, who was from the Republic. If you told Sister Philomena your father or brother had been pulled out of their car and beaten up at an army checkpoint in the middle of the night, she'd be angry and sympathise with you; she wouldn't automatically assume that they must have done something to bring it upon themselves. Girls such as the policeman's younger daughter, who was in Helen's class, or another pupil who had an uncle an Alliance MP, resented the pep talks Sister Philomena used to give them: 'This is your society, and don't you forget it. You have as much right to be in it as anyone else, and I want you all to get out there and claim the place that's waiting for you, the place you deserve.' 'Does she really think we need to be told all that?' they would say with disdain. They complained that Sister

Philomena was always bringing politics into education; Sister Philomena's supporters maintained that education was already a political issue in Northern Ireland, and that it was Sister Benedict who was at fault, for trying to deny or ignore this.

Helen's position was unusual, in that she thought Sister Philomena was right, but she liked Sister Benedict best. It made her sad to see how Sister Benedict would unwittingly annoy or alienate some of the girls, and it had happened again that very morning at assembly, when she led them in a prayer for a soldier who had been shot during the night. 'Bloody bitch,' a girl near Helen hissed, folding her arms sullenly. When Sister Philomena took assembly, she would pray 'for peace in Northern Ireland, and for all the victims of the Troubles', to which no one ever seemed to object.

Helen was surprised at how fond she was of Sister Benedict. If she'd been her contemporary, she thought, she'd probably have been her best friend. She wasn't like the other nuns. For one thing, she was incredibly untidy, as Helen herself was, and she knew how Sister Benedict struggled for that perfect order which came so naturally to the others: most of the time, she didn't achieve it. She started to rummage now on a desk piled high with books and papers. 'I know your forms are here, Helen, I saw them a moment ago.' While she searched, Helen looked around the office, at the magnolia walls hung with a photograph of the Pope, a reproduction of Fra Angelico's *Annunciation*, and a slender crucifix. She looked, too, at the nun whose life was a mystery to Helen.

The girls in Helen's class had once calculated that if Sister Benedict had been to university in Dublin for four years, in Africa for twenty years and in Northern Ireland for ten, then she must have been at least in her early fifties, although you'd never have guessed it from looking at her. They knew that she had grown up on a farm in Tipperary, and that she had been the eldest of six children.

When Helen was in fifth form, there had been a one-day retreat organised for the senior girls on the theme of the Missions. Two priests, home from Tanzania, had come to talk to them about the work they did, showed them slides; and Sister Benedict had been obliged to give a testimony of her own vocation. She had told them how happy she'd been the day she made her final vows, and described saying goodbye to her parents before she left for Kenya, knowing in her heart that she would probably never see them again 'in this world', was how she'd put it. It almost turned Helen against her, to hear her calmly describe how she'd received a telegram, telling of her father's death. 'I knew it was God's will' seemed an inadequate response to Helen; there must have been an underlying coldness there.

They were given an hour that afternoon to pray or to read their Bibles, and Helen had been sitting on a stone bench in the convent garden, her shut Bible on her knees, when Sister Benedict came up and sat beside her.

'Are you enjoying hearing the priests talk about the Missions?' she asked.

'It's interesting,' Helen said, with polite diplomacy.

'I'll be so glad when it's over,' the nun said frankly, stirring the gravel on the path with the toe of her shoe. 'I hate it, it makes me feel . . . homesick, looking at the slides, or even just hearing about it. It's strange, I feel the way so many of the Irish sisters used to feel when they were out there, a terrible sense of yearning to be somewhere else. And anyway, I don't like the way the idea of the Missions is presented here. There's still this "pennies for the black babies" mentality; this idea that we do something for them. The people I knew in Kenya gave me more in twenty years than I could have given them in twenty lifetimes. But I was deceiving myself at some level. I liked to think I was doing God's will, but it happened to coincide exactly with what I wanted to do, so it made it easy for me to see it in such noble terms. My vows were never a problem to me. Poverty: we'd had so little in material terms when I was a child, and there'd been no want of happiness in the house for it. It never grieved me not to get married and have a family of my own. When God gave me my vocation, he also gave me the gift of a celibate heart.'

Helen felt uncomfortable when she heard Sister Benedict talk in this way. It made her seem distant, and jarred with the image she had previously formed of her. It wasn't that she thought the nun was insincere, but she spoke of a reality which Helen had not experienced, and with which she could not empathise.

'My problem, I now see, was obedience. The day I was told I was being sent to Northern Ireland was the hardest day of my life. Harder, even, I think, than when my father died.' Her words were more broken now, there were long pauses between the sentences. 'I remember leaving the mission station. I remember saying goodbye to my friends. We flew from Nairobi to London. I had my rosary beads in my pocket, and throughout the flight I kept putting them through my fingers saying on each bead, "Thy will, not mine, O Lord, Thy will, not mine." I kept saying it, when we changed planes at Heathrow. We landed in Northern Ireland; it was a day in winter. I remember the physical shock of the cold when I walked across the tarmac, I remember the rain beating into me and I thought "How am I going to live here?" ' She laughed. 'When we got to the convent, there was a bowl of fruit in the parlour: small, faded-looking fruit; and it somehow got fixed in my mind, this is what you've come to. I've never been able to forget the fruit. I . . . I even thought about leaving the Order and going away again, as a development worker, but I knew that that was just the Devil trying to undermine my vocation. Because I never stopped believing in that, whatever else, and no matter how hard it became. Every morning, when I was in Kenya, I used to thank God for my vocation. Here, I pray that I'll be able to fulfil it.'

Helen tried to focus her attention on what Sister Benedict was saying to her. 'These are your forms, aren't they? You're doing French, English and History, I see.' Helen nodded. 'I see you've applied to read Law at Queen's for your first choice. Law! That's impressive.'

'My parents aren't very happy about it,' Helen blurted out, in spite of herself. She hadn't wanted to say this.

'Aren't they? Why not? Do they think you won't get the grades? Your teachers have nothing but praise. I see here that you did exceptionally well in your mock A levels last year. Why aren't your parents happy?'

'I . . . I think it's a bit hard for them to believe, the idea of their daughter doing Law. It seems over-ambitious. I'm the first person in my family to go to university, and I think they find it hard to get used to that, no matter what I'm planning to study.'

'What would they like you to do?'

'They'd like me to go to St Mary's and be a primary school teacher.' Sister Benedict raised her eyebrows. 'My mother was a teacher,' Helen added, but still the nun didn't respond, which made Helen anxious. 'I mean, she trained to be a teacher, but she only worked at it for a year or so, then she got married and stopped.' Sister Benedict was looking at her very hard now, but Helen had nothing left to say. She looked helplessly towards the window, which was still streaming with rain.

'Have you ever heard that there is nothing more important to children than what their parents have *not* been?'

'No, Sister.' She didn't know what further comment she could make about this.

'And why Law?'

'We need our Catholic lawyers in this society,' Helen said, and Sister Benedict looked up sharply at her. She thought Helen was being sarcastic, repeating the words Sister Philomena was constantly repeating to them: 'Our educated Catholics have a role to play in this society. We need our Catholic teachers and doctors and nurses and lawyers.' Helen felt confused now.

Sister Benedict stared at her for a few moments. 'Well,' she said eventually, 'if the educated Catholic middle class in Northern Ireland was bigger, it probably would make a difference, but I dare say not the difference you or indeed others have in mind.'

'I've thought a lot about this, and I know what I'm doing. I don't want to do Law just for the status or the money, really I don't.'

'I'm glad to hear it,' Sister Benedict said drily. 'But you still haven't answered my question. Why Law?'

'Because I want to do something worthwhile with my education; I want to help people. The way things operate here is deeply unfair, and I want to make a difference.'

'But you won't.' The nun pounced so quickly with her reply that Helen felt she had been set up, manipulated into saying just the thing that would allow Sister Benedict to contradict her. 'Believe me, Helen, you can throw your life away if you want, but it won't make any difference to anyone except yourself.' Helen tried to speak, but Sister Benedict wouldn't permit her to do so, raising her hand and continuing to talk.

'You want to defend people who've been unjustly accused. Fine. But tell me this, how will you feel defending people who really have done terrible things, who've planted bombs or shot men in front of their families? What even makes you so sure that you'll get into the line of work that appeals to you; that you won't end up specialising in tax law or conveyancing? Anyone else would be consoled by their salary, but you won't, you're too austere. Money'll only make it worse. Sometimes I think idealism is one of the most dangerous forces there is. I saw it myself when I was in Africa, time and time again. Girls like you, they were good-hearted, unselfish girls, but their minds were shut; it was a disaster. They went out there thinking they were going to *help* people,' her voice heavy with sarcastic emphasis now, 'they were going to *change* things. And instead what happened was they hurt others, and they hurt themselves. Look at me,' she said. 'I wanted to be a missionary, and look how I ended up, sitting here in mid Ulster, arguing with you.' The nun gestured to the window, where the rain was still pouring down.

'I don't want to go to Africa,' Helen said. 'I just want to go to university in Belfast.'

'But that's the point, you could go anywhere, do anything you wanted.' The nun was almost pleading with her now. 'I don't want to see you throwing your life away, staying in this – this horrible place.'

Helen flinched at this last phrase, as if she'd been struck in the face. 'I like it here,' she said. 'This is where I'm from. This is my home.'

Again Sister Benedict sat looking at her for a moment without speaking, then picked up a silver fountain pen, uncapped it, signed Helen's form, blotted the ink, and slid the application into a blue card folder. Speaking quietly, as though she were making a great effort to do so, she said, 'I know you're going to do very well in your exams. Tell your parents I said that if you get accepted for Law at Queen's, and I've no doubt but that you will, I'm sure you'll have no trouble with your studies there.' She picked up another form. 'When you go back to the library, will you send Nora Bradley down to me?'

She didn't look up again as Helen left the office, and it was all Helen could do not to slam the door hard behind her in anger.

It hadn't even been a proper row, she thought, as she went back through the school. When she'd argued with her mother about the same thing a few days earlier, she'd actually found it satisfying, because for the first time ever they'd argued as equals, as two women. She had understood that her mother had been judging Helen's future in terms of the failures and shortcomings of her own life, and Helen had forced her to admit that she really didn't regret the choices she'd made. 'Let me make my own mistakes,' Helen had pleaded in the end, while her mother kept saying, 'I'm afraid for you. I don't know how to explain it, but I'm afraid for you.' Remembering Granny Kelly, Helen had felt a pity for her mother far removed from the resentment she now nursed towards Sister Benedict. She remembered how at assembly a few days earlier the nun had read out the part from the Bible about how when you were young you walked where you wished, but when you were old you would stretch out your arms and another would bind you and take you where you would not want to be. She'd noticed how Sister Benedict's voice had caught as she said these words. Well, that was her problem, Helen thought. She'd had her life, and if she regretted what she'd done with it, that was her affair; it was no reason for her to meddle in Helen's plans, and spoil her life too.

When she went back to the library, she nodded to Nora Bradley, who left the room as Helen sat down and tried to settle to her work again. But her concentration had been broken, and she sat looking out of the window with all her books spread open and disregarded, until Sister Philomena came over and sat down beside her.

'How's Helen?' she said.

'All right,' Helen said.

'How did you get on downstairs?'

'I got my forms signed.'

'That's good. Put it out of your mind now.' Helen nodded. 'How are things at home?'

'All right.'

'You had an uncle died a while ago, didn't you?' Helen nodded again.

Late one evening some six weeks earlier, the phone had rung at home. Helen answered: it was Brian. He told her he was calling from the local hospital. He'd been out for a drink with Peter earlier that evening, and Peter had collapsed in the pub. He was in intensive care; the doctors said he had had a heart attack, and had a fifty-fifty chance of recovery. But from the moment Brian told her that, Helen insisted to her family that there was no hope. 'He never looked after himself, never ate properly. He has no resources; nothing to fall back on,' she said. Within three days, the doctors were saying the same thing; within five, Peter was dead.

The last time she saw him, he'd been asleep. She had sat for over an hour by his bed just watching him, and would have stayed longer, had she not been asked to leave. 'There's not much point, anyway, is there?' the nurse had said, and Helen hadn't even bothered to contradict her. If this woman couldn't see that the past hour could have been precious to Helen, that it might have been one of the most important hours in her life, there was no point in trying to explain to her, for she wouldn't understand. It was good that he had been sleeping, because they had nothing more to say to each other. Words would have been a burden. It was enough to be with him, and to watch him. She had remembered how, when they were children and they were out in the car with their father, often he would point to a group of men working at the side of the road, trimming hedges or cleaning drains; and he'd say, 'Look, there's Uncle Peter!' And then he'd pump the car horn as he drove past, and Peter would look up and see them all waving frantically out of the car windows at him. His face would light up and he'd raise his arm; he'd stand like that with his hand held high in the air until they could no longer see him.

She remembered going into the back scullery at Brian's house and seeing Peter standing by a sink full of soapy water, whistling to himself as he stacked the clean, thick plates in the rack on the drainingboard. She remembered how he used to take them out in his boat, remembered the day he'd rowed them to the island and they'd seen the sun flash on the water, seen him leaning against a tree smoking a cigarette, while the damp chicks struggled to be born.

At his wake, she'd outraged her mother by saying, 'Maybe we shouldn't be giving him a Catholic funeral.'

'What do you mean: that we should give him a Protestant one instead?'

'Maybe we shouldn't have anything. I mean, nothing religious. We should just bury him.' Her mother actually laughed at this, which annoyed Helen, so that she went on, 'He didn't believe in any of it, he thought it was all nonsense.' She said it loud enough so that the priest, who was sitting near by, would be bound to hear her. Her father gently hushed her. 'You can't have a proper funeral without prayers,' he said, stroking her hand to comfort her.

A week after the funeral, Helen went over to Brian's house one afternoon. There was no one there but Granny Kate, who was sitting in the dim kitchen, two black plastic bags tied closed with orange twine on the floor beside her.

'What's in the bin liners, Granny?'

'Them's Peter's clothes,' she replied. 'I have to get Brian to get rid of them for me. I went through them all; there wasn't a stitch that was fit to give to a charity, so there wasn't. I told Brian to keep his watch; and there's a lighter I'm going to give your daddy. Brian's children bought it for him for Christmas and I told Peter not to use it out of the house, for he'd be sure to lose it. I'd forgotten it was there until I saw it in the back of the drawer. It's all there is to give your daddy as a souvenir. There was never a man had as little.' Helen stared at the black plastic bags. As though she could read her thoughts, Granny Kate said, 'As far as the world was concerned, he had nothing and he was nothing, but he was a good man. I loved him.'

'Do you know what I think?' Helen turned to Sister Philomena, whose presence she had almost forgotten. 'I think you're working too hard. Maybe I'll have a word with your teachers and see about them letting you off homework for a while. Perhaps you need to take a few days off school completely.' This alarmed Helen.

'Oh I couldn't do that, I'd fall behind with my work. I can't risk losing any time at all.'

'But you're well ahead as it is, and the exams aren't for months yet. What if you push yourself so hard that you fall ill? Then you'll have to take time off, and just think how much you'll miss then.'

Helen insisted again that she could cope with her studies. A bell rang in the distance. 'I have to go now, Sister, I have a class.'

Sitting listening to the radio at home that night, she knew Sister Philomena was right. She felt worn out, weary in a way she shouldn't have been at her age; and she'd felt like this for years now. Both at home and at school she was constantly being told how important her education was, that she owed it to herself, to her family, to society, to work as hard as she possibly could, and she had done so. But now everybody was getting uneasy with the results, they were backing off, telling her to ease up. But as far as she was concerned, it was too late. The damage had been done.

The music on the radio came to an end, and was followed by the news. They gave the name of the soldier who had been shot the previous night, and for whom Sister Benedict had prayed at assembly. The soldier was twenty years old. Helen thought of his family. Like Sister Benedict, they would think of Northern Ireland as a horrible place. She'd not told the truth today, things at home were tense at times. Uncle Brian sold copies of *Republican News* outside the chapel in Timinstown after Mass every Sunday, and their father had argued with him about this. She heard the sound of the bathroom door opening, and the loud sucking noise of the water draining out of the bath. There was a strong, sudden blast of honeysuckle perfume throughout the house. Maybe Kate was right to want to go away. Maybe Helen would regret it if she stayed here.

She switched off the radio, and turned her attention again to her books. Only her History homework remained.

'Describe and assess the circumstances which led to the Partition of Northern Ireland.'

Chapter Thirteen

FRIDAY

Helen looked up as Owen came into the room. 'Guess who's coming in to see us this afternoon?' He stared at her blankly. 'Maguire's mammy,' she said, and Owen put his head in his hands.

'Ah Christ, no, not again,' he said. 'There's nothing we can do for her, nothing we can say that I haven't said a dozen times already. Do I ever need this on a Friday afternoon?'

'I'll see her if you like. I can actually take this sort of thing better on a Friday than on a Monday morning.'

'No, I'll do it, you can't handle something like this.' He immediately realised he'd made a mistake, and tried to mollify Helen, whose face had darkened.

'I don't want you to give her a bollocking: though God knows I feel like doing it myself at times, and I don't know how someone like you would be able to resist it.'

'It's her son who's on trial, she isn't,' Helen said, not meeting his eyes. She picked up a file, glanced at it and put it to one side. Owen ran his hands through his hair.

'Why doesn't that fucker own up to his ma and put us all out of our misery? He must think she wouldn't be able to handle it yet. I suppose she'll come round to it in time.'

'She's going to have to,' Helen said. She still didn't look at him. There was a long silence.

'Helen,' Owen said eventually, 'I'd really appreciate it if you could see Mrs Maguire when she comes in this afternoon.'

Helen raised her head. 'Fine,' she said. 'I'll do that.'

And then she said, 'Thanks,' and then, 'Sorry.' Owen shook his head and smiled.

'Christ, you're a funny woman.'

'Are you only noticing that now?'

She was glad of the banter. She felt sorry for having picked Owen up so sharply a few moments earlier, for what he'd said was uncharacteristic. She liked working with him, and always considered she'd been lucky to be taken on in a firm where there was a certain amount of work on terrorist cases. Although there were enormous quantities of legal work in Northern Ireland at the time she graduated from university, there was also tremendous competition. She'd dreaded ending up doing nothing but family law, as was the fate of quite a few of the women with whom she'd studied. She told Owen from the start what interested her most, and although his firm didn't get an enormous quantity of that kind of case, over the years what they did get he gave to her; and he did it without making a big deal about it, or suggesting that he was doing her some kind of favour. But what Helen also noticed and appreciated was that he discreetly began to withhold such work from her after her father was killed. It was never said that he was doing it to spare her feelings, and there was always a plausible reason as to why he should deal primarily with any particular case, rather than Helen. She was grateful for his sensitivity in this matter, and there'd been an unspoken agreement, too, that she would someday begin to take on such cases again. But when the Oliver Maguire job had come in, it had been at a time when Owen was very busy and Helen had suddenly little on hand.

'Listen, we'll do this the two of us, all right?' Owen had said. 'It's a bit heavy duty.'

Helen had nodded, and silently vowed that it would be a point of honour for her to see this one through.

But when she turned her attention again to her work this morning, she noticed that Owen did not do likewise, which was most unusual. He flicked through papers, sighed, rattled boxes of paper-clips, and by all this she knew he wanted to talk, so she met his eye, and looked at him quizzically.

'This is just a job,' he said immediately, apropos of nothing that Helen could see. 'Never forget that it's only work. It's how you earn your keep; how you put a roof over your head and a bit of food on the table.' Helen struggled to suppress a smile, for the phrases he used, with their suggestion of survival and necessity, didn't square with the high style in which he actually lived. She thought of his elegant house, in a quiet street off the Malone Road, and the extravagant dinners he occasionally gave there for his friends. Unlike some people she knew working in law in

Northern Ireland and in spite of what he had just said, Owen wasn't just interested in the money he made, although what he did earn he enjoyed. He saw her smiling, and he smiled too.

'Do you ever regret getting into this line of business?'

'Sometimes,' she said, and she wondered if he would ever know how much it took for her to admit even that, even to him.

'I think we all probably do. What I regret most is not being able to handle things better, deal with them in the way I ought to.' She could see now how tremendously ill at ease he was: he was circling towards the heart of the matter, and she would have tried to help him to it, if she had had any idea what it was.

'I'm not sure I understand.' Frowning, he picked up a stapler from the desk, and started to click it open and shut. She wondered if he'd made some serious error of judgement in a recent case, or if he was maybe more worried about Oliver Maguire than she had realised.

Not looking at her now, he said, 'I feel bad about . . . about the shit I put up with sometimes. I shouldn't do it. I feel ashamed of it now.'

Helen didn't say anything, but waited until he was ready to continue.

'You know that Law Society do I was at a couple of weeks ago? Something happened at that, and it's been eating away at me ever since. Towards the end of the night, I was in a group with a few people, none of whom I know well. We'd all had a good bit to drink over the evening, and then of course – well, I was going to say, the masks started to slip, but it wasn't that. That makes it sound like they couldn't help what they were doing, but they could. What they did was deliberate. I could see them looking at me from time to time, they would say things that were getting close to the bone, and then look to see how I was taking it. And then suddenly, I felt afraid, really afraid; and they could see it. And then they knew they had me where they wanted me. "Boys, boys!" one of them says at once. "Wait till I tell you this one," and he starts to tell a story about when he was at some college or other in the nineteen fifties, and about a teacher he had, that was in the B Specials. An announcement was made that they were going to admit Catholics to the college for the first time. So the man who was telling the story says about how he went up to your man's office late that evening and he's standing there in his full uniform, boots, holster, gun, the works. He's near foaming at the mouth with rage, and he says, "Do you know what this means? I'll tell you what it means. It means I'll have to teach them by day and shoot them by night!" And of course at that they all start to laugh fit to piss themselves. But I didn't laugh. I said nothing; a minute or two later I walked away and not one says to me, "You're going." '

Again there was silence for a few moments; then Owen said, 'It frightened me, Helen. I mean, this is 1994; and that they could still do that to me, and that I could still let them away with it . . . I couldn't sleep when I went home, it scared me that much. And I was angry too, of course; more angry with myself than anything. I didn't even tell Mary, I was ashamed of what she would think of me.'

'I hope you don't think you're the only person this has happened to. I bet this sort of thing goes on all the time amongst people we know, and everybody's too embarrassed to talk about it. But things like this are a matter of bad manners as much as bigotry. When someone sets out for no good reason to try to humiliate you or make you feel ill at ease in a social setting, you're often so taken aback that you don't know how to respond; and it's hard to be able to put them down without sinking to their level. You probably did as much as any of us would have done. If I were you, I'd put it out of my mind.'

'It's been eating into me for days. This has been a hell of a hard week.'

'Tell me about it,' said Helen.

She said much the same thing later that day to David, who phoned her shortly after lunch. 'Thank God it's Friday, and all that.' Owen was out of the office at that stage, so she told David about Cate, and how her family had reacted to the news. 'Tomorrow's her last full day at home, so I'll go down this evening. I'm looking forward to spending some time with them all. How about you?'

'Well, Steve isn't coming back. Or rather, he is back, but just to work his notice and then to prepare to move back to London. I'm surprised you haven't heard us shouting at each other; you don't live that far away. He told me he hadn't realised how hard it would be to settle into such a small, closed society, and that I hadn't done anything like enough to help him. I told him that this was neither fair nor true, and he knew it. And then your name was mentioned and, I'm afraid, it all turned a bit nasty and went past the point of no return.'

Helen was at a loss to know how she should respond to this. 'You don't sound too miserable about it, anyway,' was all she could think to say.

'It's been on the cards for such a long time now, that it's something of a relief to all concerned that it's finally happened.'

After she'd promised to see him some time the following week and hung up, Helen mulled over what David had said to her. He was probably right that the split had been a foregone conclusion, but that wouldn't necessarily make it any easier, now that it had happened. She admitted to herself a sneaking relief that Steve wouldn't be around in the future, as she'd never felt completely at ease with him. It hadn't struck her until now that he might have found her friendship with David intrusive, and if that was the point he was now making, she still didn't believe that it was a valid one.

She remembered a conversation which had taken place between them not long after Steve had moved to Belfast. David hadn't even been in the room at the time, he'd been off in the kitchen preparing a meal for them; and Steve had inexorably brought up the subject of her job.

'So you work with terrorists?' he'd said.

'Some of the time.'

'What are IRA men like?'

'Probably not as unlike the Loyalist terrorists as they'd like to think,' but Helen had known, even as she said this, that it wouldn't get her off the hook.

'But no, tell me.'

She shrugged. 'They're sort of ordinary, most of them,' she said, hoping to dampen his interest with the force of sheer boredom.

Steve didn't reply immediately, but stared hard at her for a few moments and then said, 'I don't know how you bring yourself to sit in the same room as people like that, much less defend them.'

'No, you don't know, and I'll tell you more than that: you

won't ever know,' she'd snapped back, surprised at her own asperity.

'Sort of chilly in here, isn't it?' David had said, when he came into the room a few moments later, carrying a salad bowl, to find his lover and his best friend glowering at each other. 'Should I maybe switch on the central heating, or are the pair of you going to be sensible?'

Remembering this, Helen reflected that she'd really told Steve the truth about the paramilitaries: for the most part they did strike her as ordinary. There were only a few who really stood out in her mind. There'd been a man called Devine, the only person she'd come across who struck her as an out-and-out psychopath, someone who loved killing for its own sake. Even if things had been peaceful in Northern Ireland, she suspected that he would have been in jail for murder anyway. As Owen had put it, 'Instead of shooting policemen and soldiers it would have been women, kids, dogs, mice, Christ knows what, so long as he was killing. The Troubles is only an excuse.'

It had been an excuse, too, for Malachy Mulholland and people like him; hoods who would have been involved in robbery and thieving to line their own pockets no matter what was happening in the country. Mulholland had been mixed up with the IRA, but in the long run they had no time for people like him, and considered them more trouble than they were worth. A few years after Helen had met him, the IRA killed him, for, they said, 'drug dealing and other anti-social activities'.

The paramilitaries didn't much like people like Tom Kelly either, and avoided them if at all possible. Kelly had killed an RUC man, pushing past the man's wife, who had opened the door of their house; and shooting the policeman as he sat on the sofa watching television. But the policeman's five-year-old daughter had been in the room and saw everything. When Kelly was arrested and charged, he broke down and wept and made a full confession. He said he couldn't live with himself because of the child; that he wouldn't have done it if he'd known she'd be there; that he could never, no matter how long he lived, forget the sound of her screams as he ran out of the house.

But for the most part, the men she came across struck her as neither particularly tender-hearted nor particularly vicious. They had squared their own consciences about what they were doing. Often they had strong political motivation, particularly once they had done a stint in prison, where they had ample time to discuss and argue about such things amongst themselves. Often they came out more committed to what they were doing than they had been when they went in. It was important to them to do their time in jail with as good a grace as possible, seeing it as a part of the sacrifices they had to make for what they referred to as 'The Cause'. In themselves they were, as Helen had said to Steve, mostly ordinary, and it was an important distinction to her whether they were from the country or the city. Being from the country herself she tended to find it easier to get on with the men whose background was similar to her own. Often she found the Belfast men too streetwise, too boisterous; and it was a distinction the men also observed in themselves, tending to make friends amongst their peers, and not feeling wholly at ease with those from a different background.

So they, for the most part, had thought through what they were doing, and knew what they felt about it. But what about Helen? Often her attitudes were inconsistent, perhaps even hypocritical, she had to admit to herself. Take her old school friend, Willy Larkin. She would often see him when she was down home at the weekend. He'd wave as he drove past in a tractor, or she might meet him in the shop at Timinstown. He'd be there with his two kids, with their open, genial faces, so like his own, he'd have his papers and his fags and a bag of sweets stuffed in his jacket pocket; and for a few moments he and Helen would chat to each other, they'd ask after each other's mothers, and she always felt the better for having seen him. But while she was talking to him, it was never in her mind that he'd done time for being in the IRA and possessing explosives; and if she did think of it afterwards, she tried not to think too deeply about where those explosives might have ended up had Willy not been caught. And if she was prepared to turn a blind eye and hold her mind back from certain things like a dog gripped by the collar, was that not, particularly in the light of what had happened to her father, the deepest hypocrisy?

So there was Devine and there was Mulholland and there was

Tom Kelly and there was Willy Larkin. And there was also, of course, Oliver Maguire.

She'd been to see Oliver earlier in the week, the day Cate had come to Belfast to stay with her.

'How's Helen?' had been his greeting, as always.

'Fine,' she answered curtly, as she opened her briefcase and took from it the documents she'd come to discuss. She didn't know why she disliked him so much. Owen couldn't bear him either, which was unusual; and frequently referred to him as 'that creep Maguire'. He was in his twenties but looked younger, and could easily have passed as a teenager. He had thick, dark-brown hair and eyes so brown they looked black. When he was with Helen, his gaze would be locked on to hers in a way she hated. He could have been a journalist, she'd once remarked to David, for he had that confrontational stare that she regarded as a hallmark of the trade, and the same capacity for single, blank questions which were difficult to answer. She wasn't above staring people down herself, as a tactic to unsettle them, but she didn't like anyone else doing it to her, especially as a matter of course.

As she explained to Oliver the papers she'd brought along, he continued to stare hard into her face, as though he were trying to memorise every word she uttered, and when at last she said, 'Here, have a look at them yourself,' it took longer than she would have thought necessary for him to unlock his gaze from her, and fasten it upon the documents which she pushed across the table to him. She looked at the crown of his head as he read, and wondered again what it was about him that bothered her so much. Maybe it was because, through David, she'd had a glimpse of the full effect of what Oliver had done. He was also a person of enormous self-possession, and that was a quality that never appealed to Helen. She noted now with some relish that his nails were bitten to the quick. She strongly suspected that he didn't like her either, that he would have preferred Owen to deal exclusively with his case. Maybe he thought that because she didn't come across as particularly sympathetic to him she wasn't going to make much of an effort on his behalf; or, even worse, he might even think that she wasn't up to the job simply because she was a woman. As he looked up again, she realised that she felt afraid to be with him, but she didn't know if it was fear on her own behalf, or on his.

'That looks all right,' he said, handing the papers back to her. 'But what about this?' and he went on to query in detail two points which had come up in their last meeting. This sort of thing happened frequently, and she always found it intensely annoying. The prisoners who were on remand spent much of their time discussing their cases with one another, pooling their not inconsiderable legal knowledge so that they knew their rights to the letter. Often they would challenge what their lawyers said to them, or make suggestions which were useful or to the point. Helen heard Oliver out, frowning at the surface of the table and not meeting his gaze. She told him that she and Owen were already aware of the angle to which he referred, but that as yet, nothing could be done.

'We'll keep you informed.'

He nodded briefly. There was a short silence. 'Oliver, I know Owen has told you, and I'm telling you again now, the forensic evidence on this is as tight as can be, you know that?'

'Yeah.'

His tone annoyed her. She took a certain pleasure in following on by saying, 'You know you're bound to get time?'

'Yeah. I know that.'

'You're going to get life.'

'You mean you know you're going to lose this case,' he said. He glanced away. 'I'll do a few years.'

'You'll do more than that,' Helen said.

He shrugged. 'Have you seen my ma lately?' he said after a moment.

He was chewing at his nails now, Helen noticed. 'No,' she said. 'Have you?' He shook his head.

Suddenly, she could see him as on the night of the killing, as vividly as if she'd been there with him when he went into the call box and booked a cab from a firm based in Sandy Row. He waited then outside a chip shop for the car to arrive, the collar of his leather jacket turned up against the cold of the night. Every so often the door of the shop would open, and a heavy smell of vinegar and hot fat would surge out; she could hear the voices of the women who worked there. He stood in the shadows so as not to be seen, only moving out to the edge of the pavement when a blue car pulled up, and she recognised the jowly face of the driver from blurred photographs of him which had been published in the newspapers after his death. He rolled down the car window and called out the false name in which the cab had been booked. Oliver nodded and got in. There was a faint smell of stale pine from the tree-shaped air freshener which dangled from the driver's mirror. Helen watched the lit streets of the city, black and slick with rain, slip past beyond the steadily moving arc of the windscreen wipers. Oliver would not be drawn into conversation; in the mirror she could see anxiety gradually flicker in the taxi driver's eyes, until the moment when Oliver took a gun out of his jacket pocket and pressing it against the driver's neck said, 'I've changed my mind. You and me are going somewhere different.'

Sitting across the table from him, Helen involuntarily raised her hand to the left side of her neck, which was as cold as though it had been brushed by a sliver of ice.

'You did do it,' she said. 'You really did do it.'

Oliver took his hands away from his mouth, and gave a little smile.

'That's what people like you keep telling me, anyway.'

'Mr Kane isn't here?' was the first thing Oliver's mother asked when Helen showed her into the office that afternoon. Helen and Owen were on first-name terms with Oliver, but Mrs Maguire was persistently formal: it seemed to make her feel better.

'He asked me to see you, as he had to leave early today,' Helen replied, aware of how hesitant and anxious the woman was. Suddenly, Mrs Maguire became aware that Helen might possibly offer a new opinion.

'Mr Kane says it's certain that Oliver'll be convicted.'

'I'm afraid so.'

'And you think the same thing?'

Helen nodded.

'But he didn't do it!' the woman wailed. This time Helen neither spoke nor nodded. She looked briefly at her watch, then glanced up at the woman.

'This is terrible,' Mrs Maguire said, 'people getting convicted for things they didn't do. Look at the Birmingham Six, how long they were in jail. Are you telling me that that's what's going to happen to Oliver, and there's nothing to be done to stop it?'

'That was a very different case,' Helen said quickly.

'Why?'

Helen paused, tempted to say the obvious: that the Birmingham Six were innocent, and then leave Mrs Maguire to draw the logical conclusion about Oliver. Instead, she said nothing, hoping this would give greater import to her words when she did at last reply.

'Mrs Maguire, I think it's best for you to try to prepare yourself for the worst. Oliver's going to get a long sentence. He knows this himself. The sooner you come to terms with this, the better.'

Most of the other solicitors they knew wouldn't have put up with this sort of thing, and she sometimes wondered why Owen bothered. There was nothing to be gained from it: a complete waste of time for all concerned, but then it was unusual for a mother to be as persistent as this. Owen was always much tougher on the clients than with their relatives. In many cases Helen admired the fortitude of the women concerned, and sometimes she thought it was more than some of the prisoners deserved. Women would be left for years to bring up children on their own, with little or no money. Helen used to see them waiting in the rain for the bus out to the jail, or taking part in demonstrations on the Falls Road on behalf of prisoners. But there was no denying it was easier for families where there was a strong Republican tradition, where a father, brothers, cousins, maybe sisters, had done time for the IRA. When the whole family believed in The Cause, there was no stigma attached to being in prison.

It was a different story for families with no such tradition. Helen had seen that at close quarters: gentle, middle-aged couples mortified at their son or daughter being on the wrong side of the law for anything, let alone this. She used to see such people sitting in the public gallery of the court. They cried. Sometimes they broke down completely, either on hearing an exact account of the crime of which their child was being accused, or when sentence was passed. When they left the court, they hid their faces in shame. It would be like that with Mrs Maguire, Helen thought, listening to her as she talked about her son's life. Oliver was the youngest of a family of four. He'd been a late arrival, seven years after the child above him. His father died when he was ten. She'd wanted him to be like the others: *they'd* got jobs, trades. 'None of them ever was in anything,' she said. Christ, how Helen hated that phrase! The soldiers had picked on Oliver when he was a teenager. They'd arrested him before now, and once they'd beaten him.

'If you'd seen the hiding he got, Miss Quinn, and he was hardly more than a child. Wouldn't you wonder how they do the things to another human being?'

'What things?' Helen said sharply.

The woman, who'd had her eyes fixed pleading upon Helen's face, suddenly broke her gaze, looked away. 'The things,' she said, as Helen stayed intimidatingly silent. 'You know the things that happen here.'

'Yes,' said Helen. 'I do.'

'Oliver couldn't have done what they're accusing him of. I know, because I'm his mother, and nobody knows him better than I do. I know his faults as well as his good points and he hasn't it in him to . . . to do a thing like that.' But her voice faltered, and suddenly Helen looked straight into the eyes of the woman sitting opposite her.

'She knows,' Helen thought. 'She knows the truth as well as I do, but she can't bear to believe it. She comes here to try to get us to hold off the day when she has to believe it.' Helen thought of her own circumstances. Two years down the line and it was still the last thing she thought about before she went to sleep at night, and the first thing that came into her mind when she woke every morning. What they'd done to her father still haunted her dreams, the thought of it could ambush her at any moment of the day. Something as trivial as the nicotine stains on the fingers of the man selling her newspapers could bring him back to her, but only for a fraction of a second, only to take him away again, and leave instead the terrible image of his going.

And yet . . .

Oh there was no danger of her losing her temper with Mrs Maguire, as Owen had feared. She wouldn't shout that her son was as guilty as hell and she knew it, so why did she come in here to waste everyone's time? No, the danger was that she would say something much worse. Oliver's mother knew full well what had happened to Helen's father. The danger was that Helen might say, 'I would rather be me than you: I wouldn't be you for anything.' *That* was the one thing Mrs Maguire wouldn't have been able to handle, and suddenly Helen realised that if she were to speak at all now, that was the only thing she would be able to say. Mrs Maguire knew it, too. The two women sat there looking at each other. At last, Oliver's mother spoke.

'It's all like a dream, so it is,' she said very softly. 'All like a terrible dream.'

Helen bowed her head and put her hands over her eyes: she loathed anyone seeing her cry. She heard the scraping sound of a chair being pushed back.

'I'm sorry to have taken up so much of your time, Miss Quinn,' the woman said. 'Thank you for talking to me.'

Chapter Fourteen

FRIDAY NIGHT

After dinner, they sat around the stove in the kitchen, drinking tea and talking, far into the night. Helen shared the sofa with Cate, who had taken off her shoes and sat with her legs curled up under her; their mother was in the high-backed chair she preferred, and Sally was on a foot stool.

'I hope it's a long time before we have to go through another week like this one,' Emily remarked.

'It wasn't so bad,' Sally said at once. 'We've been through worse than this before now, far worse.'

'That's true, aye,' her mother agreed, embarrassed now at what she had said; and she glanced shyly at Cate, but Cate blushed and looked away.

'Maybe that's the only good thing about what happened,' Sally went on. 'No matter what ever arises in the future, nothing can ever be so bad again.'

'Anyway, just think, in a couple of years we'll be sitting here picking mashed banana out of our hair. Won't that be great?' Helen said. 'I don't know about the rest of you, but I can't wait.'

'It'll be strange having a baby around the place again,' Emily said. 'I have to admit I haven't thought that one through yet; I can hardly imagine it.' None of her daughters said anything in response to this, but their silence was eloquent; and Emily knew that that was what she needed to imagine, and, as Sally had said, it wasn't the worst possibility, not by a long way.

They were all reluctant to go to bed that night. They put more fuel in the stove; they listened to the sound of the wind blowing around the eves of the house, and their talk became more broken, more desultory. Emily at last stood up, weariness getting the better of her unwillingness to be the first to break the warm, half-spoken intimacy of the evening. It was always like this towards the end of Cate's visits, and tonight, for the first time in years, Emily suddenly blurted out what she always thought at such a time: 'It's a pity you have to go away again, Cate. It would be lovely if you were always here.'

'Oh, but then I'd lose my novelty value,' Cate said, with as much irony as she could summon up. 'You'd take me for granted then, and begin to forget just how special I am.'

'She's not away yet,' Helen added. 'We still have two more magical days of her company. How are we going to stand the excitement, will you tell me that?'

Laughing, their mother said goodnight and left the room. The sisters sat in silence and listened to the sound of Emily's footsteps as she ascended the stairs; and then they could hear her moving about in the room above them, as she prepared for bed. They continued to talk, more quietly now, so as not to disturb her. 'You should go up too, Sally,' Cate said, some time later. 'I know to look at you that you're exhausted.'

'We all are,' Sally said; but she was the next to go. And now Helen realised that she was afraid of the moment when Cate would also withdraw from her company, and she would be left alone. Cate knew this too. 'I'm getting my second wind now,' she lied.

'Would you like a whiskey?' Cate shook her head, smiled sadly and patted her middle.

'Sorry, I forgot.'

'You have one, anyway.'

'I'll leave it.'

But when at last Cate did leave the kitchen, Helen poured herself a stiff drink, and sat listening to Verdi on her Walkman until it was so absurdly late that there was nothing for it but to rinse her glass, check for a final time that the front and back doors were locked, put out all the lights and go to bed too.

She lay down and in the blackness pulled the blankets tightly around herself.

When Helen was a child, sometimes she used to find it hard to fall asleep at night, and then she would slip into a fold in her mind somewhere between her dreams and her imagination. It was something she cultivated: she knew she wasn't asleep, but she could see marvellous things then, which would never have been possible had she been fully awake.

By the force of her imagination she would lift herself out of her bed, and pass through the roof of the house like a beam of light passing through water. Then she would soar, oh, how she soared, through the black night until she was high above the world, until she was as far away as one of the angels who floated beside God's shoulder in the picture at the front of the Children's Bible, where God was a vast old man with a triangular yellow light around his head, leaning above the solar system with his hand raised in blessing. The blackness of the universe was warm, soft as velvet, and studded with stars that twinkled. The Milky Way, far off, was a silver glittering belt, like flung coins.

But what Helen saw was better than a picture in a book, better than a film, because she could see and feel that the universe was alive; see the sun burning and feel its heat, see the planets, laced with moons which circled and spun around them.

Once Miss Wilson had taken the whole class, in groups of five at a time, into the windowless bookstore and, armed with a toy globe and a pocket torch, had shown them how the world rotated in the light of the sun: how day and night happen. Now Helen could see it for herself, as she leaned over the earth and the clouds obligingly swirled and melted away, leaving a globe of the world as bald as the one in the schoolroom: but alive! In turn, the countries moved into the light and day broke. She narrowed her eyes and looked at Japan: in houses with paper windows, people were waking up. She saw dim temples where monks in robes were burning incense before golden statues. She looked at China: a web of roads; rickshaws and millions of bicycles in a pure dawn light. Mountains, deserts, tangled jungles; fabulous cities, dusty villages: she could see even to the depths of the ocean, where there were shoals of coloured fish and the wrecks of ships, their treasures all spilt.

And then she would look for Ireland, where it was night. It made no difference, for with the powers she had she could see it all, see it first as an island at the edge of Europe, the seas pounding around it; then, on looking closer, the rim of mountains, the flat centre ('Ireland is like a saucer,' Miss Wilson had told them), and then, closer again, the patchwork of fields, cut by rivers and ditches. She saw dark houses, sleeping cattle, birds and night animals: the red fur of a fox, a heavy badger. She looked then to the north of Ireland, and this delighted her most of all: she saw the place where she lived. She recognised everything she saw now: the silent schoolroom, with its rows of empty desks, its nature table; the locked chapel, uncannily quiet, a red light burning before the tabernacle; familiar trees; the cold, dark waters of the lough. In Uncle Brian's and Aunt Lucy's house Granny Kate was fast asleep, pink and grey hat boxes stacked on the wardrobe which contained her immaculate suits and dresses: Helen could smell the dried lavender which hung there in lace sachets. On the lane which led up to the house a man was staggering along, sobbing and laughing and shouting at the stars, and Helen's heart contracted with pity when she looked at him. And then, strangest and best of all, she saw her own house, saw her daddy sitting on the kitchen sofa, smoking a last cigarette before locking the doors, banking up the stove for the night, and going off upstairs to bed where their mammy was reading. Sally and Cate were already asleep, and finally Helen could see herself, as though she were looking down on her own bed, where she was curled up, drowsing, waiting for sleep and feeling safe, so safe and so happy, not knowing that when she was a woman, it would break her heart to remember all this.

For now when she lay longing for sleep, a different image unrolled inexorably in her mind, repeated constantly, like a loop of film but sharper than that, more vivid, and running at just a fraction of a second slower than normal time, which gave it the heavy feel of a nightmare.

But this was no dream: she saw her father sitting at Lucy's kitchen table, drinking tea out of a blue mug. She could smell the smoke of his cigarette, even smell the familiar tweed of his jacket. He was talking through to Lucy, who was working out in the back scullery: she'd been doing the dishes when he arrived, and he told her to carry on with what she was about. He glanced up at the clock and said, 'I wonder what's keeping Brian that he's not home yet,' and Lucy replied, 'There's a car pulled up outside now, but it's not Brian's, by the sound of it.' And as soon as she spoke these words he heard her scream, as two men burst into the back scullery, and knocked her to the ground as they pushed past her; and then Helen's father saw them himself as they came into the kitchen, two men in parkas with the hoods pulled up, Halloween masks on their faces. He saw the guns, too, and he knew what they were going to do to him. The sound of a chair scraping back on the tiles, 'Ah no, Christ Jesus no,' and then they shot him at point-blank range, blowing half his head away. As they ran out of the house, one of them punched the air and whooped, because it had been so easy.

And at this point, in an abrupt reversal of the gentle descent of her childhood, Helen's vision swung violently away, and now she was aware of the cold light of dead stars; the graceless immensity of a dark universe. Now her image of her father's death was infinitely small, infinitely tender: the searing grief came from the tension between that smallness and the enormity of infinite time and space. No pity, no forgiveness, no justification: maybe if she could have conceived of a consciousness where every unique horror in the history of humanity was known and grieved for, it would have given her some comfort. Sometimes she felt that all she had was her grief, a grief she could scarcely bear.

In the solid stone house, the silence was uncanny.

One by one in the darkness, the sisters slept.